Scenes From a Bar

Marisa Rae Dondlinger

Published by Marisa Rae Dondlinger, 2018.

This is a work of fiction. Similarities to real people, places, or events are entirely coincidental.

SCENES FROM A BAR

First edition. March 27, 2018.

Copyright © 2018 Marisa Rae Dondlinger.

ISBN: 979-8224246724

Written by Marisa Rae Dondlinger.

For my mom, who always believed.

My dad, who always hoped.

And Andy, who walked beside me each step of the way.

Chapter 1

Casey – September 21, 2012

"Remind me why I'm doing this?"

"Because it could be fun," Cadie offered.

"Unlikely," I countered, swerving through the early evening traffic. Driving on the narrow streets of the eastside of Milwaukee was like playing a game of *Paperboy*. A new obstacle—a biker, a stroller, a delivery truck—comes out of nowhere every two seconds. "He just so..."

"What?"

"Geeky. Can someone in their thirties still qualify as geeky?"

"Most people stopped with the labels after high school."

I sighed. "I can't understand why he would agree to this either. We have nothing in common beyond sharing a few friends. We've barely spoken. In fact, I think he tries to avoid talking to me."

"Maybe he's intimidated by you. It's not like he'd be the first man—" A blood curdling scream interrupted what was likely another misinformed rant by my sister about how men have worshipped me since the day I was born. Despite our divergent lives—she was a married mom and I'm single, single, single—she still acted like we were teenagers competing for dates. (Not that that ever happened...) At the onset of puberty, I bought stock in the teenage mythology that being pretty and popular would lead to happiness while Cadie devoured books like bite-sized doughnuts. Twenty drama-filled years later, I've learned that seldom does male attention come without any dangerous strings attached, but I had as much chance of convincing Cadie of that as one would in getting Muslims to accept Jesus as their savior. "Hold on."

I could hear my niece, Jayden, relaying through heavy sobs, some cataclysmic event. At all of three-years-old, she reveled in drama, fighting victoriously with some internal beast to ensure her life played out like a soap opera. The uncanny similarity between our emotional makeups made me protective towards Jayden and also fearful of her future.

"I'll let you go," I said, easing my beat up Jetta into the glove-tight fit between two oversized SUV's. "I'm at the bar."

"Promise me you'll give this date a fair shot."

"Promise."

"No stories of drug-induced hallucinations where you claim to have psychic abilities—"

"But I can predict the future!" Cadie hasn't smoked a cigarette let alone anything illegal and thus discounted my powers entirely.

"—rants about how all men are cheaters, emotionally impaired or intellectually incapable of discussing anything other than sports."

"So try not to be me?"

"Be you," Cadie allowed, "but be *nice*. Remember, geeky guys make the best boyfriends. They care about making you happy."

"You would know," I teased. My brother-in-law Chris was nice enough, but if I was forced to marry him I would have Googled the most effective and least painful suicide options on our honeymoon. He wasn't exactly a thrill a minute, but neither was Cadie.

"Hilarious. Call me tomorrow."

I rummaged through my purse for a piece of gum. I was five minutes late to meet Joshua Shaw, but I wanted to make sure he showed up first. Who was Joshua Shaw? That was the million dollar question, second only to why I agreed to this date. Although not technically a blind date—we've hung out through our mutual friends Haden and Rachel—we've never engaged in any meaningful conversations. At least I don't think we have... I wouldn't testify to that fact under oath given that most of the times I saw him—weddings, parties, bars—involved copious amounts of alcohol. But after years of running in similar circles, I knew very little about Joshua.

On the surface, Joshua couldn't be further from my type. He was cute-ish, but not in a stop, turn, trip over your feet sort of way. He worked a look—hipster meets computer geek meets pseudo-intellectual. Translation: he always wore t-shirts and jeans, plastic-rimmed glasses, had shaggy, curly hair and a perpetual five o'clock shadow. He spoke with the casual arrogance fit for an Ivy League classical literature professor (or some other completely useless subject), which made it obvious he thought he was smarter than his audience.

But my therapist admonished me to be more open with the men I date. So here I was, as open as Target on Black Friday—come one, come all!

I sighed as I looked into the rearview mirror. Fashion was the center of my world and thus I felt a bit depressed knowing that the details of my outfit would likely go unnoticed. I chose something casual and yet alluring: dark skinny jeans, a black lacy tank top and black leather vest, both of which I designed myself, and a thin leopard belt for a hint of fun. All set off rather nicely against my long, dark brown hair and sapphire eyes.

Joshua, on the other hand, didn't spend two seconds deciding on his wardrobe. I saw him through the bay window as I approached Mission Bar, crouched over and tapping on his phone. Dressed in what appeared to be a faded Jimmy Hendricks t-shirt, a pair of skinny jeans and converses, he could pass for anywhere between 18 and 35. (Maybe if conversation ran dry we could debate whose ass looked better in skinny jeans.) Was this an issue specific to my generation—the reluctance of men to change their style as they aged—or a problem since the dawn of time?

The bar was shaped like a horseshoe and Joshua sat at the tip of the left side. He didn't notice me enter. Not that I minded. Five years ago I was vain enough to need that appreciative gaze. But I've learned that if physical attraction forms the foundation of a relationship, it will collapse around the same time my body finishes metabolizing the night's liquor. At this point it felt nicer to be heard than seen, but I only experienced that once in my life and I doubted it would ever come to fruition again.

I tapped Joshua on the shoulder and gave my best can-you-believe-we're-doing-this smile.

He brushed his curly hair out of his eyes, adjusted his glasses and smiled. A nice smile, I had to admit. But the slight blush that crept up his neck like a sunburn told me he had no idea the effect it had on women—a perfect blend of disarming and charming.

"I, uh, didn't know what you wanted to drink so I thought I'd wait. This is water."

"And here I thought it was tequila," I teased, sitting on the barstool next to him.

He looked at me for a moment before laughing. He tapped his fingers against the glass, making a soft bass noise. "No, that's your expertise."

Was that an insult or a compliment? He *was* smiling. "Meaning?"

"New Year's Eve last year at Mo's? Ring any bells?"

Most of that night was a blur but I did recall consuming copious amounts of tequila, followed by plenty of singing and dancing. I had a vague recollection of Joshua being there, but, per usual, didn't remember talking to him. "Yes, well, that was New Year's Eve. I don't traditionally consume a liter of tequila in one night."

"So what do you drink on an ordinary Friday night?"

"Vodka and tonic, please," I answered.

Joshua signaled the bartender—a tall, clean-cut guy with a face like Tom Cruise in *Top Gun*—and ordered two. The bartender looked at Joshua with mildly concealed boredom, but his face broke into a wide smile with bedroom eyes when I spoke. I turned away. I'd seen far too many looks like that in my life to be impressed.

Joshua swiveled his stool so that he was facing me. Yep, it was definitely a Jimmy Hendricks shirt, but at least the shirt was snug enough to reveal a pair of toned biceps. I detested baggy shirts on men, which usually failed at disguising a paunch. Not that Joshua had to worry; he had the wiry body of a marathon runner.

"So..." he said.

I felt vaguely self-conscious and a bit nervous. Usually I could talk to anyone, but I was stumped for conversation. My mind kept returning to the question of why I agreed to this date. How had my life morphed from being the girl every guy wanted to the girl married friends pitied? I finally had my life together: a successful career, modest savings, a clean(ish) lifestyle. Why wasn't that enough? Why did my married friends view being single and in my thirties on par with cancer? Treatable, sure, but very bad luck.

"I was under the impression you never really liked me," I blurted out.

Joshua's head snapped back, as if I had slapped him, making me feel like an asshole. Maybe this was why I couldn't sustain a healthy relationship. I used to think being single was my choice, but perhaps I had become too bitter and outspoken that men didn't want to be *tied down to me*. I vowed to sweeten up, if only to make this night bearable.

"To be honest, I never knew you well enough to form an opinion. I thought that was what tonight was about."

"I'm sorry. Sometimes I say things without thinking...I think for a reaction." I barked out a laugh. "Say the most offensive thing and see how people respond. Fun times!"

"It's fine," Joshua reassured me. But as he looked around the bar, I could tell he felt uncomfortable. In fact, my money was on him leaving within the next five minutes claiming he left the oven on or forgot to feed his dog. At least then this charade would be over.

"Seriously, can we start over?" I gave him my most dazzling smile, that, to be fair, had led a few men astray. "Besides, it would give Rachel far too much satisfaction if she found out I offended you in the first five minutes."

He took the bait, leaning forward and whispering conspiratorially: "I'm supposed to text her every five minutes with updates."

"Why am I not surprised?"

Rachel was a perfectionist and a busy-body, which made her a lethal over-achiever: wife, attorney, volunteer, cook, party planner, interior designer...you get the point. We went to high school together but categorically avoided each other. Rachel participated in every sport, club and committee, whereas I drank and experimented with boys—both worthwhile pursuits in my mind. She thought I was trailer trash and I thought she was faker than a set of silicone implants. I graduated high school thinking I'd never see her again. But while in law school, she vacationed at a resort I worked at in Key West with my best friend Haden. As luck would have it (cue sarcasm), Haden and Rachel fell in love and married, ensuring Rachel a permanent place in my life.

Why she orchestrated tonight's date was beyond me, other than to further her naïve hope that if I got married I'd spend less time with Haden.

"I'm kidding," Joshua said. "But I am required to call her later."

"You met Rachel in law school, right?" Joshua nodded, more or less confirming that he had endured years of Rachel bitching about me. She probably had a Power Point presentation listing my faults with supporting anecdotes. "I'm curious, what do you guys have in common? You're so laid back and nice and she's…"

"It's hard to understand our bond if you haven't been through the trenches of law school."

I suppressed an eye roll at his self-aggrandizing statement. Upon graduating high school, counting breaks, it took me nine years to earn my degree in fashion design. Along the way I obtained an associate's degree as a pastry chef, perfected my bartending skills and had countless flings with unsuitable men. A post-grad degree was neither possible nor desirable. Not that someone like Joshua would understand.

"We were in the same study group first year," Joshua continued. "Finals were intense. Imagine three hundred students studying around the clock for three weeks, subsiding only on caffeine and junk food."

"I don't think I studied twenty-four hours in all of high school."

He smiled—with or without condescension? That is the question! "She kind of had a nervous breakdown—"

"No!" I leaned forward, eager for more juicy tidbits. "What happened?"

He pushed his glasses up on his nose and inched closer to me. "Well the day before our last final, we were quizzing each other and she got an answer wrong and just lost it. She ran out of the library crying, leaving her laptop, books, notes—everything—behind. We went back to studying, assuming she'd return when she calmed down. Well, she didn't. She called me drunk later that night, babbling about how she's positive she failed all of her exams and was going to drop out of law school—not even show up for the exam the next day."

"Wow. Rachel hardly ever gets drunk. She's always so dignified, sipping her wine." I said *dignified* out of deference to Joshua's friendship. Annoying and self-righteous was much more accurate.

She looked down at Haden and my drunken antics like we were auditioning for the *Jersey Shore*.

"Probably because of that night. I stayed up with her all night, plying her with coffee and helping her study. To this day she credits me with the B she pulled out in criminal law."

"Wow. Most guys would've hung up the phone and gone back to bed." I experienced first-hand the willingness of some men to leave behind a drunken girl without a second thought.

He waved off my compliment. "I can see how some might find her...aggravating, but we've always been there for each other. Friends like that are hard to find."

"I'm sure she *can* be a good friend," I hesitated, "but I doubt that will happen with us. She blames me for Haden's bad behavior. If he's drunk or high or out all night, it must be my influence."

"She definitely has some trust issues, but the fact that she knows you've dated married men before doesn't help."

My hand froze in mid-air, leaving my drink perched mere inches from my mouth. I wasn't sure how much he knew, so I stayed quiet.

"I'm sorry," he quickly amended, having the decency to blush. "That's not any of my business."

I smoothed my hands over my thighs, rolling out the invisible creases in the fabric. At least I confirmed that anything I told Haden was directly relayed to Rachel. I suspected this was the case, but it still pissed me off. Thankfully Haden only knew the abridged version of my ill-advised affair, and well after it ended. I had enough forethought to know that having an affair with Rachel's married boss wasn't something I should broadcast.

"Well now I know why she's so keen on fixing me up!" I joked, while flagging down the bartender in a not-so-subtle change of topic. "Do you want one?"

"Sure," Joshua agreed, strumming his fingers against the bar. "You're rubbing off on me. I don't usually make such rude comments."

I ordered two more drinks. "Don't worry. I've said way worse."

"Well, I'm sorry. I feel terrible—"

I put my hands on top of his. "We're even, okay?"

"Okay." He let out a long breath and smiled. It was kind of endearing how much he cared about not offending me. A common theme in the men I've dated is a distinct lack of interest in my emotional well-being. I spent years out of touch with my own emotions, pretending to be that cool, flippant girl and consequently dated men that piled their emotions (and emotional awareness) into a vault and threw away the combination. It took me a long time to realize that my sensitivity—I have enough emotions to fill the void of a dozen emotionally stunted men—combined with a selfish man doesn't make for a happy relationship.

I wanted a guy who listened *and* shared his feelings. But what would that relationship look like? Passing tissues while watching chick flicks? Having weekly dinners with his mom/best friend? Attending couples therapy to ensure each person felt heard? No thank you. I wanted the simplicity of a confident, ambitious man, but with an emotional IQ to match. Did that man exist outside of Hollywood?

"What are you up to these days?" Joshua asked. "Still bartending?"

"Nope, not since graduating from design school a couple years ago," I stressed, swallowing my annoyance. I could show at Paris Fashion Week and Rachel would still see me as a bartender. "I manage Kipp-Lerner a couple days a week and spend the rest of the time in my studio."

He shook his head. "I've never heard of Kipp Lerner."

"It's a clothing boutique in the Third Ward. I apprenticed for Kipp while in school. He sold a few of my pieces and it grew from there. Now I have a little section in the store with my clothes."

"Wow," he nodded, looking equal parts impressed and surprised. "It would've been nice for Rachel to brief me on this new part of your life."

"You wouldn't actually expect her to tell you anything that would make me sound successful, would you?"

"Tell me how you got into design," he diplomatically soldiered on.

"My mom taught me how to sew when I was little. I used to make clothes for my dolls, but by high school I was designing for myself. I'd buy fabric from JoAnn's or rip up clothes from Goodwill and make new pieces. But it took me awhile to realize I wanted to make it a career."

"Are you wearing any of your designs?"

"This tank-top and the leather vest." I unbuttoned the vest to show the subtle embellishments stitched throughout the black tank-top, giving it a textured look. I looped my thumbs through the leopard belt, arched my back forward and even pouted a bit to give the full effect of my mock couture pose. I held the pose for a good three seconds before laughing.

"It's very, what's the phrase...fashion forward?" Joshua said the words slowly. His face turned the color of licorice, betraying a combination of pride over finding the correct words and embarrassment that he actually knew them. "My ex was obsessed with *America's Next Top Model* and *Project Runway*. Despite my best efforts to tune them out, I learned a few things."

"I like the idea of you watching those shows," I admitted. "It sheds light into an unknown side of your personality."

"You know, it takes a real man to watch Lifetime television."

I laughed. "Duly noted."

"I'm curious, though, tell me more about this personality assessment you've made of me."

"It's hardly an assessment," I objected.

"Stop delaying and give it to me straight."

"Okay," I warned. "You come off like a serious intellectual, happy to play the role of witty observer."

And this assessment comes from?"

"Oh, you know, just seeing you out. You're always watching, never truly participating. When I think of you, I always imagine you in a doorway nursing a drink while the party unfolds or talking to a small group of people. I can't tell whether you think everyone is lame or you just don't know how to let go and have fun."

Joshua peered deeply into his own drink. He wore the exact serious, inscrutable expression I was trying to describe!

"Like tonight," I continued. "You chose to sit at the end of the bar. That's fine, of course, but when you're in the middle you meet more people, have more fun."

"I'm shy," he explained, rubbing the palm of his hand against the whiskers on his chin. "I've never been comfortable in large group situations."

"Yeah, I don't get shy from you. Cautious, maybe? Like you're not sure exactly where you fit in so you hover on the outside. You'd rather wait for people to approach you than the other way around."

"Cautious," he repeated, letting each syllable roll around lazily inside his mouth. "Yeah, I could see why you might think that."

I leaned forward and placed my hand on his knee, knowing full well that the angle gave him a nice view of my cleavage. (True to form, Joshua's eyes widened as he felt the gravitational pull of my breasts. I abruptly sat back up. Why was I acting like a tease? What was wrong with me?) "Why are you so cautious?"

Joshua leveled his gaze at me. "I'm not sure the best way to break this to you, but for most of my life, I've been what you beautiful people would call a dork or a loser."

"No!" I said in mock-disbelief.

"Yes!"

I found his self-deprecation refreshing. "And here I thought I was sharing a drink with the quarterback of the football team."

"Ha! School was like a warzone. I definitely wasn't hanging out there after hours."

"I'm sorry," I said, backtracking a bit. I struck my interested pose—head tilted the left, fingers strumming my lips, eyes perched wide open—to let him know I was curious about the tales of his lonely youth.

Joshua's eyes narrowed. "You really want to hear?"

"Of course!" Extracting a little humbleness from a man was never a bad thing. "I'm an excellent listener—one of the reasons I made so much money bartending."

"I must warn you, it's quite traumatic, the moment where one realizes they were never destined to be cool."

"I have no idea what that's like," I deadpanned. The truth was I probably didn't. I assumed that everyone had friends in high school because that was my experience. The easiest part was socializing. (I might have been valedictorian if socializing was graded.) Sure, not everyone was popular, but the geeks had geeky friends right? Even Cadie had a few friends.

But my life was far from a cakewalk. Rachel and her posse ridiculed me for being poor. I told myself they were jealous. Money couldn't buy them the attention I got from guys. But that didn't stop it from hurting. "Seriously though, I want to hear. It will help ground me."

"Yes." Joshua's voice dropped an octave lower as he looked directly into my eyes. "Someone as beautiful as you occasionally needs to be brought back down to earth."

The compliment threw me slightly off guard. "So tell."

Chapter 2

Joshua – February 13, 1987

It was a little before five in the morning, pitch black outside except for the halogen glow of the streetlights that seeped through my bedroom curtains. I was wide awake, having hardly slept. I spent half the night underneath my comforter, flashlight in hand, rereading the latest Spiderman comic book. I desperately wanted to go watch cartoons, but I knew the noise would wake up my dad and he would get mad. I often heard—usually weaved into my daily conversations with my father—how tired he was, how much his body ached and how I needed to study hard so that I never ended up working in construction.

I stayed in bed, listening to my rapidly beating heart. Today was a big day. HUGE. It was our class Valentine's Day party and I was going to tell Betsy Gliebe that I loved her. My mom laughed when I told her. *You have a crush Joshua; that's not love.* But she was wrong. Betsy was the only girl smart enough to beat me at Around the World in math. She also hated gym class, constantly coming up with reasons she couldn't participate in whatever torture-driven sport Mr. Heiglman devised. Best of all, she was nice to everyone. I *loved* her.

I quietly crept over towards my desk. The valentines sat in an orderly, alphabetical pile. My mom made me write a valentine to every person in my class, but I made sure Betsy's was special. I drew a picture of her lying on her stomach on the gym floor, legs bent upwards at the knee with her ankles crossed. She leaned on her right elbow and held a book in her left hand while twirling strands of her beautiful brown hair with her right hand.

My inspiration for the picture came two weeks ago when we both sat out of gym class. Betsy claimed a severe stomach ache, while I was still ailing from a sprained ankle courtesy of a deathly flag football the day before. It took me two days to get the correct coloring of her acid wash blue jeans and another three to detail all the tiny pastel flowers on her sweatshirt. Viewing the finished product, I knew that skipping my allotted hour of television after dinner was worth it. Betsy deserved perfection.

I wrote *I love you, Joshua* in the bottom right-hand corner. Maybe we could start hanging out during recess, fake sick together during gym class or play video games after school. The possibilities were endless.

DESPITE THE FRIGID temperature, the school yard bustled with kids. They shrieked and laughed in glee, utterly unaware of their runny noses, frozen extremities and chapped lips. Why weren't they cold? I cocooned myself in a hat, scarf and mittens, as well as my snow boots, and I still shivered inside my mom's heated car.

I tried to open the car door in an attempt to make a quick escape (as I did every morning) and failed (as I did every morning).

"Aren't you going to give Mommy a kiss?" Her voice raised an octave with hope.

I told her numerous times that I was too old for kisses but she was persistent. My age wasn't the real reason. On the first day of school, John Bertha walked by our car as my mom kissed me goodbye. No problem would have arisen had my mother given me an ordinary peck on the cheek. But my mother's kisses included holding my cheeks in a vice grip, pulling my face within an inch of hers and saying: *You're my precious boy. Mommy loves you.* Of course, the window was open because it was one of those scorching end-of-summer days and so John caught every single word. Now whenever John saw my mom he started slobbering all over his hand, making kissing noises. His partner in crime, Kenny Longfa, called her my girlfriend, as in, *Don't forget to kiss your girlfriend!* My mother either didn't notice or didn't care. She had selective hearing.

"M-o-o-m-m," I complained, as I cautiously glanced out the window. "I have to go!"

"Quick one!" She smacked her lips against both cheeks, but it was enough for me to taste the Cheerios we both ate for breakfast.

"Did you give your girlfriend a Valentine's Day kiss?" Kenny asked as I sat down at my desk. On cue, John brought his forearm up to his mouth and drooled on it like an excited puppy. Kenny sat on top of my desk, inching his face close to mine and roughly grabbing my cheeks. He smelled like a mix of day-old sweat and cat litter. "What's this?"

"Looks like a love bite," John sneered, coming up from behind.

The taunting caught the attention of the rest of the class, who laughed along in their seats. I looked over at Steve—my only real friend—but his head was buried inside a book. I wasn't mad. It only made the teasing worse if we both got involved. We implicitly agreed to fight our own battles.

"What's going on?" Ms. Schaefer asked as she entered the room. All-in-all she was a pretty good teacher. She gave us candy during tests ("brain food"), allowed us to earn pizza parties and brought in movies as a teaching tool.

"Oh, honey." She smiled in an amused yet insulting way. This look would be more appropriate for confronting someone stuffing their mouth full of chips, mid-aisle, before checking out at the grocery store. The look asked: *Have you no shame?* "Why don't you run to the bathroom and clean up?"

Thoroughly perplexed, I ran to the bathroom where I noticed with horror that my mom left a perfectly formed red pout on each cheek. I was a walking cosmetic ad! I angrily scrubbed the lipstick away while cursing my mom. It's as if she tried to make my life harder!

But my anger melted away as I walked back to class and saw the red paper hearts decorating the hallway. Today was our Valentine's Day party. Today, I would give my picture to Betsy. Pretty soon I wouldn't remember this as the day my mother gave me a facial tattoo, but rather the day Betsy became my girlfriend.

SHORTLY AFTER A FREEZING recess, Ms. Schafer announced it was time to exchange valentines. Each person had a huge red envelope taped to the front of their desks. My envelope had my name in bubble letters and each letter was filled with silver glitter. I also drew several action sequences from my Spiderman comic book. I felt rather proud until I looked around the room and realized only the girls used glitter.

Ms. Schafer, as well as the two "den" mothers, stood in the front of the classroom by the display of cupcakes, cookies and juice. They gazed at us with frozen smiles.

"Now remember, absolutely NO running! We will hand out the valentines in an orderly fashion like well-behaved young adults." Ms. Schafer gazed from left to right, trying to intimidate each student. "Once the valentines are all passed out, we can enjoy some cookies and juice while we read the messages. Okay? Ready? Go!"

A flurry of activity ensued as twenty-five boys and girls ran from desk to desk, forgetting all warnings. I saved Betsy's valentine for last, carefully slipping the picture into her envelope.

I was about to tuck into a chocolate cupcake with pink frosting when two disturbing things happened. First, I reached into my envelope and pulled out a single valentine from Steve. I set the valentine aside and peered into the envelope. Empty! How was this possible? My mom made me write out valentines for every single person in my class, including people I didn't like, because it was *required*. But an arsenal of voices interrupted my thoughts.

"Joshua's in loooovvvee!!"

"Joshua likes girls?"

"And it's not his mom!"

"Betsy and Joshua, sitting in a tree, k-i-s-s-i-n-g!"

"Everyone be quiet!" Ms. Schafer yelled. She touched her thumb and her index finger to her temple and stared at the ground.

"I thought Joshua was a fairy."

"I said QUIET!"

I crouched, shell-shocked, in my seat. I breathed through my nose, trying to keep the tears at bay.

"I am very disappointed in the way each and every one of you has acted. Joshua made Betsy a beautiful valentine, expressing feelings of *friendship*"— Ms. Schafer had that part wrong!—"and instead of admiring his artistic abilities you acted like spoiled children. This is not how you treat a fellow classmate."

I looked towards Betsy's desk and saw her crouched in a position not unlike mine. Her usual glowing cheeks shone scarlet red. The lump inside my tummy grew with the knowledge that I caused the one person I cared about pain.

"Betsy, do you have something to say to Joshua?" Ms. Schafer stood behind me, resting her hands on my shoulders. Betsy tucked her hair behind her ear and focused her eyes directly on me. Her beauty was startling. How could I have ever been so naïve to think she could love me? Why did I think drawing a picture would make her see me differently than everyone else?

"But Ms. Schafer," she protested, her angelic face scrunched in confusion. She cleared her throat, which sounded like a bomb being shot out of a cannon into the quiet night sky. "I never asked him for this picture."

Ms. Schafer reflexively tightened her grip on my shoulder. "No, you didn't," she conceded warningly, "but it was a very nice gesture."

"I *won't* thank him." She looked pained at having to contradict Ms. Schafer. Normally a goody two-shoes, Betsy took this moment to make a stand. "I don't want anyone to think that...that we're in love."

"Give it back," yelled Kenny, evidently enjoying my humiliation. "Give it back! Give it back!"

The other students quickly joined in.

Betsy stood, carrying my picture in her shaking hands, and slowly walked towards my desk. Ironically, in my daydreams she walked towards my desk in a similar slow-motion vignette. Yet, in those moments she wore a brilliant, beaming smile. But her face now was as grim as a pallbearer.

She set the picture on my desk. I looked at her, trying to find any semblance of the girl who was nice to everyone, but she refused to make eye contact. I pushed her out of the way and ran out of the classroom.

I was the class joke. I had no real friends. I deserved to be alone.

Chapter 3

Joshua – September 21, 2012

"That was the moment I officially woke up," I finished explaining. "I no longer had any grand illusions that I would one day be homecoming king, the star athlete or date the popular girl. My status as a loser was solidified early on."

I shrugged to let Casey know that none of this mattered anymore. Everything worked out in the end: I had good friends, a respectable job and even got laid a fair number of times once the millennium hit and geek became more chic than shit. Beyond the occasional bout of crippling insecurity, my past was exactly that, *my past*.

Casey's forehead wrinkled with concentration. "I've got it!" she gasped loudly—as if she were in an episode of *Murder She Wrote*—before grabbing my shoulders.

"What?"

"We should look this Betsy chic up, see if she's in town and then give her an eyeful of what she missed out on."

Casey looked so adorably eager to vindicate me that I almost went along with her terrible plan just to keep her entertained. I knew Casey had this effect on men—she could persuade them to walk into a burning building—but it was a lot harder to resist when the attention was directed my way.

"I don't think so," I chuckled. "Knowing my luck, Betsy would still be perfect."

"Nope, no way." Casey emphatically shook her head. "I'll tell you a secret. The hot girls always end up fat, strung out, working a shit job or marrying the wrong guy. Beauty doesn't guarantee happiness. Something always goes wrong. Trust me, *I know*."

"Objection. Speculation." Casey eyed me like a bruised banana and my face flamed in return. This wasn't a court of law. Objecting only made me sound pretentious and boring: two personality traits Casey already identified and rejected. "But even worse, what if she has a horrible life but still thinks I'm beneath her?"

"Then she's not worth your time," Casey said.

"Exactly." I lined my empty glass up next to hers. "Want another?"

"Yes...but I need a change." Casey strummed her index finger against her lower lip, plucking it like a guitar.

I'd known of Casey for years, but always from afar. She was the center of attention—like a magnet, people were drawn to her—and I lived on the fringe. But tonight I was able to study her in close proximity. I had the exclusive view of her supple lower lip, which she highlighted with every strum. It looked juicy and ripe, stained the color of a freshly picked strawberry.

"Tequila?" Casey asked, issuing a subtle challenge.

I came into tonight game for anything, but Casey's demeanor—the witty banter, jokes and easy confidence—made me even more nervous. I had no idea what a night of drinking with Casey would hold, but I had to make the most of it. Hell, maybe a few stiff drinks would level the playing field.

"One shot," I conceded warily. "I had a bad breakup with tequila."

She laughed. "My most stable relationship has been with tequila."

"You can do better."

"I could do worse."

It was impossible not to return her smile. "So now that you've heard about my pathetic youth, tell me how the other half lived.

What problems troubled the beautiful and popular? Beyond chipping a nail or staining your cashmere sweater."

"Oh God, you too?" Casey groaned. "My sister Cadie suffered from the same delusions. Instead of trying to improve her lot, she sat around complaining about how easy the popular kids had it."

"You went to high school together?"

"Unfortunately. She was a year above me."

"How could she have made her life better?"

Casey threw her hands up in the air, as if I should be able to guess the innumerable ways her sister could have moved up in the high school pecking order. "Oh, I don't know, she could've wore clothes that fit her body instead of baggy dresses like a nun. She could've flirted a bit. Maybe, God forbid, she could've got drunk at a party."

"I always wanted a sibling," I confided. I remembered begging my parents to have another child. When I was young I wanted someone to play with, but as I got older, I wanted someone else to help relieve some of the pressure. It's hard to be an only child when your parents pin all their hopes on you, manipulating your decisions to fulfill their unlived dreams.

"Consider yourself lucky."

"So you and your sister aren't close?"

"Growing up? God no," she shuddered. "She was a huge geek. No offense."

I held up my hands. "None taken."

"But things changed when she left for college. She stuck by me during some really hard times. Besides, her geek-filled years paid off: she has a great job, husband and an amazing little girl. And I, well, I finally have my shit together but it took ten years too long."

"Some people just take longer to work out what they're supposed to do with their lives."

Casey studied me carefully. "It's amazing that you can espouse such truisms without even a hint of bitterness. It's my fault for never taking anything seriously for the first"—she smiled and looked at the ceiling—"twenty-five years of my life."

"I didn't know you back then," I said magnanimously. "Maybe you would've been the one hot girl that was nice to me in high school."

"You wouldn't have liked me much in high school...had we ever talked." She caught herself and blushed slightly. "There I go again!"

"You're too hard on yourself. You're a bit wild, but you've always been nice to me." I carefully omitted the times she acted conceited, flippant and distracted. Tonight was a new beginning.

"Thank you," Casey said quietly. I held her gaze for a moment before the bartender interrupted us with two tequila shots.

"Tequila time!" Casey clapped. She looked at the miniature glasses as if a sip would provide eternal youth. "What should we shoot to?"

"Your story."

"What story?"

I shook my head to let her know that shining those beautiful brown eyes my way wasn't going to get her out of divulging a few secrets. "The story about your less-than-perfect high school existence. The one that makes me say, thank God I wasn't popular! That sounds terrible!"

Casey tapped her shot glass against mine and flipped it smoothly into her mouth, not even flinching as the tequila met her taste buds. How did I fare? Nowhere near as suave. I barely swallowed half the shot when my throat caught on fire, causing an unflattering coughing fit.

"Finish up," she said, pointing at the remaining tequila. "Then I'll give you the inside scoop on being popular. You might be surprised."

Chapter 4

Casey – December 26, 1996

My mouth tasted bitter and stale, like I took too many swigs of cough syrup. I cautiously rubbed my temple. It felt like someone was trying to hammer a nail between my eyebrows. I opened my eyes and saw several neon stars stuck to the ceiling. This insignificant detail alerted me to my location: Alicia's bedroom floor. The stars gave off a slight halogen glow, but the effect was muted by the grey light creeping in through the shades. It must be daytime.

Last night came to me in pieces, like a movie missing several slides. Christmas at my house. Aunts, uncles, cousins and one set of grandparents all crammed into our tiny Cape Cod. The usual merriment people experienced around the holidays didn't exist in our family. I'm pretty sure the only reason we got together was to reargue the merits of long-held grudges. No one ever changed their mind, but depending on how much liquor was consumed, new additions were made to the story to further enhance the offense in the mind of the wronged party.

The night started with an argument between my dad and Uncle Jimmy about a poker game they played over twenty years ago. Uncle Jimmy claimed my dad cheated by hiding cards under the table with gum. My dad was still seeking his winnings. When the argument turned into a spirited wresting match—seriously two middle-aged men pregnant with beer guts?—I escaped outside with my cousin Alan and a bottle of Wild Turkey. This was far from my first-time drinking, but it was my first date with Wild Turkey. The first gulp tasted like poison, but as the alcohol infiltrated my system it merely felt like there was a volcano erupting in my throat.

The night got hazy from that point. I remember not making it to the toilet and throwing up in my sister's open dresser drawer instead. And again in the neighbor's garbage. At some point I fled the three blocks to Alicia's house.

"You're awake," Alicia's said from the doorway. I carefully lifted my head and watched as she plopped her butt down on her bed without an ounce of grace. Alicia wasn't fat, she was…curvy. And perpetually on a diet to achieve that Kate Moss cocaine chic look.

"I don't even want to know."

"Okay," she taunted me. "I won't tell you how you showed up, reeking of puke and babbling about how you needed to use my phone because you wanted to call Nick Androse, go over to his house and fuck him senseless."

"No!"

"YES!" She threw one of the decorative pillows at me. It weighed a pound, but it felt like a cement truck had barreled into me.

"Did I call him?"

"Like I would let you." She grabbed a cigarette and lit it. Alicia's parents recently divorced and her mom was in a depressed fog. Hence, she wouldn't notice if we started a meth lab in her kitchen.

"*Please* put that out." I pulled the blanket over my head in a feeble attempt to block out the smoke. My stomach contracted and my throat burned, alerting me that another round of puking was imminent.

"I saved you from a lifetime of embarrassment and you want to deny me a cigarette?" Alicia sighed dramatically and cracked open her bedside window. "You better get your shit together. Kyle Orcher is having a party tonight and, according to Jenny Blaylock, who he is apparently with this week, Nick will be there, and…wanted to make sure you were going!"

"What?" I yelled, ignoring the searing pain that bolted through my head as I jumped onto the bed. Nick was a senior. That fact alone should've ensured our paths never crossed. But since Thanksgiving I've seen him *everywhere*. So far, I had nothing substantial to report. Nick barely strung three sentences together when we talked. But the killer smile he flashed me each time we passed in the hall was worth way more than words. Bottom line: this invitation from Nick, through Kyle, Jenny and Alicia was a BIG deal.

"Yep. We're going to Kyle's house tonight." Alicia said Kyle's name in a dreamy tone ordinarily reserved for the likes of Brad Pitt. But Kyle's looks were far too clichéd—tall, dark hair, blue eyes—to attract me. Not that this logic stopped the rest of the female student body from spreading their legs on command.

I preferred Nick's soulful grey eyes, honeydew hair and muscular forearms. It was during baseball season last spring that I first noticed Nick. I became mesmerized by the subtle popping of the muscles in his arms as he swung the bat, the fluid way he fielded the balls and the cocksure grin he gave as he rounded home plate.

"So what else did Jenny say?"

"About you?" Alicia picked up two bottles of nail polish and held them under her desk lamp to figure out which one had yet to expire and turn into clumpy colored water. "Not much."

"Not much?"

"Jesus. I didn't transcribe the conversation. The important part is he wants you there, okay?"

But that wasn't true. The most important part was determining his intentions: friend, hook-up, girlfriend? I hadn't the faintest clue how to act, which only made me want to puke...again.

EVEN THOUGH I WAS ONLY a sophomore, I successfully infiltrated the upper-class social circle via the old adage: fake it 'til you make it. Thus, I faked confidence with each breath: faked having fun by laughing with the right people; strutted down the hallway like it was my personal runway in the designer knockoffs I sewed out of cheap scraps; and faked falling for the desirable "it" boy when the right opportunity presented itself. It was confusing at times where my real feelings began and the faking ended, but being wanted by the guys and envied by the girls was worth it.

But my gut told me I wasn't faking my feelings for Nick. I didn't want to be with Nick because it was advantageous. Admittedly, he was rich, good looking and popular, but I was drawn to him because he seemed so loved. His parents cheered wildly for him at all his games, always waiting afterwards with a hug of congratulations. Seeing Nick interact with his family made me recognize the emptiness in my own. What would it feel like to be adored?

My parents quit trying to figure me out early on, likely concluding that I resulted from a mix-up at the hospital, an alien brainwashing or Immaculate Conception. They spent most of their time working or watching television. My dad worked as a manager at an electronics store while my mom was a secretary. At night, my mom sat on the kitchen counter eating Ritz crackers with peanut-butter while watching her soaps on the twelve-inch television in our kitchen. My dad lounged on the recliner, watching sports. They rarely said a word to each other or us. Neither of my parents excelled in the art of conversation.

Needless to say, I wasn't shocked when I called home to tell my mom about Kyle's party that she failed to notice I was gone. It wasn't until Cadie stole the phone and screamed at me about puking in her dresser that my mom intervened.

"Casey," my mom said in her fake I-won't-stand-for-any-of-your-crap parenting voice. "Did you—Christ I can't believe I'm asking you this—throw up in your sister's dresser last night?"

"Of course not!"

"Then why would she say that?"

"Because she blames me for her pathetic existence."

"I had to throw out two of my favorite shirts!" my sister screeched in the background.

"Good!" I retorted. I wouldn't apologize. It was an accident. She'd understand that these things happened if she ever partied. "Tell her to throw out all of her clothes."

I could picture my mom standing in the kitchen, wearing her grey sweatpants with the hole in the right knee, staring at the ceiling, begging God for patience. "So then who puked in her room?"

"There were tons of people there, most of them drinking," I pointed out. "It could've been anyone."

"I can't imagine how someone would mistake Cadie's dresser for the bathroom."

"See, it couldn't have been me. I know exactly where the bathroom is."

"True." My mom's silence lingered, either giving me time to fess up or, more likely, lost in the latest episode of *Melrose Place*.

I answered a few logistical questions and hung up. Did I feel bad for Cadie, sitting home alone, scrubbing puke from her drawer? Nope. Cadie's problems were the furthest thing from my mind. Unlike her, I had a life, and it was just about to change for the better.

WE PULLED ONTO LAKELAND Drive looking for Kyle's address among the large houses, but it proved unnecessary. His house was the only one with every room lit up like a Christmas tree. Cars lined the street, forcing us to park a block away.

Alicia pulled out a bottle of vodka from underneath her seat. She chugged and handed the bottle to me. I did the same, suppressing the urge to gag as my stomach violently fought against consuming more liquor.

"How do I look?" Alicia asked, inspecting her face in the rearview mirror.

"Hot."

"My face looks blotchy."

"Stop."

"I wish I was beautiful like you," she grumbled. "You don't even appreciate it."

I ignored her and stepped out of the car. Alicia accused me of being beautiful as if I stole something from her; like if I didn't exist maybe God would've given her my bone structure, curves or lush hair. As if!

The nervous pit in my stomach expanded with each step as we trudged through the snow-stained sidewalk. As excited as I was to see Nick, I wasn't confident about how to act. Nick was eighteen—practically a man! Everything I knew about boys didn't apply. Should I approach him or play it cool? I needed some more liquor to quash this insecure voice inside my head.

Three boys I didn't know stood outside the front door smoking. I smiled and walked inside as if Kyle and I were best friends. My entire house could've fit in the three-floor entryway. I definitely wasn't in Kansas anymore.

We made our way to the kitchen where my friend Shannon, a junior, lay on the kitchen table while Kyle squeezed Jell-O shots onto her bare stomach.

"HI!" Shannon squealed as we entered. "You HAVE to have one of these shots. They, like, don't even taste like liquor but are super potent!"

Kyle reached over Shannon's body and handed me two shots. I gave one to Alicia as I appraised the room. Rachel and Julie, both juniors, sat at the kitchen table flirting with a couple of basketball players. Rarely friendly and always gossiping—I wasn't sure whether they hated me because I was poor, beautiful or a sophomore—they waved with fake smiles. Their attitude turned on a dime, but they organized a lot of the social events so I smiled and waved back.

"Time to pay the toll," Kyle said to me.

I lay down on the counter and pulled my shirt up just enough to reveal the faint hint of my lacy purple bra. Kyle squeezed out the shot and placed it over my belly button, causing instant goose bumps to form on my stomach. The red liquid jiggled, making my pasty white stomach appear translucent.

Kyle gazed mischievously into my eyes before bending down and taking the whole shot in his mouth. Although I couldn't see Alicia, I felt her anger crackling and seething like a fire behind me. But it wasn't my fault. I would've looked like a total prude if I said no.

Unfortunately, karma is a bitch because at the exact moment Kyle's lips sucked the shot off my stomach, I heard Nick's voice. I wasn't sure whether I looked like a fun girl or a complete slut. I jumped off the table...directly into Nick. I ran my hand through my dark hair, leaving only half of my face exposed (supermodels never showed their entire face when acting provocative).

"My turn?" Before I could respond Nick lifted me up like a ragdoll and laid me on the table. He pulled up my shirt, but instead of stopping at my bra he rolled it up to my neck and laughed.

An intense coldness covered my heart as he placed the shot between my breasts. Time slowed as he licked the rim of the Jell-O shot, pricking my heart with his tongue, before swallowing the entire shot.

I opened my eyes—I hadn't even realized I closed them—to see a satisfied smile on Nick's face. Is there any better high than seeing someone you've fanaticized about gaze at you with wanton lust? I think not.

"More shots!" Shannon yelled. She clumsily poured Fleishmann's vodka into plastic cups, getting more on the kitchen counter than in the cups. We all slammed another shot.

"Let's go upstairs," Nick said as he grabbed my hand.

I heard hoots and hollers well before we entered the back room. Nick opened the door to reveal half of the basketball team sprawled on the L-shaped couch and the floor. Three girls were sprinkled between.

It was only after we sat on the couch that I noticed the noises emitted from the television. Faint moans, whimpers and a few ecstasy-filled screams invaded my ear drums. I looked up to see a blonde woman bending over the end of a chair, being taken from behind by some oversized—*in every sense of the word*—man. Her tits, which looked more like inflatable balloons than breasts, bobbed up and down, alternatively smacking the chair and her face. *Gross.* Was this the crème della crème of the senior social scene?

I glanced at Nick. His eyes were glued to the screen, but he didn't look excited or embarrassed. In fact, he looked bored. Obviously! How dumb was I? He probably saw this video like a million times.

"Having fun?" I whispered. He turned and his face broke into a smile, melting me to the core.

"Are you?"

"I'm here with you. That's a start."

Our eyes locked and for one exciting moment I thought he was going to kiss me. Instead, he put his arm around me and pulled me close. He smelled of Hugo Boss and soap. I closed my eyes and committed the smell to memory. But closing my eyes made me keenly aware of my racing heart. *Clap-clap-clap-clap.* It sounded like a leg of the Triple Crown was taking place inside my chest. Thankfully, the woman's climatic screams on the television masked the caged animal inside my chest.

"Nice!" Blake Christianson called out as the guy came all over her tits. This started an outpouring of grunts from the rest of the basketball team. Nick sprang forward and let out his unique grunting noise. The team sounded like they were performing an ancient mating call.

The video thankfully ended. Nick tucked one finger inside my belt loop and directed me out the door and into an adjoining dark room.

I walked towards the window and gazed into the Orcher's snow-filled backyard. Nick came up behind me and rubbed my shoulders. It was a forgone conclusion that if I turned around we would kiss. It was an interesting paradox to suddenly hold so much power.

But just as I was mulling my options, Nick wrapped my hair in his fist and pulled my neck backwards, reasserting control over the situation. I half-expected him to pierce my flesh with his razor sharp teeth and start sucking my blood. (I recently watched *Interview with a* Vampire.) Instead, he licked my neck like a lapdog, working his way to my lips.

Just as I was embracing his kiss, Nick picked me up, cupping my butt, and threw me down onto the bed. A second later he was on top of me. His erection played a game of darts with the zipper of my jeans, rubbing and banging against me furiously. Despite the stabbing pain of his penis, the lushness of the bed felt like a cocoon, lulling me to sleep.

A moment (or several) later he flopped onto his back and pulled me on top in one swift motion. I felt dizzy and sat up. Nick took my momentary reprieve from kissing as an invitation: he whipped off my shirt, popped open my bra and squeezed my breasts as if he was a gynecologist checking for lumps. I looked down at him but he swayed across my field of vision. I pinched my leg, willing myself back into the moment but the fog continued to roll in. My grip on reality was fading. I felt like I was watching a plane take off, knowing there was nothing I could do to stop it.

Nick pushed my head down towards the opening of his jeans, which were conveniently unzipped. Keeping one hand tangled in my hair, he used his other hand to pull off his pants and boxers. His penis sprang up towards me at a ninety-degree angle, like a guest that showed up late to the party and wanted to make sure everyone noted its appearance.

"Put it in your mouth," he instructed, knowing I wouldn't object. I mean, he was *Nick Androse*. Who would say no?

I hadn't gone down on a guy before but I had a clear picture of what was required. I stared at it, willing my mouth to discover its God-given natural ability to give blow jobs. My biggest concern, in light of my queasy stomach, was that I might gag and throw up.

I bent over, grabbed his penis with my hand and inhaled. *Ugh*. It tasted sour, like I was sucking on a sweaty gym sock flavored popsicle. I'm not religious, but I starting praying for him to come, the spinning to subside, my stomach to settle and feeling to return to my jaw.

"Now," he grunted. I moved my head out of the way as goo sprayed out in large, thick clumps. Nick stretched out comatose on the bed with a small content smile on his lips. He looked adorable. I bent down to kiss him but he pushed my head away. "Whoa, what're you doing?"

"Kissing you," I replied, confused by his abrupt change in attitude.

"Think about where you mouth was," Nick sneered. "That's pretty fucking gross."

I covered my mouth with my hand and mumbled an apology.

Nick grabbed tissues from the bedside table and began cleaning the residue off his stomach and groin.

"That was fun," Nick grunted, pulling on his clothes. "We should hang out again sometime."

The word *sometime* hung in the air as Nick walked out of the room,   gracefully   extracting   himself   from   the   situation without…giving me anything! I wasn't sure what I wanted, but I knew I deserved something more.

I rested my head against the sweet relief of the pillow as numerous thoughts ran through my head. *Did Nick like me? Did I do a good job? What did he mean by "hang out sometime"?*

I suddenly feared that Nick viewed this as a one-off. I'd be shunned by his friends, labeled a slut. Everything I worked towards—building the illusion I was happy, beautiful and popular—would evaporate. All the parties, the boys chasing me and the jealous glares from girls would cease. I would become a stupid, poor nobody before I ever showed everyone I was someone to aspire to.

I felt achingly hollow, deliriously drunk and painfully alone. It was a new level of despair. I cuddled up against the pillow as tears seeped from my eyes. I would cry tonight, I vowed, but starting tomorrow, I would put on a brave face. One bad drunken sexual escapade would not define my high school experience: I was born to be beautiful and popular. Nick Androse be damned.

Chapter 5

Casey – September 21, 2012

"I'm sorry that happened to you," Joshua soothed as he rubbed my hand. It should have been awkward, but it felt nice—nice to be comforted for once. "What a jerk."

Ah, Nick Androse: the first asshole kind enough to show me what men were capable of taking—if you let them. Let me be clear. I despised Nick, but the way Joshua received the story underscored the fact that it was a lot more serious than I thought at the time. I was more concerned with what people would think if they knew I randomly gave out blow jobs than I was with the emotional consequences. It wasn't until working with my therapist that I understood how that encounter molded my expectations for men. I wished I had the maturity back then to peer deeper into why I was so upset. I knew something was wrong but I pinned it on the surface concern of my wavering popularity. Perhaps if I told someone I could've avoided a good number of one-night stands, emotionally havocked relationships and drug binges.

Or maybe I would've been messed up anyways. I wasn't exactly a square before Nick.

"It's not a big deal," I reassured Joshua. "It's similar to how people hate to hear celebrities complain about the paparazzi. No one cares. It's the same with me on a smaller scale. I was pretty and popular. If I had to put up with a few assholes, so be it."

"That's a terrible analogy," Joshua retorted. His mouth tugged downwards in a slight frown. "People are taking pictures of celebrities, not forcing them to engage in lewd sexual conduct."

"Is that another one of your attorney phrases?"

Joshua pulled off his glasses and peered at me. "You can tell yourself it was normal, but I'd call it date rape. At the very least it was statutory rape since he was eighteen and you were fifteen."

"You're the one who wanted to know about the darker side of popularity," I reminded him.

"This is just one more reason you should've hung out with the geeks: we would've never treated a girl like that."

His comment was laughable. "Assholes come in all shapes and sizes. Men feel entitled to a beautiful woman regardless of how they look."

"Maybe as adults," he conceded. "But as a teenager? I would've been way too intimidated to even talk to you, let alone..."

"You never know," I said gamely. "I might have found your nervousness cute."

It was a generous compliment since I knew I wouldn't have given him the time of day in high school. Hell, we met years ago and I've barely given him five minutes to impress me.

Joshua wasn't conventionally handsome. But upon closer inspection, the combination of his facial features made him a perfect candidate for the eccentric beauty featured in Calvin Klein campaigns. (I had a habit of deconstructing people's looks to determine what type of fashion campaign would fit best in the hope that one day I'd cast my own show.) He had straight teeth but a smile that slanted right, brown eyes set two millimeters too far apart, razor sharp cheekbones, unkempt hair that curled onto the rims of his black plastic glasses and stubble that darkened his complexion. (There was something about a flaw on an otherwise beautiful face that drew me to a man.)

I struggled to remember why I was so reticent in the past to get to know him. Was it his quiet demeanor, my bad taste in men or circumstantial barriers? I blamed it on the latter, specifically his friendship with Rachel. I wrongly assumed Joshua's voluntary association with her meant he was equally uptight and annoying. But his kindness and humor, both surprising traits of which I was oblivious to before tonight, proved my first impression wrong.

"You're lying," Joshua grinned. "You would've ignored me like the rest of them."

"Alright, fine. But it would've been my loss."

"Finally!" Joshua slapped the bar with the palm of his hand, giving me a front row view of his courtroom theatrics. "My mom assured me during high school when I couldn't get a date that those girls would eventually realize their mistake. I'll call her later tonight and let her know my day has come!"

He *really* was funny. Joshua would never be considered cool in the traditional sense, but his confidence came from knowing it was finally cool to be different. He wasn't trying to rewrite the past. Growing up was all about fitting in and being an adult was about standing out. Joshua was finally in his element.

"So no exciting prom night for you?" I asked.

"No,"—he scratched his chin comically as if trying to recall an important date—"I think for prom I was involved in a pretty heated *Grand Theft Auto* tournament."

"Never heard of it."

"Wow. And you were popular?" Joshua gasped. "It was only the coolest video game for Nintendo 64."

"You don't still play, do you?" I knew I jinxed things by admitting I found his quirkiness attractive. A swift wind came into the bar and transformed him from geek-chique to a lifetime member of the Dungeons & Dragons fan club.

"I've cut down to about an hour or two a day," he said with a straight face. "I'm kidding! I lost interest in college."

"Probably right around the time you starting getting laid."

"Are you sure you didn't have lunch with Rachel to get the goods on me?"

"Trust me; there's very little in the world that could get me to voluntarily have lunch with Rachel." An open bar and a threat from Haden was it.

Joshua smiled but refused to dignify my comment with a response. Thank God for his smile, otherwise I'd be quite lost as to whether he enjoyed my company. "You're right though, playing video games didn't seem so important once I got a girlfriend."

"Tell me about her. She had to be something special for you to break your vow of chastity."

"Is it considered a vow of chastity when it's forced upon you?"

"Fair point," I conceded.

"But yes, she was special."

I clapped excitedly. I loved hearing stories involving firsts: first kiss, first time having sex, first time getting fucked up. Unlike my deflowering story—five solid pumps from a sweaty Bobby Witten in my bed the summer before junior year and my virginity was kaput—they are usually filled with angst-ridden emotion and hilarity. "Spill. I want every detail."

"Every detail?"

"Don't worry. You can't shock me."

Joshua looked at the ceiling in quiet contemplation. "We'll see."

I, for one, was quite intrigued.

Chapter 6

Joshua – September 13, 2001

Classes resumed today but everyone walked around like zombies. As students, we desperately wanted to crawl back into the cocoon that held our previously naïve and luxuriously protected lives. We resolved to imitate normalcy by pretending our country wasn't under attack, we weren't terrified about the future, getting an A in Psychology still mattered and that scoring some liquor and weed for the weekend was a priority.

A few pretty girls passed the bench where I sat in the quad reading. At least the part of my brain that registered girls was still working. (Who was I kidding? My brain was monopolized by women for a good ten years.) Living in Minneapolis, however, didn't help. Women in every shape, size and color flaunted their beauty. The warm weather ensured an ample display of skin: toned calf muscles spilled out of skirts, soft mounds of cleavage peeked beneath tank tops and tight t-shirts exposed taut stomachs.

Get a grip, I scolded myself while subtly adjusting my shorts. Was I really so shallow that I could sit here fantasizing while countless people mourned the loss of their loved ones? Maybe it was a coping mechanism. It certainly was a lot easier thinking about hot girls than the fact that three thousand people just senselessly died.

A guy in ripped jeans and a black t-shirt with the words GOT WEED? printed in neon pink letters handed me a flyer advertising the Candlelight Vigil at Northrop Mall tonight. I shoved it in my backpack and walked to my dorm.

My roommate Kellan sat on the futon watching television. He rarely attended class. He was more interested in socializing, drinking and meeting girls—not that I was complaining. He invited me along everywhere and somehow managed to make me feel like he enjoyed my company as opposed to treating me like a charity case or a scientific object of study.

"There you are," Kellan greeted me. His face registered surprise each morning when I headed to class and he seemed equally perplexed when I returned home as to where I went all day.

I handed him the flyer. "We should go."

"Of course. Everyone's going." I had no idea who the "everyone" was. Our social life was a revolving door of new people. I had a hard time keeping track of names, but Kellan seemingly knew everyone on campus—particularly the hot girls. He flopped down on his bed. "I'm exhausted. I'm going to nap before we go."

It was a mystery to me as to why Kellan was always tired. He never did anything. But what did I know? Maybe being cool was exhausting.

IT WAS ONE OF THOSE perfect fall evenings where it was still warm enough to wear a t-shirt but the way the prickly breeze flirted with my neck hinted at the treacherous winter to come. It was too nice for such a somber event; like having a funeral on a blue sky, sunny day.

Kellan and I weeded through the crowd on Northrop Mall. Conversations about the attacks flushed in and out of my ears: a girl spoke of knowing someone who was in the second tower; another girl's father got stuck in traffic and missed his flight—on one of the planes that crashed; and finally two guys, discussing whether they would've jumped or waited to burn to death.

I closed my eyes, letting the guilt wash over me. No one depended on me. Yet here I was, unharmed, while those people in the towers with spouses and young children would never go home again. The unfairness sickened me.

Kellan joined a small group of students. Unlike most people, they weren't discussing the attacks. They bantered about the nuances of college life that two-days-ago seemed of utmost relevance: what to major in, what dorms had the best food, who was pledging what frat or sorority and which bars had a lenient ID policy. The normalcy melted on my tongue like the first bite of freshly baked chocolate-chip cookies.

Kellan made introductions. I smiled and pretended to commit everyone's name to memory while secretly knowing it had a five-second shelf-life.

But I was quickly proven wrong when Aubrie captured my attention. She wore an oversized sheer black tank-top, tight jeans and black laced up combat boots. As she waved, my eyes immediately homed in on her lacy purple bra, which clung to the ample curve of her breasts. Not wanting to stare, I forced myself to look at her face. I saw a friendly smile that contrasted her efforts to toughen her exterior: heavily lined eyes and bloodstained red lips. Her black hair was long with purple highlights.

In a moment of boldness, I sat down next to her. I no longer felt in control of my body: the evolutionary urges of mankind overpowered the cellular makeup of my normally insecure brain.

"So this sucks," I said, opening with what was probably the biggest understatement ever uttered in the history of humankind.

"What?"

"Everything, I guess," I said, struggling to sound coherent. "I don't know what to do. We didn't experience the attacks firsthand and so I don't really think we own the right to speak about it. But it also seems disrespectful to talk about anything else."

I ran my hand through my hair, convinced she thought I was a total idiot. And yet, she smiled at me. We read a study in my intro psych class that talked about how girls were programmed from a young age to smile in social settings, even when not happy. Naturally, I wondered whether her smile was a result of social programming or she found my rambling endearing.

"I don't know if there's a right or wrong thing," she said. I was instantly struck by the contrast between the sweetness in her voice and the severity of her appearance. "I think the point is to feel our feelings..."

I nodded along, resisting the urge to play devil's advocate. I'm pretty sure if I felt happy with the attacks she would change her viewpoint on "feeling my feelings." But I stayed silent. I'm not an expert on women, but I know they don't find it attractive when you point out flaws in their logic.

Unfortunately, my little self-diatribe ensured that I committed the only other unforgivable sin when talking to a beautiful woman: I stopped listening. Before I knew it, without any idea where the conversation left off, she asked: *What do you think?*

"I think you're right," I answered nonchalantly.

Aubrie cocked one eyebrow towards me skeptically, but was polite enough not to expose me as a fraud. Instead, she pulled a cigarette out of her purse and lit it, cupping her hand over the cigarette to prevent the wind from extinguishing the flame. Until tonight I never found smoking seductive. But every motion Aubrie made—her pouty lips tightening against the thin cigarette, the slight sucking noise while inhaling, the slow release of the smoke from her mouth—caused a barrage of erotic images to fly through my head. Like one of those children flip books, I saw myself taking Aubrie in every position: on top, from behind, standing up.

"So where are you from?" she asked.

I crossed my right leg over the left to hide any evidence of my thoughts. "Oconomowoc, Wisconsin."

We carried on for the next half-hour, trading biographical information interspersed with funny anecdotes, until the Vigil began. It was easy. This isn't to say I wasn't second-guessing my responses or scrutinizing her facial expressions for clues. But I felt comfortable enough to say a resounding *yes* when she asked me to grab coffee afterwards. Even if I was making a fool of myself, she was worth it.

"MY ROOMMATE IS OUT," Aubrie said as we walked into her dorm room after grabbing coffee. Immediately I was confronted with the smell of perfume and shampoo combined with the staleness of sleep, dirty clothes and cigarettes. It was shocking to realize that women could smell so sweet and yet nauseatingly familiar. "She sleeps at her boyfriend's place. I've met her, like, twice."

The room was narrow, but long; two matching closets sat on opposite sides, followed by two beds and then a set of built-in wooden desks. Clothes lay piled on the ground next to mounds of shoes and boxes of Ritz crackers, strawberry Pop Tarts and Captain Crunch. Posters of Janis Joplin, Bob Dylan and Joan Jett decorated Aubrie's wall. Aubrie pinned several black and white photos to the corkboard behind her desk. They were not the typical arms-around-each-other-smiles-pasted-on-faces pictures. The people never faced the camera and it was hard to tell if they knew they were being photographed.

"Did you take these?"

Aubrie winced. "Yes, but they're shit."

"I wouldn't know. I'm better at drawing pictures than taking them."

Aubrie reached behind a book on her shelf and pulled down a bottle of Smirnoff vodka. She handed me a generous pour in a coffee mug. "You're an artist?"

"Not really."

She sat on her desk chair, but leaned forward, giving me a liberal view of her breasts. They looked so big and luscious and...there.

A few moments passed in silence, for which I took ownership. Lulls in conversations gravitated towards me like models to athletes. Why didn't I tell her that I was an artist? How drawing was like breathing to me. How I'd major in art if my parents hadn't threatened to withhold tuition payments. But that would probably just make me sound pathetic and immature.

"Do you have any hobbies?" On second thought, maybe discussing my art would've been the better route.

She laughed gently and nodded her head towards the wall behind her. "Photography."

"Right." How did she manage to make fun of me and yet sound polite? "Anything else?"

Aubrie lowered herself next to me on the bed. She took a sip from my glass and slowly licked her lips. "I'm a fan of drinking and making new friends."

People usually decry *Why me?!?* when going through a major life crisis, not when something exciting happens. Yet those were the first words that came to mind: *Why me?* I wasn't ready. I mean, trust me, physically I WAS READY. But mentally I was like a man lost wandering in the woods. I assumed I would have a traditional romance where we would start by kissing and progressively move our way around the proverbial baseball field until approximately three months later, we both agreed it was time to go *all the way.*

But this? She would know very quickly that I never kissed a girl let alone had sex. A blinking neon billboard would flash overhead:

WE'VE GOT A GRADE-A VIRGIN HERE! Could my ego recover from such a beating?

Aubrie pressed her supple lips against mine. Four words galloped through my brain: *I can do this*. She slowly licked my bottom lip from side-to-side with her tongue, turning my mind to putty.

She eased me down against the bed and climbed on top. Perched on all fours above me, she looked at me like a ravenous animal before returning to my mouth. I pressed my hands against her butt, slowly massaging her closer. She offered tiny moans in response, which caused my ego to temporarily soar. A moment later she sat up, pulled her tank-top off and threw it to the side. Pictorially she was perfect: soft curves and a tiny waist.

"Should I take off my shirt too?" I wanted to murder the geeky, insecure, high-pitched voice that echoed off the walls. The moment stood painfully still, so much that I was sure students smoking outside in the courtyard asked each other: *What's she doing with this loser?*

"Sure," she whispered.

I moved my hands from her butt and cautiously explored her breasts. They were a combination of soft and heavy that no picture could capture. One of her breasts popped out of her bra and she laughed. "Take it off."

I reached around back, confident I could accomplish such a measly task. I ran my fingers under the entire length of her bra and yet I was unable to find anything resembling a hook, fastener or a clip.

"It's in the front," she breathed into my mouth between kisses. My hands raced around to the front and, *voila*, the full weight of her breasts released into my hands. I could've gazed at her all day, but just as I began taking mental snapshots, she flipped off the light.

I felt her hands around my waist as she pulled off my jeans and boxers in one swoop. (Did she attend a class on efficient clothing removal? I didn't see it offered in the student handbook.) I heard the soft rustle of fabric as she removed her remaining clothes.

"Hi," she said, lying down next to me. If she got shy right now nothing would happen. I certainly couldn't get us from point A to B without a little guidance. I mean, I *knew* the mechanics but I wasn't sure exactly how to navigate the terrain. "So, there's some condoms in the bottom desk drawer..."

I stood up too fast and jammed my big toe into the foot of the bed.

"Damn!" I grabbed my foot in my hand and started to rub it to relieve some of the pain while jumping around the room on my other foot.

"Are you okay?" she asked. I realized too late that jumping up and down naked and moaning in excruciating pain wasn't the most attractive way for a woman to view a man's body before sex.

I froze, my manhood on display in the soft moonlight, and pointed at the desk. "Condoms in here?"

Aubrie laughed. "Yes."

I found the *opened* box of condoms—a twenty pack with approximately fifteen left—and quickly slid one on. I kissed Aubrie to help the full excitement return—the toe incident understandably dampened my mood—before easing myself into her.

"Not there!" She bolted up, hitting her head against the closet wall.

"What?" My voice cracked, hitting a pitch that Mariah Carey would envy.

"Wrong place...let me help." She slowly guided me inside of her. The sensation was so utterly mind-draining that I was able to momentarily forget I tried to have anal sex on my first time out of the gates.

The next minute was filled with hazy pleasure. I became an object moving towards something bolder and bigger. An explosion followed, making my solo endeavors both juvenile and underwhelming.

Before tonight I balked at the adage that sex changes you. How can friction with another person cause such a dramatic change? But I felt like a new man. Gone was the wimpy, insecure boy afraid of disobeying his parents. In his place arrived a confident, smooth-talking playboy ready to take on the entire female population on campus.

Okay, okay, that was a *bit* of an exaggeration. But I did feel different. This beautiful girl had chosen to seduce me. This knowledge alone gave me the courage to ask the only question on my mind: "Again?"

LOVE CANNOT BE DESCRIBED accurately with words. It is so intense and raw that words become impotent. Pressed for words, the Alexandre Dumas quote, which first moved, then baffled and later angered me, came to mind: *True love always makes a man better, no matter what woman inspires it.*

Aubrie, both the idea of her and her essence, inspired me to finally accept myself. My confidence grew. I participated in class. I started running and lifting weights. I stopped questioning why Kellan wanted to hang out with me. I decided to minor in art and major in pre-law (otherwise known as the Great Compromise in my house). Aubrie's influence pulled forth the man I was always wanted to be but could never generate alone.

But as I grew, Aubrie remained an enigma. She was emotionally complex and yet elementary in her needs; beautiful but obsessed with her perceived flaws; smart but insecure; generous with her affections but selfish with her possessions; and craved information about me like a crack addict but safeguarded her secrets under lock and key. But she was my enigma, so I ignored my apprehensions.

As time passed, the riddle of Aubrie continued to grow as she became more mysterious and distant. After months of sleepovers in her dorm room, Aubrie stopped extending invitations. And when I asked her out? Well, she had to study for a test (I would distract her if we studied together); go to the gym (she didn't want me to see her sweat because she felt fat); and she had her period (harking back to Victorian time, she wasn't fit for visitors). You get the point—probably a lot faster than me.

It came to a head on a Friday night before Thanksgiving break. Winter came early and with a vengeance, dumping a foot of snow on the ground. Needless to say, I wasn't surprised when Aubrie declined my invitation to go to a house party.

"I'm not going out in this snow," she said with an exaggerated yawn. "But you should go. I would hate for you to miss out just because I'm lazy." I could hear in her voice the false enthusiasm my mother often exhibited during high school while encouraging me to attend the Friday night football game...alone.

Kellan glared at me as I hung up, but to his credit refrained from saying anything nasty.

A few hours later we were suitably drunk and left the house party for a frat party that one of Kellan's buddies pledged. The party was held in a damp basement that smelled of sweat, sex and beer. The music thumped off the walls. A small group of coeds danced, while others talked in small circles or groped one another in the corners. As I looked around the room, I felt a twinge of guilt for hanging out at a party geared towards fostering hook-ups.

But just as I was about to call it quits, a familiar figure caught my eye. Leaning against the wall, not more than ten feet away, was Aubrie. To her credit, she was not kissing the guy who had his arms locked around her waist. But the inch or so of real estate between their mouths suggested they were either about to kiss or taking a break.

I walked over and stood next to her. Aubrie's smile melted like an ice cream cone left out in the sun. She quickly recovered her bearings, however, and led me outside through a set of glass doors.

"What are you doing here?" Aubrie asked, swaying before me. I grabbed her waist to steady her before I realized I was holding her in the exact spot as that asshole inside. I let go and she stumbled backwards. I watched with little guilt; it was no longer my job care for her.

"Me?" I sputtered. "What about you?"

"You just don't get it, do you?" This was Aubrie's favorite phrase. She launched it at me like a grenade regarding anything from picking out the wrong candy at a movie to not understanding why she couldn't tolerate her parents, even for a night.

"I get that you're cheating on me."

"I didn't cheat!"

"Stop lying."

"I'm not lying. *I*"—Aubrie pounded her heart before punching me in the heart—"did not cheat on *you*."

"So what do you call ditching me to hang out with another guy?"

"I'm trying to be nice."

"Nice?" I repeated.

"I don't want to date you anymore." Aubrie stared at me with a hardness I didn't know she possessed. "Get it now?"

One would think the last few minutes, if not the last few weeks, would've prepared me for these words. Yet hearing her cold delivery crushed me. Aubrie looked similar to the girl I spent nights up memorizing and yet subtly altered. Her features became blurry as she slowly transitioned from my girlfriend into a liar and a cheater.

I walked into the snow-filled back yard. Aubrie called my name but I refused to turn around. As the pangs of loneliness and anger swirled through my bloodstream, I took comfort in the thought that she was feeling the same agonizing pain. After all, we loved each other. Those feelings don't go away overnight.

I laughed bitterly. I imagined Aubrie standing there feeling cold, drunk and alone. Hopefully she would feel like shit for a long, long time.

Chapter 7

Joshua – September 21, 2012

"Every story you tell ends up with me calling your girlfriend a bitch."

"I've dated a few women of that persuasion."

"Are all your stories so depressing? You're dragging the night down."

"Right," I mocked Casey. "Because hearing about how you were sexually assaulted at fifteen left me feeling warm and fuzzy."

Casey stopped mid-sip and laughed. "Did you just say warm and fuzzy while simultaneously hugging yourself?" A trickle of tequila ran down the side of her mouth. She wiped it off it with the back of her hand and continued to laugh. "Say it again!"

"No."

"Please!" She tilted her head and gave me a lascivious smile, intended to make me cower to her ridiculous demands. A few years ago that smile would've annoyed me—the sheer assumption she could get whatever she wanted simply because she was beautiful—but really I was just bitter that she never shone her gaze my way. Sure, she was beautiful, but I realized tonight it was her playful personality and outlandish commentary that kept men interested.

I rolled my eyes before wrapping my arms around my shoulders and moving side-to-side in a pitiful self-hug.

"Warm and fuzzy," I groaned. I was not below embarrassing myself to keep the glow in her eyes directed my way.

My performance earned more laughter and a round of applause. "So did you guys ever talk about the breakup?"

"Not really. I thought she cheated. She denied it," I shrugged. "Not that it mattered. She obviously didn't want to be with me."

"Ah," Casey sighed. "Wouldn't it be great to have the ability to travel back in time and share some wisdom with your younger self?"

"I doubt you'd listen. There are some things in life you just have to learn for yourself—even if everyone else tells you it's a mistake."

As I spoke the words, I hoped they didn't apply to tonight. At my request, Rachel set up this date, but not before warning me against getting involved with Casey. I'd listened to Rachel's complaints about Casey and witnessed her irresponsible and selfish behaviors, but I couldn't shed my attraction for her. I felt a fizzle of nervous energy whenever we were in the same room even though we rarely spoke. Tonight was about finding out whether there was something to substantiate my attraction. Regardless of how tonight ended, I would no longer have to wonder what if.

"So did you become one of those relationship-phobic man whores because of Aubrie?"

"Man whore is a bit harsh," I hedged. "But I was devastated. I didn't have another girlfriend until junior year."

"That's a long time to go without sex."

A slow grin spread across my face. "I didn't say anything about sex."

"So you admit you became a man whore!" She wagged her index finger at me. "I knew it!"

"Not even close," I retorted. "My biggest problem then, and now, is that I'm too much of a gentleman."

"That's not a bad thing. Gentlemen are a rare breed."

"I suppose. But sometimes it backfires. Before Amanda there were a few girls who put me in the friend zone because I took too long to make a move."

"Amanda being...?"

"My ex-girlfriend."

"Blonde hair? Petite?" Casey asked.

I nodded.

"I think I met her at Haden's New Year's Eve party a few years ago."

"Maybe."

Truthfully, I forgot Casey met Amanda but I didn't forget that Casey was at the party. She showed up looking beautiful in a long, silky black dress that amplified her curves. She held hands with a man that had movie star looks and the body of an Olympian. Together their beauty was blinding, like looking directly into the sun. *How obvious*, I thought. *She's so vain.*

Later that evening I walked in on them in the bathroom with a few lines of coke sitting on the sink. They stared at me with veiled disgust. I quickly excused myself, angry at them for not locking the door and at myself for regressing to that bumbling, insecure boy.

The night turned, however, when Casey's date ditched her and I was forced to give her a ride home. I was partly annoyed—playing taxi didn't figure into my plans with Amanda—but Casey looked too worn out and sad for it to last long. Besides, a part of me loved playing Casey's savior. I wanted to help her, make her smile, make her forget—if only for a moment's attention.

"Wasn't she with us last New Year's?" Casey asked.

It was the night the Grim Reaper appeared in our relationship. "At Mo's."

"Yes! But if I remember correctly, you spent the night in the corner, sober, while Haden babysat you."

"He didn't babysit me."

She held her hands up, palms forward. "It's okay if you don't like drinking. I love it, but not everyone has the same hobbies."

"Drinking is your hobby?" I laughed.

"Hobby? Extracurricular activity? It's nice to have an area of my life where I can consistently reach my goals."

"Haden and I had to stay sober because the girls decided to get drunk and relive their sorority days."

"Ugh, sororities," Casey lamented. She squished up her nose as if she smelled something nasty. "So you and Amanda dated awhile?"

I hated having this conversation. When you date someone after the age of twenty-five the question of marriage inevitably comes up. People ask it casually, as if inquiring about the weather instead of the most intimate part of your life. *We'll get married when we're ready,* I answered robotically. Turns out, I never felt ready. "About two-and-a-half years."

"I assume you don't want to talk about it."

"Not really."

"Well, at least not yet," Casey said and took another swig of the tequila. "It's a rule of mine to not talk about a breakup unless I have at least five shots to dull the pain."

"Depending on how often you talk about it that might make you an alcoholic."

"You know the old adage, divide the amount of time you dated in half and that's how long it will take you to get over it?"

"Okay," I said, playing along.

"Well, I divide the relationship into quarters. You should be able to spend the first quarter drinking as much as you want without judgment."

I burst out laughing at the ingenious reasons Casey created to foster her drinking "hobby." "What a convenient rule for you."

"Not just for me," she argued. "*Everyone* benefits."

"Well, I'm officially depressed."

"Why?"

"Using your logic, I still have another year of mourning."

"When did you guys break up?"

"She moved out at the start of summer." It was over long before that, but I was too much of a coward to end it.

"Hmm…" Casey used her index finger and drew numbers on a make-believe chalkboard, pretending to solve a math equation. "You're right. But on the upside, you have another four months of drinking without judgment."

"Then we need more drinks!" I signaled to the bartender.

"Well, there are two caveats to the rule."

"Please tell."

"First," she held up her index finger with a serious face, as if ready to lecture me on a world crisis like AIDS in Africa. "It depends on who was the dumper and dumpee. It's significantly less time, potentially none, if you dumped her because you already mentally prepared for the breakup. Second, men tend to need less recovery time than women."

"Whew!" I wiped my brow dramatically with the back of my hand. "The next year of my life just freed up since I broke up with her and I'm a man."

She gently rested her hand on my forearm. "In that case, I'm going to be honest with you. You're drinking way too much." The bartender set down two more shots and she grabbed them both with a conniving smile. "I better drink this for you."

"Alright, fine," I laughed. "You're right. I'm distraught. I need liquor."

She set the shot down in front of me. "But another one of my rules is to never drink on an empty stomach. We need to order food, stat."

"Does that mean you're ready to transition drinks into a dinner date?" I chided her. "Rachel said you were forward, but this? Wow. Maybe we should slow down."

"Shut up. You need to eat too. It's not like you have any extra weight to absorb the alcohol." She looked at my stomach as if I just returned from a concentration camp.

"Are you calling me scrawny?" I challenged. I considered myself more toned than skinny, but the painful reality was that people tended to view me as the latter.

"No, you're just weight challenged." Casey grabbed the menu stuck between the salt and pepper shakers on the bar. She opened it and held it up to our ears, shielding us from the other patrons. "Do you want to hear a secret?"

"Always."

"I'm going to order some greasy food. My official reasons are that we need to fatten you up *and* greasy food is the best way to avoid hangovers."

"You're the expert..."

"Naturally," she agreed. "The real reason is that I've been craving fried food, but"—she stuck out her lower lip and pouted—"as a woman, I'm regulated to salads on a first date. If questioned, I'll deny everything."

I winked at her. "You're secret's safe with me."

Casey turned to the bartender and ordered fries, sliders and cheese curds, a Milwaukee staple. "Anything else?"

I shook my head. "So has anyone ever been stupid enough to break your heart?"

"Of course!" she cried. "Who hasn't had their heart broken?"

"Give me names. These guys need a good ass kicking."

She arched her right eyebrow at me. "From you?"

"Seriously, tell me about it."

"About what?"

"The first time you got your heart broken," I said. "Fair is fair."

"So my rondevu with Nick doesn't count?"

"No way! Getting accosted while drunk should piss you off, not break your heart."

"And why exactly do you deserve this information?" Casey asked.

"The fact that I told you how I pranced around naked directly before losing my virginity means nothing?"

"That *was* embarrassing," she mused, strumming her bottom lip with her finger. "The least I can do is give you my own humiliation and neurosis on a silver platter."

Casey's face became animated as she got lost in her story. She put such enthusiasm into each sentence that it was hard to tell if she was confessing for the first or the millionth time. Either way, I felt lucky to enter another sliver of Casey's world.

Chapter 8

Casey – December 21, 2002

Professor Know-it-all held the pathetic honor of emceeing my two-bit graduation ceremony. He spoke with vigor, giving advice to the "new culinary geniuses" entering the marketplace. Ironically, that was not the phrase he used to describe me during one of our treasured tete-a-tetes. "Lack of ambition" and "utter disregard for this profession" took a front seat over the rhetoric that now flowed from his mouth like a sonnet.

Generously put, my life was at a crossroads. I could officially work as a pastry chef, but I didn't have any job offers. Even more troubling was that I developed a hatred of baking. The smell of sugar, flour and frosting made me gag faster than chugging a bottle of Wild Turkey. And the crème de resistance: Alicia kicked me out of her apartment last night. Effective January first, I was homeless. *Happy New Year to me!*

Despite living together the past two years, Alicia and I grew so dramatically apart that even the republicans and democrats had more in common than us. She studied constantly (due to a grave misstep by becoming premed) and no longer had time to get drunk, high or date. Thus, she crucified me for having fun.

Here's a random sampling of her hypocritical lectures: *Do you know what all that drinking is doing to your liver?* At twenty-one, I cared little. *You're frying your brain by smoking so much pot.* My pre-med friend was the same girl who crafted a bong out of a Diet Mountain Dew bottle so we could take hits before an assembly on the evils of drugs. *You need to stop hooking up with so many guys; otherwise no one will marry you.* That's right. Alicia became a born-again virgin. Apparently, you made a vow to God to remain pure until marriage and—*poof!!*—you became a virgin again. The biology behind it seemed a bit dubious, but *I* wasn't the one studying to be a doctor.

Oddly enough, Alicia failed to reference these grievances when she kicked me out.

"I found out that you and Kyle Orcher"—she paused to wipe the snot dripping from her nose with her sleeve—"hooked up at Rich Shelton's going away party."

I was about to deny Alicia's accusation when a blurry image of Kyle and I making out around the bonfire skirted into my memory. I remembered finding Kyle funnier than he was in high school. So when he kissed me, I thought: *Why not?* It never occurred to me to say no because Alicia liked him years ago.

Not quite understanding the stakes—the lack of rent alone should've made me fall to my knees and repent—I stood my ground. "We kissed. It was nothing."

She burst into tears. Like witnessing a breakdown on *The Real World*, it was hard to watch but even harder to turn away. "If you had spent two seconds paying attention to me, you would know I love him. I still keep our picture by my bed!"

In fact, I *had* noticed the picture and found it incredibly disturbing. Who keeps a picture of someone they barely knew from high school sitting on their bedside table? Even if "happily ever after" existed outside of Disney movies, it wouldn't include the exchanging of vows between a born-again virgin and an advertising associate with a penchant for nose candy.

Alicia gave me two weeks to pack my stuff. She hasn't spoken to me since.

As I sat alone at graduation, with no job prospect beyond bartending and homelessness on the horizon, it was easy to feel depressed.

AS I STROLLED ACROSS the stage, Dean Shefton handed me my diploma and Professor Know-it-all shook my hand without making eye contact. I walked down the steps and continued out of the auditorium.

"Casey!" I heard a familiar voice echo off the walls of the hallways. I turned around, surprised to see Cadie.

She wore an ill-fitting grey business suit, a pink button down shirt with far too much starch in it and no makeup. Why was her hair in a bun? She looked like a washed out librarian.

"What are you doing here?" Given our differences, I'm surprised Cadie didn't cut ties with me the moment she moved out. But Cadie was loyal to a fault. She called and visited with the commitment of a probation officer.

"I figured I'd come since Mom and Dad couldn't make it." Cadie shuffled her weight from one two-inch wedged heel to the other. "Are you upset they're not here?"

My parents were in Green Bay visiting my Aunt Beth and Uncle Nicolas. When I asked if they could reschedule because of my graduation, my mom reminded me they planned to come to my graduation last spring. (I failed my internship because my boss was a sexist asshole and wasn't allowed to graduate.) *We can't schedule our lives around yours. How were we to know you were actually going to graduate this time?* Touché, Mom, touché.

"Let's get a drink," I said, ignoring her question.

Five minutes later, we sat in the corner of a sparsely populated dive bar where I unleashed upon Cadie my latest string of problems.

"I have an idea," she said when, three vodkas later, I finished complaining. "I was at a dinner party last week with Chris' family and met a family friend who recently invested in a small hotel in

Key West. They updated it and added a swanky bar overlooking the beach, but they're having a hard time finding bartenders."

"Why? I'm sure there's like a million immigrants down there willing to work for almost nothing."

"He wants attractive bartenders." Cadie's brown eyes—identical in color but missing my long, thick eyelashes—bore down at me from across the table. "Beautiful women and men who will give the illusion that by staying there they are just as beautiful...or at least have the opportunity to bed someone beautiful."

She cringed while delivering this speech. Growing up we claimed opposite roles: Cadie was smart and I was beautiful. Duality of roles was not allowed. As a result, Cadie oversimplified the advantages of my looks and I repeatedly fulfilled my duties as the vapid beauty and family slacker.

I sighed. "So essentially I'd be doing the same thing I'm doing here?"

"Yes. But it would solve a few problems," Cadie pointed out. "You need money. Check. You'll be homeless in two weeks. Check. You need time to sort out your life. Check. Need I go on?"

Cadie used logic as a lethal weapon. "Can you?"

"Well, you do like to party. I hear Key West has quite the scene."

"You should've made that your first reason."

"Do you want me to have Chris call him?" Cadie asked. Chris was Cadie's boyfriend. She met him during her accounting internship two summers ago at Deloitte & Touche. In a fit of post-adolescence rebellion, they began secretly dating during her internship. For an accountant, he wasn't bad. Best of all, Cadie became a moderately fun human being around him.

"What do I have to lose?" I asked rhetorically, before realizing those words always foreshadowed the loss of anything even vaguely important. My only comfort was that my life was in shambles. I could jump on a plane tomorrow and not miss a single person or thing. Although, as I looked across the bar, I realized I might miss Cadie. Not enough to stay, but a little bit.

THE SUN SHONE BRIGHTLY through the grimy, yellow-tinged blinds, oppressing my fragile eyes. I congratulated myself for being only remotely hung-over. I cut myself off at three drinks last night—my first night in Key West—knowing I had to wake up at eight this morning for orientation.

I stretched my legs and quickly found the edge of my twin bed. The room was the size of a walk-in closet and the bed occupied most of the space. A narrow five-row dresser sat on the opposite wall.

The apartment was fit for squatters. It had a damp and musty smell that no amount of Febreeze could eradicate. Only a small trickle of water came out of the showerhead and I feared that the toilet would purge its contents if I deposited anything beyond piss. On the upside, I rented it by the week and it was close to work.

I appraised last night's damage in the smoke-stained bathroom mirror. My makeup was a bit smudged but overall I looked good. Alicia threatened that my partying would eventually wreak havoc on my looks, but I didn't care. I knew with age came wrinkles, sagging breasts and cellulite. But I was vigilant about drinking water, always wearing a bra and never eating late at night. Besides if you couldn't party while young, when would you?

After washing up, I put on my favorite jean shorts (cut and distressed by *moi*), flip-flops, a white tank-top and my pink string bikini—just in case we got out early.

As I walked onto the beach, I noticed a tall guy with broad shoulders, a narrow waist and floppy brown hair sitting in the sand near the bar.

"I'm Haden," he said with a delicious British accent and decidedly un-British like orthodontist enhanced smile when I approached.

"Casey," I replied, noting his bloodshot eyes as he removed his sunglasses. Ah, a kindred soul. I warmed to him instantly. "Rough night?"

"I'm still half way up the flagpole."

"A man after my own heart," I joked as a middle-aged balding man wearing khakis and a salmon colored polo shirt approached us with a clipboard and a grim face. He had a paunch and very skinny arms.

Frank, whose personality I could immediately tell was as exciting as watching a documentary on the mating habits of snails, was the general manager of food and beverage. He spent the next two hours going over the rules, menu, attire and work philosophy in his nasally, yet monotone voice.

"What time do the shifts start?" I asked when Frank finished.

"I'll need you both on nights. Starts at six. So"—he rubbed his belly in a circular motion reminiscent of a perverted Santa Claus—"any other questions?"

A wicked smile from Haden let me know I wouldn't be bored working the night shift. Sun, partying and a bit of work—the future looked promising.

BARTENDING IN A TROPICAL paradise was by far my easiest and most enjoyable job. It was like Christmas year-round down here. Customers were perpetually happy and tipped generously. All I had to do was make drinks and conversation—two skills I mastered in high school.

One evening in March, however, uprooted my cushy existence. I met John, the man that would calculatingly steal, use and dispose of my heart. He came alone and ordered a Dewar's on the rocks. As a veteran bartender, I prided myself on my ability to read my customers. John had a leave-me-the-fuck-alone sign pasted to his forehead. I complied without a second thought.

Okay, fine, I'll admit I found his brooding sexy. John had dark blonde shaggy hair and an ungroomed beard, reminding everyone he didn't care enough to own a comb or a razor. His dark, heavily-lidded eyes stared mournfully into his glass looking for answers.

On his third visit, I caved. I leaned forward and rested my forearms on the countertop in front of him. "Who are you running from?"

"Am I that obvious?" His voice was deep and gritty, like a bulldozer plowing into cement. "It's actually a thing, not a person."

"Are we playing twenty questions or are you going to tell me?"

"I'm writing a book." He shook his head in disgust. "But at this point it's just a collection of anecdotes that I don't even find amusing anymore."

"That's impressive. I could never write a book."

"Neither can I," John groaned. "I wasted the last two years in Boston, telling myself I couldn't write because there were too many distractions. But I've been here a week and have yet to write more than a few incoherent pages. So, at this point, I'm thinking the problem is me."

John picked up his empty glass, turned it over and shook the last remaining drops into his mouth. His despair seduced me; he was on the brink of genius or utter destruction.

"I'd offer to talk through your ideas, but I'm not much of a reader."

"I used to be full of ideas," he mumbled while vigorously rubbing his forehead. "I thought writer's block was for hacks. I was so smug."

"Have you published anything I might have read?"

"I thought you didn't read. So how's that possible?" John asked, cleverly exposing me as an idiot and himself as a good listener.

"I was talking about the books they assigned in school."

"Uh-huh," John laughed, causing his dark eyes to crinkle.

"I'll have you know I've read three books since moving here."

"What books might those be?" His cocksure grin warned me that this was an intellectual test, but I was too stubborn to backtrack.

"I can't remember the names."

"Hemingway or Faulkner, perhaps?"

"Nope," I said icily, suddenly feeling like I was the butt of the joke.

"I published a few short stories when I was in grad school," he continued. "But nothing since. I set a goal to write my first novel by thirty. Well,"—he glanced at his watch—"I don't think I'm going to make it."

"When do you turn thirty?"

"Next month."

I poured him another shot and offered up the only piece of advice I found useful. "I think you need to relax for a few days and have some fun. You're putting too much pressure on yourself and it's stifling your creativity."

"I spent the last couple of years partying on my parent's dime, hoping my ideas would magically find their way onto the page. Relaxing isn't the answer."

"But relaxing here is different," I argued. "Inspiration is everywhere."

John flicked his eyes towards me with the most gorgeous smile I'd ever seen. His whole face came to life underneath his disheveled beard. "When's your next day off?"

"Sunday." I had off one day per week, which was fine by me. Working, paying cheap rent and eating here for free, I already had quite the nest egg.

"Spend it with me," John said with the confidence of a man who never heard the word no.

"On two conditions."

"Women and their conditions."

"First, you need to shave." This was a selfish request. I hated kissing guys with facial hair. It felt like making out with sandpaper. "Second, I make the plans."

His mouth gaped open. "Shave? Are you serious?"

"It's your career, not mine." I started wiping down the counters, confident my I-don't-care attitude would seal the deal.

"I'll shave," John conceded as he threw down some money on the bar. He granted me one more glimpse of his killer smile. Clearly, he was born with too many teeth. "But you better be worth it."

I spent the rest of the night playing back my conversation with John. I had never really fallen for a guy like in the movies—spent sleepless nights thinking about him, wrote bad poetry, dreamed of our wedding—but maybe this time was different. Maybe I moved to Key West because I was destined to meet John.

I MOVED IN WITH JOHN after that first date. My infatuation with men usually lasted a few weeks, but John was a drug I became addicted to on my first hit and thereafter craved like a seasoned junkie. His touch sparked nerve endings and caused pleasurable shivers to course through my body in even the most innocent places. Simply being near him ignited a powerful, mind-numbing lust. It felt like our bodies were destined to be one. Love was the only explanation.

But rest assured, our love wasn't generated exclusively from great sex. When I talked, John listened. He procured my thoughts about books and politics, whereas no one else ever asked. Somewhere along the line it was decreed that because I was pretty and liked to party my opinion on anything beyond the choice of bar was worthless. But John saw a beautiful, fun *and* smart girl. I wanted to believe him, but like an anorexic who saw only fat, I drowned in intellectual comparisons with Cadie from an early age. *Beautiful gets boring,* he said one night. *I need more.* I relished the inference that I contained the illusive *more.*

A few months into our relationship, however, his constant "insights" into my life led to our first big fight.

"What are you wearing?" John asked, peering over the edge of the bar as I washed glasses.

"A t-shirt and shorts." I could wear what I wanted as long as the important parts were covered, but not *too* covered.

"Yes. But where did you get it? I've never seen anything like it."

I looked at my dark blue shirt, which was cropped with a thick band of black cotton just above my belly button. I hand painted different cities I wanted to visit on it in black. I sewed the shorts together with three different fabrics—plaid, beach print, solid dark blue—that each made up approximately one-third of the short.

I shrugged. "I made it."

John stared in disbelief. "To save money?"

I threw down the rag and turned to face him. Given his privileged upbringing, I'm sure nothing as desperate as making clothes crossed his mind. "It's a hobby. I *enjoy* it."

"How long have you been doing this?"

"A long time," I spat back, ready for a fight. Not all of us grew up with access to Daddy's credit card.

He rolled his eyes. "Could you be more specific?"

"My mom taught me to sew when I was like six. In high school I took some home-ec classes and learned how to manipulate different fabrics, work with a dress form and tailor clothes. I started copying designs from magazines and making them myself." It was the only way I could afford the latest styles, but I wasn't going to give John the satisfaction of knowing just how poor I grew up. He was already on a different planet than me as far as sophistication. "It's not really something I go around advertising."

"Maybe you should," he countered. "You have a *gift*."

John pronounced the word *gift* like he was the one bestowing it upon me. The man loved to hear himself talk. He drunkenly doled out bullshit advice to customers at the bar like he was Oprah, but his willingness to interfere in my life was gut-wrenching. He told me he loved me as I was, but clearly that wasn't the case if he wanted to fix me.

"Thanks for the advice," I replied.

John heaved a sigh and crossed his arms, annoyed that I blew off his praise. John wasn't one to let things die on someone else's terms. Along with being sexy, smart and a great drinking partner, he was stubborn, arrogant and always had to have the last word.

"You're always reading those fashion magazines. And now I find out you know how to make clothes. It seems pretty obvious you should go to fashion school." John waved his arms dismissively around the bar. "You don't want to tend bar for the rest of your life, do you?"

I glared at him. The hypocrisy! Regardless of whether bartending was below my intellect, at least I was working instead of living off my parents.

"Does this have to do with your parents visit next week? Do you want to show Mommy and Daddy that your girlfriend isn't some gold-digging whore?"

"Goddamn it!" John yelled, sending spit balls of whiskey towards me. "You know what your problem is? You push away anyone who wants to help. I'm not perfect. Believe it or not, had I not met you, I don't think I could've written this book. But I accepted your help. I have no fucking clue why you won't let me do the same for you."

Some might say it was pure stubbornness to let John walk away. But I think it was fear: that he was right about me; that he knew me better than I knew myself; and that he saw talent in me as a designer. Maybe I did want something more than bartending. Maybe my relationships were always short and toxic because I pushed people away before I became vulnerable. Maybe John really was trying to help because he cared about me, rather than fulfilling some selfish, snobbish ideal he had for a partner.

I turned to Haden—coworker, confidant, drinking buddy—wanting to ask him whether John's accusations rang true. Haden was honest, but he always laced it with a dash of his impeccable British humor which helped me laugh through the pain. But the prospect of two of the men I cared about most assaulting me with brutal honesty was too daunting of a task. Instead I walked over to Haden and hugged him.

"Do we hate John now?"

"No," I murmured, nuzzling my head between his sculpted shoulder and pulsing neck.

"What was the fight about?"

I stepped back and leaned against the margarita machines. The dull hum soothed both my head and my heart. "John thinks he knows everything. It never bothered me before but when he started criticizing my choices...well, it pissed me off."

"I hate when girls tell me what to do," Haden agreed.

"John thinks I have talent designing clothes. He says I'm wasting my time bartending and should go to fashion school."

Haden scrutinized my outfit. "He must really fancy you because you look like absolute shite to me." I slugged him in the gut, which was as solid as a brick wall, and ended up causing sharp pain to reverberate through my wrist. "You need to remember that John's rather posh. He doesn't think about how money might pose a problem in accomplishing these fancy dreams."

"Exactly," I said, shaking my head. "He can muck around for two years pretending to write a book while his parents bankroll his adventures. Meanwhile the rest of us are just trying to eat."

"Answer me this, do you want to design clothes? Is it your passion or just something you're cracking at?"

I loved making clothes. The entire process—sketching the design, finding the right fabric, sewing and tailoring—was cathartic. But was I any good? I had no clue. A bevy of girls emulated my style in high school but was that really evidence of talent? It could've been my looks or personality the girls coveted. I hated that John put an idea into my head that was probably never possible.

"It's a waste of time to think about because it's not a realistic possibility for someone like me."

"Remind me doll," Haden drawled. "What kind of person is that?"

"I'm twenty-one, poor and work at a bar. I have no formal training designing clothes and no means to go about getting it."

"That does sound rather bleak," Haden deadpanned, before pulling me close. "John cares about you. Run along and apologize before it's too late."

I opened my mouth to protest but I realized Haden was right: John was only trying to help. But tonight's argument exposed some major hurdles in our relationship, namely the financial and family divide we so studiously ignored. How was I supposed to explain to John that becoming a fashion designer was an unrealistic dream? I grew up in the old and poor section of a newly gentrified suburb. No one expected me to amount to anything.

I wasn't capable of putting my fears and insecurities on a platter when I knew it would cause him to leave. Pretty girls were a dime a dozen; he could easily find one without baggage. The less John knew, the better.

"I'm sorry," I whispered when I crawled next to him in bed. I wrapped my arm around his stomach and brushed the faint hairs that trailed down towards his boxers. I made rash promises to God—I would volunteer, drink less, even call my parents—if John forgave me. Seconds later John turned around and cupped my tear-stained face.

Nothing was ending tonight. I had earned John's love for at least another day. It was the only salvation I had ever known.

FROM THE OUTSIDE, OUR relationship proceeded seamlessly for the next six months. From the inside, however, a subtle shift took place after our first fight when I took the blame and he accepted it without question. The shift in the power dynamics was so minute that it was hard to tell whether it really existed or was in my head. I ached to ask him what he was thinking, but refrained. I would not be the *what-are-you-thinking* girl.

Our relationship felt like we constructed an end table from IKEA without following the directions: we were left with an extra screw and I had no idea where it went or how to stabilize it. I had a lingering feeling we missed a crucial step by not talking about the fight.

One night in October as we were closing up the bar, however, I broached the topic with Haden. "Do you think John and I have a healthy relationship?

Haden laughed uproariously. "You think I have any clue what a healthy relationship looks like?"

"Right. Forget I asked."

"Not sure what you see in him to be honest," Haden mused. "But you seem happy enough."

"What wrong with John?"

Haden stared at me, his sky blue eyes questioning whether I really wanted to hear the answer.

"He's a bit of a wanker," Haden finally said. "Moody as shite. Always has to be the center of attention. If his book isn't going well, he mopes all night."

I learned to work around John's moods, figuring out when to leave him alone and when to coddle him, but I had no idea anyone else noticed them.

"But you love him, so I'm chuffed," Haden continued. "Besides, he has good bits. Hilarious when he's drunk and forgets he's a big shot writer." Haden nudged me with his shoulder. "Why do you ask?"

"I'm a wreck," I said, exhausted by my self-inflicted drama. "Some days I'm certain he's going to leave me and other days I feel like we're really happy. There's just something about him I don't trust."

"You're thinking too much. I'm quite confident that if there isn't a good spat every few weeks, women make something up." I rolled my eyes. I forgot I was seeking advice from the world's least evolved man. "But drama always leads to a good shag."

"Sex isn't the problem."

Haden grinned winningly. I was immune to its effects but it made women whip off their clothes faster than drunken college girls celebrating Mardi Gras. "Case closed. Good sex equals a happy relationship."

This was the word of the Lord, according to Haden.

JOHN ASKED ME TO SPEND Christmas with his family and I gladly accepted. I felt vindicated: John invited me because he loved me. But even through the happiness of the moment, despair lurked in the background. Like Rochester's crazy-ass wife locked in the attic in *Jane Eyre* (I was forced to skim the Cliff Notes in high school), the feeling that this love was transitory haunted even the best moments.

As we boarded the plane for Boston, I was a ball of nerves. My insecurity rose exponentially over the last twelve hours because John finished the first draft of his book last night. I tackled him with kisses of congratulations, never once asking what would happen when he was done editing. Would he stay in Key West? Would we move to Boston?

Although we never talked about the future after our big fight, I couldn't erase the knowledge that John needed a girlfriend who was more than a bartender. I feared that John's accomplishment in finishing his book highlighted the fact that I spent the same amount of time bartending, sunbathing and drinking.

"You're my muse," he said after we had sex last night. My head lay on his chest and I could hear the rapid strum of his heart slowly subside. I nuzzled into the nook of his shoulder, safe in the knowledge he considered me indispensable.

Today, however, my feelings wavered between crippling insecurity and needing a modest amount of reassurance about the future. Was I still indispensable now that he was done writing? Perhaps I provided motivation or ignited a spark but John was far and away the most intelligent man I'd ever met. We both knew he didn't *need* me.

I reclined my seat and pulled on my facemask in an attempt to escape my thoughts. But the darkness left me feeling haunted. I either transformed into a paranoid, insecure girlfriend or John was hiding something from me. Both possibilities left me feeling sick.

I'VE NEVER BEEN ONE to damper a party, but it seemed a little excessive that there wasn't a moment from when we touched down in Boston, outside of sleeping, that John wasn't high on something. We drank all of Christmas Eve and Day, even showing up for mass stoned out of our minds. (The wafers tasted delicious!) Yesterday, we met up with his friends Dale and Jen to celebrate "Boxing Day." A latecomer brought some E, which my body normally takes to with a passion, but mixed in with the liquor and the weed, I felt sick, not sexy.

This afternoon, thankfully our last day, we partook in the endless mimosa special at brunch with his sister. Afterwards, I collapsed into bed only to have John wake me a couple hours later to head to the next party. My head spun faster than a tilt-a-whirl and my stomach felt emptier than a coke addicted model. I wanted to stay in bed for the next twenty-four hours.

I felt completely out of sync. Since when was I too tired to party? Why was I tracking John's drug and alcohol consumption like an undercover DEA agent? Why was I spending every waking moment obsessing about our future? I put the pillow over my head and took three deep breaths. This had to stop. John loved me because I was a fun, go-with-the-flow girl. With my last few ounces of energy, I vowed to channel her.

When we got to Dale's place, a condo in Back Bay, the party was already in full swing. We moved through the rooms, a stylish loft with dark wood floors, white furniture and plum accent walls, but quickly got separated during a bevy of introductions.

I found the makeshift bar, mixed a vodka and tonic, and went in search of John. I saw him through the floor-to-ceiling windows that led out onto the balcony. He was smoking weed with a group of people. *Surprise, surprise.*

"It's amazing, absolutely amazing," I heard him say in the slow drawl he adopted when high. I sat down on a bench that abutted the windows. John's back was to me, but his voice was as clear as a radio announcer. "I don't want to oversell it, but I think it's a bestseller."

"What's it about?"

I froze, my curiosity putting all my senses on high alert. John was as secretive as the Illuminati about his writing. *You'll read it when I'm done*, he assured whenever I asked for a sneak peek.

"These two broken, incredibly fucked up people meet on vacation and fall into this intense sexual relationship. The book is about the aftershocks when they move back home. That might even be the title: Aftershocks!" John ran his hand through his shaggy hair, giving the others a moment to *o-h-h* and *a-a-h* over his clever title. "The man grows from the experience, turns his life around, but the girl never moves on. She becomes obsessed with losing her one chance at love."

The vodka in my stomach recoiled and shot half-way up my throat. *Was he talking about me?*

"Sounds moving," a Twiggy-inspired girl swooned.

"Sounds a bit autobiographical," Dale hedged.

"Casey inspired the premise, but everything else was pure genius from up here." John tapped his head twice.

"Who's Casey?" Twiggy asked.

"The girl I was seeing down in Key West."

His words sucker punched me. The girl I *was* seeing. Was; as in over, done, finished. A heated debate raged in my head. Fact: John was drunk and stoned. Fact: John was anal-retentive about grammar.

How to reconcile? If he was sober I would trust the preciseness of his words. But drunk and high and sleep deprived? God only knew.

"Is it going to be hard to leave her?" Jen asked.

I stepped outside, peering directly into John's glassy eyes. "Well?" I demanded.

John squeezed my shoulders. "Of course it will be hard. But we both knew I was down there to write my book..."

The unsaid words swirled around us like cigarette smoke. My emotions—confusion, stupidity, anger, regret—paralyzed me. The dark recesses of my mind hinted at this separation for months, but I listened to my heart which wanted to believe that love conquered all.

John led me inside to a bathroom, where my hurricane of emotions boiled down to anger. I felt angry at myself for not having the guts to broach this topic earlier, angry at him for leading me on and angry we were breaking up in a cramped bathroom, while a soundtrack of laughter and joy seeped underneath the door.

"When were you going to tell me you were leaving?"

John shrugged. "I don't know. I haven't even booked a ticket yet."

"You don't know?"

"Of course not," John soothed, trying to hug me. "That's why I didn't say anything. Why ruin our last few weeks, you know?"

John grinned, as if his logic eviscerated his deceit.

"You used me!" I hissed, pushing him away from me. "You never cared about me."

John rolled his eyes. "Don't play the victim. You knew the score. I was there to write. I never expected to fall in love, but it happened."

"You talk about our relationship as if it's completely out of your control."

"That's funny coming from you," John shot back, sounding a lot more sober. "You go through life without a care. You have no plans, no goals, no aspirations. You take whatever comes your way. It makes it hard to believe you care much for me."

"I've opened up to you more than anyone," I argued, failing to understand how he could pin our demise on me. "You know I love you."

He laughed wickedly. "Your definition of opening up is on par with a sullen teenager being questioned by the cops. I know nothing about you, really. Your family, your friends, your life back in Wisconsin—you never talk about it." He shoved his hand over my mouth to stop me from interjecting. "Casey, you're many things, but open isn't one of them. You may think you love me, but you're too immature for love."

I shook my head, unwilling to concede his point. He came from the perfect life—supportive family, money, good schools, loyal friends—which made it impossible for me to share my history with him.

"You think you know everything, but you're just as fucked up as me. Oh, but wait, that's right, you end up better off for having met me. Isn't that how the story ends? When were you going to tell me you pilfered our life into a novel?"

"It's called creative license," John snarled.

"You're right; because if it was real life you'd have to tell everyone what an asshole you are."

He stood there, smug and unrepentant, unwilling to concede he used me even a bit. I pushed past him and flung open the door.

I left the party, fully expecting John to follow. He didn't. Why do men always chase women in the movies? Men *never* chase after me.

I hopped in a cab, swinging by John's parents' house to get my stuff, before going to the airport. I managed to switch my ticket to a flight that left at six the next morning.

Using my sweater as a pillow, I curled up against the plastic airport chair and cried. I had no idea who I was anymore. My relationship with John proved I was insecure, paranoid, weak and unable to entertain the simplest conversations about my past or future. A year ago I sat in a dark auditorium, depressed, homeless and directionless. Beyond a change of scenery, nothing had changed.

I was nothing more than the pretty girl guys used to pass the time. Despite my best efforts to love him, John confirmed my worst fear: I was easy to love and leave.

Chapter 9

Casey – September 21, 2012

"Did anything ever come of John's book?" This was always the first question when I talked about John.

"You haven't read *A Lifetime Affair* by John Adam Glanvilt?" I asked mockingly. "It's a classic."

"Hmm…I must have missed that one. Would you recommend it?"

"I'm not the best person to ask," I allowed, tracing the rim of my shot glass with my thumb. "Reading it was excruciating. John exposed the most intimate parts of our relationship for public consumption. He got the last word and there was nothing I could do. I felt powerless."

Joshua nodded. "I always thought it would be tough to date a singer or a comedian, knowing they used your relationship as material. You'd feel so exposed. It'd be hard to be yourself."

"But that's the thing; I had no idea he was writing about us. He was so secretive about his writing and I respected that. I was an idiot."

"You should take it as a compliment," Joshua suggested. I raised my eyebrows. This was a theory I hadn't heard before. "He found you intriguing enough to write a story about you. He made you timeless."

"He didn't exactly paint me in the best light," I pointed out. "John described me as a beautiful but troubled girl who used alcohol and drugs as a way to escape her past."

"There are worse descriptions."

"Like?"

He inched closer and whispered, "Rapist; murderer; child abuser. You know, my usual clients."

I giggled. "When you put it that way, I look like a role model."

"I'm just saying there are worse things in this world than being portrayed as a beautiful, free-spirited woman."

"True," I conceded. More than anything, John's book showed me how naïve and insecure I was back then. I was so convinced he was perfect that I never challenged him on anything. I was afraid that if he knew the real me he would leave. It disgusted me now. "I got the ultimate revenge anyways."

"Which is?"

"He never published another book. At least, I haven't found one under his name. By taking away his muse, I took away his ability to write."

"Your eyes just grew five sizes in excitement!"

"Maybe that's a bad thing," I said with an impish smile. "I should move on. You know, wish him well and all that."

Joshua laughed. "I don't think you mean one word."

"Guilty," I admitted.

"Did he come back to Key West?"

"Yeah, for a week or so. He came to the bar every night, but Haden, lovely, sweet Haden, wouldn't let him near me."

Haden became my bodyguard, best friend and roommate as a result of the breakup. It was the best gift John ever gave me.

Joshua's mouth gaped open. "You never talked?"

"I couldn't. When I saw him it felt like my heart was breaking all over again." I clutched my stomach at the memory. At the time, I felt so sick with anxiety and longing that I could only eat saltines and drink 7-Up. "I'm not sure if it was the eight-year age difference, my immaturity or the fact that nothing was ever expected of me growing up, but John was right when he said I wasn't ready for a relationship or a career."

I didn't normally reveal such intimate thoughts—and never on a first date—but with Joshua it felt natural. I felt like I could tell him anything and he would try to understand; like he could anticipate every harsh thought I'd ever had about myself and was ready to counter it. Patience was embedded in Joshua's mannerisms—the way he leaned forward as I talked, the concentration in his eyes—as if he understood life was hard and merely being heard sometimes made all the difference.

"I didn't know who I was at twenty-two," I continued. "I was too spontaneous, just looking to have fun, but I've learned that I'm really rather deliberate. I need time to digest an idea before making a decision—especially when it comes to relationships or my career."

"I'm a lot like you relationship-wise but too often with my career I've made decisions to please other people."

"For example...?"

"Law school," he said and then convulsed into laughter. "I used to dress up in a suit when I was younger and act out the court scene in *A Few Good Men*. My parents thought this was adorable and made me do it whenever we had people over. From that point on, if I expressed an interest in anything else, they would gasp and say, 'But you always wanted to be an attorney!'"

"Ah, so their threat to withhold tuition payments worked?"

"Well, well, well, Ms. Byrne." A huge smile spread across his face. "I'm impressed by your memory."

"You only told me the story a half-hour ago," I deadpanned.

"Yes, but it was a minor detail. I deal with attorneys who can't remember major details such as where the crime occurred or the weapon used."

"Maybe I missed my calling," I retorted, swatting him playfully.

"Please don't go to law school. It's the only good piece of advice I can give you."

"So how'd you end up there?"

He shrugged. "It was a compromise. They paid for my art minor as long as I promised to go to law school upon graduation."

"Wow. Do you resent their involvement?" I thought of my parents who begrudgingly paid a small portion of my tuition for pastry school at the local community college. After I graduated (never once baking a cake for profit), they refused to give me another cent. I funded my design career from some unlikely sources (and not always the healthiest), but I was proud I never once had to beg my parents to follow my dreams.

Joshua's parents, however, sounded like tiny dictators. He must have learned to hide the crazy, because no one living in that type of regime can be this calm and collected. I needed to find out his baggage stat.

"I think," he started, carefully choosing his words, "they had my best interests at heart. As an artist, they worried I would never have money to buy a house or have a family."

"I hope your parents know they have an angel for a son." I meant it too. It's not something I can say about myself.

He shook his head. "They got their wish. I'm an attorney, but they never anticipated I would become a public defender and make a pittance defending criminals."

"At least you have job security. I mean, crime isn't going anywhere."

"I'll use that argument next time they get on me about changing jobs."

"Does that happen often?"

Joshua barked a laugh. "Once a week—if I'm lucky? But it was worse when I was with Amanda. They were allies in their mission to see me married with children and a six-figure job."

"You're better off without her," I muttered. "Even I know it's a cardinal sin of relationships to take the side of your boyfriend's parents over his."

"Agreed." He dumped some cold cheese curds into his mouth. "Million other fish in the sea, right?"

"Not even close. You live in Milwaukee where most people paired off during their early twenties. But on the upside, you're a man. Men are desirable at any age. I, on the other hand"—I pouted my lip—"am damaged goods. More likely to be killed by a serial killer than married, right?"

"Yes, things do look rather dire. I'd give up on love and just start trying to get pregnant from one-night-stands." Joshua cupped his hand to his ear. "What's that noise I hear? Tick-tock, tick-tock. I think it's your biological clock."

"I know you're kidding, but I swear, Rachel has conveyed that very sentiment to me."

"Forget Rachel," he said. "She thinks marriage and kids are the be-all end-all to life. It's Rachel's goal to marry off all her single friends."

"And here we are," I mused. "Pawns in her master plan."

Joshua's cheeks flushed. "The night hasn't been completely terrible, right?"

I smiled but quickly changed the subject. When something was going as unexpectedly well as this, I found it best not to discuss it.

"When I met Haden, I never would've pictured him happily married, working a steady job, wanting kids."

"Why?"

"Honestly? He was too much of a party boy," I said, flashing back to the day I met Haden at orientation. His sky blue eyes were bloodshot and he sipped his coffee from his cup like it was the Holy Grail. When he admitted he was still halfway up the flagpole I fell in love with his British charm. I knew I found a kindred soul. "His essence has slowly chipped away so that I only get glimpses of the real Haden. And only when she's not around."

"You sound bitter."

"Well, I do have a reputation to uphold as the bitter, single woman."

"We need to get you some cats if you're planning on going all the way with this single woman cliché."

"And an endless supply of Chunky Monkey."

"That too," he laughed. "You know, we first met at Haden and Rachel's engagement party."

I vaguely remembered Joshua being there, but I was too preoccupied with the problems in my life, namely applying to fashion school and figuring out how to pay for it, to pay him much attention. It wasn't until the wedding that I had a clear memory of him.

"Don't worry," Joshua said, resting his hands atop mine. It sent a pleasurable and surprising shiver up my arms. "I wouldn't have remembered me either. I was so depressed at the time that I tried to become invisible."

"What was going on?"

"Everything. Law school, parents, girls," he explained. "Dealing with Rachel's wedding just made everything worse."

"Most congenial bride, right?" Rachel's numerous meltdowns rivaled that of a two-year-old being dragged from a candy store. I thought she was going to kill me on her wedding day when she saw I altered my dress by cutting a slit up the side. "I still think it's odd that she made you a bridesmaid."

Joshua laughed. "You know, she only did that because Haden asked you to be his best man. She didn't like you very much back then."

"She doesn't like me now!"

"She likes you," he assured me without much conviction.

"How about we get another drink and you tell me why I didn't meet this Joshua at the wedding. I'm starting to wonder whether we've wasted years barely speaking."

He stared into my eyes. "I was thinking the same thing."

Chapter 10

Joshua – August 22, 2006

Summer was officially over. Underclassmen swarmed the formerly desolate campus like gnats, displaying smug superiority in relation to both their youth and freedom. I leaned against a tree on Bascom Hill, right outside the law school, yearning to warn each student that walked past not get too comfortable. The life of sporadic lectures and barhopping would end. In four years' time, they too would have to find a meaningless job or join the ranks of overachievers and aimless wanderers in grad school.

After my first year of law school, I felt inspired. I rocked my finals and felt excited to start my internship. But after a summer spent babysitting corporate brats and mollifying equally arrogant attorneys, I was ready to throw in the towel. When I wasn't staring at the clock, I was usually horrified by some legally unethical idea the partners concocted. My only salvation came at night, when I sat on my porch and drew.

"Yoo-hoo!" Rachel plopped down next to me, pulled off my sunglasses and peeled open my right eye. She looked like a Disney princess with her bubbly smile, enormous blue eyes and lashes that fluttered like blades of grass in the wind.

"How can you be so upbeat at such a depressing time?" I grunted.

"It's beautiful outside and I'm wearing a fabulous dress that accents my highlights." Rachel had no middle point; when she was up, she acted like she was on ecstasy, and when she was down, she was an avalanche of emotions. It was best to catch her on a good day.

"I might quit," I said, a hollow threat.

Quitting law school would create an emotional wound the size of the Grand Canyon between my parents and me. My parents listened and commiserated when I complained about my unbearable internship with Foster & Foster, but when I told them I applied to Rhode Island School of Design, their sympathy evaporated faster than a snow storm in Florida. Quitting wasn't an option. Apparently, I would never forgive myself! In the ongoing battle of their happiness versus mine, they once again manipulated a victory. I revoked my application to RISD and now sat on Bascom Hill cursing my life.

"Stop it. This year will totally be so much fun!" Rachel sounded like a cheerleader straight out of the Valley instead of a rich girl from suburban Milwaukee. "Besides, I have some news that will brighten your day."

"Do tell."

"I'm engaged!" Rachel screamed at such a high pitch that the statute of Abe Lincoln perched atop the hill probably covered his ears. She held out her hand and revealed a rectangular shaped diamond that sparkled in the sunlight.

I bolted upright in a mixture of surprise, confusion and alarm. It's amazing how people can be so intelligent in one area and completely idiotic in another. Rachel was delusional if she saw this *fling* with Haden going anywhere beyond the bedroom, let alone down the aisle for a lifetime of marital bliss. "That was quick. I mean, you only met him in, what, May?"

She was also depressed, undernourished, sleep-deprived and virtually celibate. She wasn't exactly in the right place to make a sound decision about the long-term potential of a man. But what was her excuse now?

"I knew the second our eyes locked that I would marry him." She covered her hands over her heart like the virginal Sandra Dee in *Grease*. Meanwhile, I probably looked like a portrait of a steel worker during the Great Depression. My outlook was grim, but I didn't want to ruin her moment.

I hugged her. "Congratulations."

"I have something to ask you." Rachel pulled back, her big Barbie blue eyes never leaving mine. "Promise me you won't act all macho, okay?"

"I think you're safe," I laughed.

"Because titles don't really matter," she continued. "Weddings today are so modern."

"Uh-huh."

She hesitated. "You're one of my best friends and I can't imagine my wedding without you. Please, please, *please* say you'll be a bridesmaid."

Come again? Questions burst through my brain like fireworks. Are men allowed to be bridesmaids? Isn't there someone else she'd rather ask? Why me? "You know I'm not gay, right?"

Rachel rolled her eyes. "Of course!"

There was no way out. I was incapable of saying no to anyone important in my life. Most recently, my mother tearfully pleaded with me to continue with law school. (Show me a man that can say no to his crying mother and I'll show you a man with no soul. I had a very bitter soul but at least it's there.) So, of course, I said yes.

Rachel tackled me with hugs.

"But I'm not doing any of that girly wedding stuff." I gently untangled her limbs from my body. "I'll go with you to your cake appointment, but only because I love cake."

"I promise," Rachel vowed, as she rested her head on my shoulder. "This is going to be the best year of our lives."

TWO WEEKS PASSED AND the only thing that changed in my life was that I was knee deep in legal work. Despite my desire to sleep through the weekend, I was unhappily headed to Rachel's engagement party. When I tried to bail she pulled the first of many guilt trips, stating that as her bridesmaid I was required to attend. I told her if my attendance was required we needed to come up with another word for my role in the wedding. She told me to stop acting like a nineteenth century repressed English male.

I walked directly into my worst nightmare: large groups of a people huddled talking, but none of whom I recognized. Although I was a far cry from the insecure boy that left my parents' house for college, there's only so much progress a person can make in a lifetime, let alone five years. I still got that bubble of anxiety when I walked into a party alone. My heart seized and I started to perspire excessively. Tonight was no exception.

I fled to the bar and ordered a drink. Looking around at the women in pretty dresses and the men in suits didn't help my waning confidence. I felt like a complete misfit in my jeans, Woodstock t-shirt, sneakers and Brewers cap. When Rachel told me the party was being held at The Social, a casual bar/restaurant by the capital, I assumed the dress code would match the locale. I was wrong.

"Joshua!" Haden yelled as he pulled me in for a half-backslap, half-hug every man has mastered except me. A gorgeous brunette stood by his side sipping a drink. "How are you, mate? Thanks for coming."

"Congrats. I'm really excited for you guys."

"Yeah, it's brilliant," he beamed. "Kind of fast, but when you know, you know, right?" He passed out shots to his friend and me. "To love."

"You're turning into such a sap," the girl teased.

"Sad you missed your turn?"

"Inconsolable." Hands down she was the most beautiful woman I'd ever laid eyes on. Her face was sculpted like a fashion model with high cheekbones, a swan-like neck and juicy lips. Her olive skin and dark brown eyes matched the oak bar, while her raspberry colored strapless dress showed off chiseled collarbones, a flicker of sensuous cleavage and long toned legs.

"Joshua, this is Casey," Haden said, catching my admiring glance.

"Hi!" Casey flicked her eyes towards me and her face broke into a smile that would've caused Henry VIII to start a war. Her voice was energetic and captivating. I felt like the Elephant Man.

"She's my best mate and best man at the wedding."

"Seriously? I'm Rachel's bridesmaid." As soon as the words left my mouth, I knew I sounded like an idiot. "I told her we needed to give it another name."

"Too feminine?" Casey hedged as Haden was pulled into another conversation.

"Just a tad."

"I have to admit, I was a bit surprised when Haden asked me. But then again, he's not very conventional."

"He followed convention by marrying young," I pointed out.

"But it's not exactly conventional to propose after only three months."

"Seriously, what's the hurry? Why not just date?"

Casey's lips curled into a delicious smile. "You like her, don't you?"

"Who?"

"Rachel. Otherwise you wouldn't care so much."

My mouth gaped open. I had secret crushes on plenty of girls, but Rachel was never one of them. "Absolutely not," I fumed. "Never."

"Hmm...very defensive. Perhaps a touch too much?" Casey statements proved the rule that beauty was always in direct proportion to craziness. The more beautiful a woman, the more bullshit and drama you encountered.

"Don't worry, I won't tell Haden," Casey laughed and walked away.

I turned back to the bar. Frankly, I found both her and Haden annoying; they had a confident, come-what-may air that only beautiful people possessed.

Rachel squeezed my arm. "You came."

"You didn't give me any choice," I retorted.

"How have you been?" She titled her head to the side and frowned; an expression perfected by blissfully happy people when forced to address someone less fortunate.

"Don't worry about me." I pulled my glasses off and rubbed my eyes. "I won't let my bad mood ruin your and Haden's night."

I looked over at Haden who was in the midst of doing a round of shots with Casey and a few other people. They laughed uproariously, swallowing liquor like water. What was it like to live so carefree?

"I can't stand that girl," Rachel said, following my gaze. "I went to high school with her. She's completely unbearable."

"Who?"

Rachel glared at me like I suffered a brain injury. "The only girl in the room that looks like she stepped off the cover of a fashion magazine."

"She doesn't have anything on you."

Rachel's eyebrows furrowed. "Right. That's why it's my engagement party and they're spending every minute together. Any other person would've taken a step back once Haden and I got engaged. But not Casey."

"Have you talked to Haden about it?"

"He doesn't get it," Rachel muttered. "*We're friends*, he says, like I'm crazy for thinking there might be something going on. I mean, they lived together in Key West! And then she moves back here with him? That's weird."

"Do you really think something is going on?"

Rachel paused. "No. I mean, I wouldn't be marrying him if I thought he was cheating on me."

"Well that's your answer," I said, thankful for an easy out.

"Yeah, but the problem is they're best friends and I can't stand her. She pretended to not remember me when I saw her in Key West. We went to high school together! It wasn't that big!" Rachel spoke quickly as pent up rage spilled out of her mouth like lava. "She only talks to Haden. It's like I don't even exist. The other night Haden went to shower and instead of talking to me she picked up a magazine. A magazine! Can you believe that?"

Before I could answer, Rachel's dad appeared with a microphone and called both Rachel and Haden forward. As he spoke my eyes wandered to Casey. She leaned against the wall, whispering and laughing with the guy next to her. She stood not more than five feet away from Rachel's dad but blatantly ignored his speech. She was rude and yet undeniably gorgeous—exactly as Rachel had described. Casey suddenly looked directly at me, as if she could feel my eyes assessing her. She waved with a cocksure grin on her face. I turned away, feeling like a voyeur.

After his speech, I walked upstairs into the restaurant to find a bathroom. A moment of panic engulfed me mid-piss as I wondered whether I'd be asked to give a speech tonight. I had no idea what the protocol was for engagement parties, but it wasn't worth enduring Rachel's wrath. I zipped up and quickly ran out of the bathroom and directly into a woman walking past.

"Bad experience?" she quipped after I apologized.

"No, I'm—" I started to craft a plausible explanation but quickly quashed that line of thinking when I noticed how cute she was. She was short with a toned body, snub nose, tiny mouth and crazy curly brown hair. "Have you ever been to an engagement party before?"

"Yes."

"It's my first one. I'm an engagement party virgin," I babbled. "Anyways, do you have any idea whether members of the wedding party are supposed to give a speech?"

"Are you the best man?"

I started laughing. I already looked like an idiot, so there was no use hiding anything now. "No," I said with mock pride, "I'm a bridesmaid."

"You're lying."

"I wish I was."

She chewed on this information before shrugging. "Only in Madison, right? But I think you're safe. Speeches are usually just for the wedding."

"Thank God," I sighed. "I'm Joshua, by the way."

"Leah."

"Leah, can you do me a favor?"

She raised one eyebrow.

"I don't know anyone at this party. Any chance you'll come have a drink with me?"

She grinned, exposing a set of dimples. "I'm not legal. I won't be twenty-one for another month."

"No one downstairs is checking. Besides, I'm going to be a lawyer. If there's any trouble I'll be the first to argue in your defense." In probably the strangest and greatest five-minute exchange in my life, she told me to the lead the way.

We got a drink at the bar while Leah told me about majoring in international studies and creative writing. She was leaving next semester to study in Rome and thus "not really on the market for anything serious." I quickly assuaged her fears that I had any relationship designs. Between law review and classes, time was a precious commodity best not wasted on women.

"I would be a terrible boyfriend," I concluded.

"Bullshit." She shook her head but kept smiling. "If someone important came along, you would make time."

I considered her point. With Aubrie, I gave up sleep, skipped class and ditched my friends to hang out with her. Then again, maybe my feelings for Aubrie were an aberration, a teenage fantasy, because I hadn't felt that deeply for anyone since.

"My father gave me some advice: the person who cares less controls more," I said. "If you love someone, you'll do whatever necessary to be with them. If you don't care, you can dictate the terms of the relationship."

"Odd how it's usually the guy that cares less," she mused.

"That's a bit sexist. It's the person that has already had their heart broken that cares less. Too much scar tissue."

"Is that what you're doing? Staying busy so you don't get hurt?" Leah stood on her tip-toes and slowly inched her way towards my mouth. Her kiss worked as an IV, sending excitement racing through my veins. She pulled back, her brown eyes lit up with the promise of a night's debauchery. "Do you want to leave?"

Was the question rhetorical? I grabbed her hand and walked towards the stairway without saying goodbye. I made an appearance. That would have to be enough for Rachel. Besides, I was sick of compromising my desires for other people. I needed some fun too!

We walked outside into the velvety arms of the Indian summer. I turned down the alleyway and saw Casey smoking a joint with two other guys. A lazy smile perched on her lips as we walked past. "Leaving so soon?"

"Something came up," I replied.

Fifteen minutes later, as I fell into bed with Leah, Casey, Haden, Rachel and my parents were no longer on my radar. Nothing was. My mind was an abyss. I was engulfed in pleasure.

LEAH AND I CASUALLY slept together for the rest of the semester. No plans or pressure was involved. There were no fights, accusations or questions about who we saw or what we did with our free time. I wasn't expected to take her out for romantic dinners, and she wasn't required to listen to my tirades of resentment towards law school and my parents. We might have uncovered the first functional friends with benefits relationship.

"Do you think what we're doing is destructive?" I asked her one night in early December after having sex. "That it's messing with our relationship schema and we'll never be able to have a healthy relationship again?"

She shivered and snuggled into my chest. "You think too much."

"It just feels too easy; there has to be some major drawback. Otherwise everyone would do it and the institution of marriage would end."

"Not everyone can have meaningless sex," Leah answered. "You have to be either so exhausted that you have no desire to grow emotionally or so hurt that you're incapable of forming new emotions or attachments."

Having observed her mainly in four states—having sex, sleeping, joking around or drunk—I often forgot she was incredibly smart. But then she would belt out some profound statement well beyond her twenty-one years and I was left to wonder where all her emotional intelligence came from. It was at those rare times when I wondered whether Leah and I got the timing wrong and she was supposed to play a larger role in my life.

"Which one is it for you?"

"The second," she finally admitted as she rose to put on her clothes. "I think you're a combination of the first and the second, which makes you a uniquely tortured soul."

Leah left me to ponder my emotional ineptness. I was no longer a shy, insecure boy but neither was I a confident and ambitious college graduate. I was something in between and frankly, I didn't like this person. Too much of my life was dictated by other people. But I didn't know how to change my path without creating a level nine earthquake on the Richter scale.

My ambivalence scared me. Even at my worst moments, I always worked hard, confident something better would come. But now I was no longer sure my life would get better, that staying in law school was the right decision or that I had any influence over my future. My life felt predestined. Why exert any effort?

I turned over and tried to erase the hopeless thoughts that lingered in my head, but they wormed themselves into my dreams. Indeed, my life left little room for escape and the one avenue, Leah, was leaving in a month for Rome.

IT WAS A BRUTALLY COLD March day. Sleet swirled onto the pavement, thirty mile per hour winds slapped my face and the sun continued its boycott. People hurried past, wrapped up like presents in long coats, hats and scarfs. But as I strolled down Jefferson Street, on the way to meet my parents for lunch, I felt immune to the elements. I wanted to savor every ounce of joy before my parents systematically picked it apart, line by line, like an auditor.

Moments ago, I was offered a summer internship at the public defender's office in Milwaukee. Unlike the overwhelming dread I felt each morning walking into at Foster & Foster, watching the action at the public defender's office fueled adrenaline in my veins. Amidst the chaos—phones ringing, files stacked six-foot high on the floor, attorneys racing to court—I felt a sense of comfort. *I belong here,* I thought. I had the grades to audition for all the top firms, but I wanted in on the real action.

I saw my parents through the window, already seated at a table. My dad was dressed in a polo and khakis, while my mom wore a yellow sleeveless dress. They looked ready for a summer barbeque rather than a snowy day in March. My parents knew I was here for a job interview, but they didn't know it was for the public defender's office.

Let the blood bath begin.

I shook my dad's hand and hugged my mom. A huge smile spread across her face, while tears sprang from her weary eyes. No matter how much time I spent with my mother, it would never be enough. Despite several attempts, they could never have another child. Consequently, my mom clung to me as if I might suddenly disappear like her other miscarried babies.

"What's the big news?" my mom asked after we ordered.

I sipped my water. "I was offered a summer internship with the public defender's office."

Silence engulfed our table.

My father cleared his throat. "I thought you wanted to work at a firm in Milwaukee."

"I never said that." His eyes widened at my quickness to contradict him. It's not like I grew up requesting permission to speak, but it was an unspoken rule that he had the final say.

"I thought that's what we decided when things didn't work out at that firm in Madison," he argued.

"No. That's what *you* decided. I agreed to finish law school, but I want my job to have meaning." I wanted to tell him how the interview process for the public defender's office already loosened the chains of depression that held me down this past year. It provided a glimmer of hope that maybe I could be happy as a lawyer. But that would've required me to open up about my feelings—something unprecedented and likely futile to the outcome. "I worked on The Innocence Project this year and was really moved by the way I can use my degree to help people. People accused of crimes need better representation, but all the top students want to go to the big firms and make money. That doesn't interest me."

"Making money doesn't interest you?" Sarcasm oozed from my father's mouth like saliva from a rabid dog.

"Money is necessary," I acknowledged. "But as a single guy, I don't need much."

"You don't know the value of a dollar to decide what you can survive on. We've spoiled you."

I looked pointedly at my dad. "I'll work there this summer and if I like it, I'll move forward. If not, I'll figure something else out."

The server delivered our food, providing a nice distraction. My mom and I ate with gusto and talked about books, Rachel's wedding and, her favorite subject, how she wished I would visit more. My dad seethed silently.

As we stood in the mahogany lobby, ready to say our goodbyes, I felt weighted down by my father's disappointment.

"Just think about what we said today." My dad always talked in the plural, as if he and my mom were a team, even though she hadn't said a word. "I think paying your way since birth requires you to consider our opinion."

It always came down to money with my dad. It was the great equalizer. The subject of money hovered over our house and, like a ghost, stayed with our relationship long after I moved out.

After saying goodbye to my parents, I found a quiet bar for a celebratory drink. In one way, the lunch was a success. It was the first time I refused to give in to my parents' wishes. On the other hand, my heart felt bruised with guilt. But maybe that was my fault for giving them so much power, for allowing them to make my life a joint endeavor well into my twenties. I needed to accept our relationship—controlling, manipulative, guilt-laden—and move on. Taking this job was a first step towards establishing my independence. They might not be happy but they would learn to live with it.

MOTHER NATURE FORGOT it was April in Wisconsin. It was sunny and seventy degrees, by all accounts a perfect day to get married. I sat in my tuxedo on the bench outside the art museum and marveled at the beauty of the pale blue sky kissing the deep blue of Lake Michigan. I wished I could spend the day lying in the grass drawing the scene: runners, walkers and bikers of all ages and races juxtaposed against the lake and the sky.

Two people in the distance, however, cut through my thoughts like a thinly serrated blade piercing skin. The man stood behind the woman with his arms wrapped around her waist. She leaned into his embrace. Her long dress was slit up the side and flapped slightly in the light wind to reveal two toned legs. The intimacy was palpable.

Two people cuddling on the lakefront wasn't extraordinary, except that the two people here were Haden and Casey. As I watched them, it was hard to accept that they were just friends. Should I tell Rachel what I saw?

As if sensing my moral dilemma, Haden and Casey turned around and started walking directly towards me. Haden called my name, but I couldn't respond. It felt like I was being held under water, unable to breathe or speak, left only with the thought of wanting to escape.

"Everything good, mate?" Haden clasped his hand on my shoulder, maybe a little too roughly. Was I paranoid? "Have you taken sick?"

"I'm fine," I grunted. "Just getting some air."

"And I thought I was the one who had to be nervous," Haden snickered.

"Don't be so hard on him," Casey cooed. "I get the feeling he's not exactly enjoying being part of Rachel's show."

Casey linked her arm through Haden's and gave me what I'm sure she intended as a sympathetic smile. Wrapped up in Haden's arms, however, it came across as wicked and insincere.

"Neither am I," Haden complained. "I was happy running off to Vegas but she wanted the big wedding."

"As long as you're marrying the right girl, it doesn't really matter where you do it, right?" I asked, needing some reassurance and fast.

Haden smiled. "That's the easy part, mate."

A few moments later, as I climbed the stairs to Rachel room, I resolved to let go of whatever I saw outside. I had no proof. My gut told me something was off, but a gut feeling wasn't enough to ruin Rachel's day. Haden wanted to marry Rachel. Rachel loved Haden. If it was enough for them, then it had to be enough to calm my conscience.

DURING THE COCKTAIL hour guests were allowed to wander through the museum. I ventured down an empty hallway, inspecting the art and dreaming about how it would feel to have one of my pictures hung for public consumption. I felt a rush of serenity, like sleeping in your own bed after being away from home. I could almost smell the fresh paint, hear the scrape of the brush against the canvas and feel the energy of an idea being transformed into art.

I became mesmerized by one painting with extremely dark colors and frantic brush strokes that went against the grain of the canvas. The colors, however, bled together and became brighter towards the right edge—the proverbial light at the end of the tunnel. The subtext reminded me of my life this past year. The dark colors going against the grain represented the energy I put towards making everyone else happy, while the bright colors showed the possibility of happiness when I stood up for myself.

The painting made me realize that by constantly choosing sides, my parents or my own, I was destined to be miserable. No one was blameless for how my life stood today. As much as I dreamed of being an artist, my parents raised me with an ingrained understanding that a dependable career was necessary. I *chose* law school. But working as an attorney didn't mean I had to forego art. Quite the opposite, I needed to cultivate a space for it separate and apart from the toxic emotions my parents caused. Most of all, I needed to embrace the common ground that existed between us—live where the colors bled together, where it wasn't too cold or too hot.

It felt like minutes, but an hour passed when a guard told me dinner was starting. I ambled back into the reception and took my seat next to Sophie, Rachel's sister and maid-of-honor, at the head table.

Sophie was single-handedly the only reason I survived the bridal shower and the bachelorette party. (Yes, I went. Don't ask.) She looked exactly like Rachel—blonde hair, big blue eyes, petite—but that's where the similarities ended. Whereas Rachel was exuberant, hard-working and controlling, Sophie was chill and accepting. Her response to Rachel's constant wedding freak-out's: *She'll get over it.*

We'd been forced to spend quite a bit of time together the past twenty-four hours since Rachel introduced a no-date policy for the weekend's events. Rachel insisted she needed our full attention in case of an emergency and then proceeded to seek reassurance that she wasn't a bridezilla. (Her word, not mine.)

"I still can't feel my face," Sophie complained about the tedious two-hour group photo session that followed the ceremony. She pushed her face towards mine. "Seriously, slap me. It won't hurt."

"It could be the mass quantities of alcohol you drank."

"Good point."

Rachel sat down next to Sophie and took a long swig from her monogrammed champagne flute. "Can you believe her? She has no shame."

"Who?" Sophie asked.

Rachel gestured towards the hallway directly to the left of the head table. The lake was behind us and the guests sat in front, making us the only ones privileged enough to witness Casey and a man furiously making out against the blocked wall. His hand was halfway up her dress, giving me an excellent glimpse of the bare curve of her butt cheek.

"They're having fun," Sophie shrugged and turned away.

My eyes, admittedly, were a bit harder to pry away. His hands were buried inside her dress, while his face hungrily attacked her neck. *Lucky asshole.*

"It's rude," Rachel seethed. "It's bad enough that she brought a married man to my wedding, but now she's practically screwing him in the hallway."

Along with feeling jealous and admittedly turned on, relief coursed through my veins. Rude or not, Haden was not the object of Casey's desires.

"Look, they're gone," I pointed, hoping they either finished or found a private spot. "Besides how do you know he's married?"

"Haden told me."

"At least she got to bring a date," Sophie whispered to me.

Rachel stopped talking as Haden and a surprisingly coiffed Casey appeared. Casey wore the same lilac colored, strapless floor length gown as Sophie, but it had a slit up the right side of her leg that ended roughly two inches below her hip—convenient for last minute groping sessions.

Casey smiled smugly as if she knew we were talking about her. There were so many reasons to dislike her—she was cocky, mean to Rachel, morally flexible—but my body disobeyed my mind. Casey's presence was like a minefield, causing explosions wherever she went. I pried my eyes away from her, reminding myself that distance was the best defense.

AFTER DINNER, SOPHIE and I had the thankless task of moving the gifts into the limo.

"Let's have a drink before we go back in," Sophie said when we finished. I sat next to a mound of presents while Sophie expertly uncorked a bottle of champagne so that it fizzed out the window. "I'm so happy this wedding is over. Rachel's been unbearable since she got engaged."

"Yeah," I agreed. Sophie nestled her head onto my shoulder as we both sipped champagne. "She's always been intense, but I think the wedding brought out her worst."

I was finding it hard to focus. Sophie's dress billowed forward slightly, giving me a direct view of her soft, milky cleavage.

"Do you think Haden and Casey are sleeping together?"

"What?" I coughed up some champagne.

"Rachel asked me this morning."

What was the protocol here? Would the truth help? They were already married.

"Casey's the type of girl that craves attention and Haden likes to shower girls with attention," I hedged. "They flirt but I think they're just friends."

"I wish I would've given her your answer. You read people really well." Sophie faced me, her eyelashes fluttering over her blue eyes. "Are you sad we won't see each other now that the wedding is over?"

"It doesn't have to be the last time," I gambled.

Sophie and I clambered for each other, furiously kissing. Like a choreographed dance, her body instinctively reacted to my touch: she arched her back as I squeezed her butt, her nipples stiffened like two eraser tops when I rubbed them, and her legs parted like the Red Sea as my fingers traced the inside of her thighs. Four lonely months passed since Leah left for Rome. I greedily breathed in every inch of Sophie like a man given water in the desert. I wanted her. I needed her.

As she pressed a condom into my palm, her large grin mirrored mine. We kissed, both aware of where this was headed and eager to arrive at our destination.

TWENTY MINUTES LATER we made the walk of shame back into the reception where Rachel was dancing blindfolded with a bouquet of roses. When the music stopped, Rachel threw the bouquet behind her head. She was so turned around, however, that she ended up throwing the bouquet into the crowd instead of the single women gathered on the dance floor. A few seconds later, the crowd parted to reveal a smiling Casey holding the bouquet. Everyone clapped and hollered as Casey curtsied.

Casey and Rachel hugged, barely touching one another during the embrace. Their relationship was akin to the cold war between the U.S. and Russia. There would be no common ground. Ever.

"Get out there!" the boisterous woman next to me commanded. She grabbed my left hand as evidence. "You're not married."

"What?"

"They need all the single men. Go!" She pushed me forward, causing me to stumble onto the dance floor. I joined the circle of reluctant men, but inside I was freaking out. *Had I zipped up my fly? Did I have lipstick on my face? Stains on my pants?* It was too late to check.

"I'm too sexy" by Right Said Fred blared from the speakers. Haden danced blindfolded in the center of the circle, gyrating his hips comically to the beat. I reluctantly swayed from foot-to-foot, snapping my fingers without an ounce of rhythm. I was so consumed with embarrassment that I didn't notice the music had stopped. The garter landed on my right foot. I picked it up and inspected it like a dinosaur fossil.

"It's you and me, babe," Casey said and threw her arms around my neck. Everyone cleared the dance floor except for Haden, Rachel, Casey and me as "Time in a bottle" began to play. "Isn't it odd that the two people who didn't want to play ended up winning?"

She sounded more bored than bitter. My first impulse was to feel guilty, as if I orchestrated this dance, but that was quickly replaced with annoyance. I may not be as handsome as her usual dates, but there were other people, like Sophie, that I'd rather spend my time with too.

"Mmmm," I muttered.

"Are you having *any* fun? I heard Rachel didn't let you bring a date."

"You knew about that?"

"Haden tells me everything."

"Naturally."

"I told Rachel it was selfish to not let you and Sophie bring dates." She sighed dramatically giving me an opening if I wanted to comment. I didn't. "But that's how Rachel is; she's so insecure that the thought of being alone for a single second on her wedding day was too much to bear."

I felt torn. Her sympathy caught me off-guard. I wanted to defend Rachel but I agreed with Casey.

"It's fine," I said truthfully. Sophie turned out to be the best date possible. "At least you got to bring your boyfriend."

Casey laughed and her entire face lit up. She fluttered her long eyelashes while two rows of perfectly aligned white teeth smiled up at me.

"Oh, he's not my boyfriend."

I raised my eyebrows but she stayed silent, letting her coy smile fill in the gaps.

"You and Haden seem close," I ventured.

Casey briefly flicked her eyes towards Haden and Rachel. The smile fell from her face. "He's my best friend. I'm not sure what I'd do without him."

I twirled her around so that her back was to him. "Did you ever date?"

"Haden? Seriously?" Casey rested her head against my shoulder and started laughing. Her breath tickled and tantalized my neck.

"Well, you know what they say, women and men can't be friends without...sex getting in the way."

She convulsed into laughter again. I momentarily forgot that she was laughing *at me* and felt quite pleased for entertaining her. "You've watched *When Harry Met Sally* too many times. After living with Haden—sharing a bathroom, seeing his laundry list of girls parade through, his disgusting eating habits—trust me when I tell you there's absolutely no sexual attraction."

"Fair enough. And just so you know, I've only seen *When Harry Met Sally* twice; both times I was forced by a girlfriend."

"I almost believe you," she teased. "But based on your logic, you and Rachel must have a history."

"No-o-o," I said. "We're just friends."

"But you said—"

"That logic doesn't apply to Rachel," I interrupted.

"Because she's too frigid that the sex would be terrible?" she happily volunteered.

"No. There was never a spark. She's too..."

"High maintenance?"

"No."

"Emotionally unstable?"

"No."

"Calculating and controlling?"

"No!"

"Ugly?"

"Stop it!" Casey must suffer from multiple personality disorder. She changed from snobby to sweet to funny to bitchy in mere minutes. "She's like a sister. It's just how it is."

"Checkmate. You've proved my point," she bragged and kissed the tip of my nose. "Thanks for the dance, sailor."

Casey sauntered off the dance floor, leaving me utterly confused. It was the Casey effect: she dazzled men with her looks and witty banter, made them feel desired and left them wanting more. But it was only a game to her.

"How was the dance?" Sophie asked, coming up beside me.

"I wish it was with you." I pulled Sophie close and we started to dance, causing my thoughts of Casey to evaporate.

"I'm happy right now."

"Me too."

And that was the truth. Finally.

Chapter 11

Joshua – September 21, 2012

"Wow," Casey repeated, shifting her body away from me. It was the fourth time she said it since I stopped speaking. "I suppose I should thank you for your honesty. Although, if *I'm* being honest, it's kind of dickish to give me such a detailed account of why you thought I was a bitch."

"It wasn't all bad," I protested. "I also found you beautiful and charming."

"Not all bad?" Momentum built in her eyes as she crafted her case against me. "You thought I was vapid, selfish and morally bankrupt, willing to do anything to be the center of attention. Did I miss anything?"

"Please don't prove my first impression right and make this all about you," I grumbled, not exactly pleased with the resurgence of Casey's selfish side. "I told you that story so that you'd understand why you met a very different Joshua years ago. I was severely depressed; unhappy with every aspect of my life. You could've been Mother Theresa and I probably still would've thought you were a bitch. And you were so beautiful and happy. I envied the easiness with which you flowed through life."

Casey pressed her lips together, opened her mouth, and then closed it. "You're right." She squeezed my knee. "I'm a bit sensitive because, depressed or not, you're not the first guy to find my personality"—she grinned—"troubling; just the first guy to give details on a date."

"I was always good at standing out—just never in the right way."

"I can't believe you thought I was having an affair with Haden," she mused. She munched distractedly on a few fries, swallowing more ketchup than fries. "Even worse, you thought it was going on during the wedding!"

"It wasn't that crazy," I argued. "You guys were inseparable. Plus, Rachel said you moved back to Wisconsin because of Haden. I assumed you were in love with him."

"Oh. My. God." Casey sighed dramatically and rolled her eyes. "Never. I realized I needed to stop dreaming about design school and actually make it happen. Haden's decision to leave gave me a much needed push."

"Fair enough," I said. "But then you brought a married man as your date to the wedding! You weren't exactly a beacon of virtue."

"Ugh. Tom." She collapsed her head into her hands, before peering through her fingers with a pained look. "He was a mistake—a brief mistake, thankfully. But in typical Rachel fashion, she greatly exaggerated and misinterpreted the situation."

"So what was the real story?"

"First of all," she said with bravado, "he was separated. So I don't think I did anything wrong." Casey held my gaze, challenging me to argue otherwise. I refrained. She was right; married and separated were vastly different concepts. "Second, we dated for like a nanosecond."

"How long is a nanosecond?"

"A month, tops!" she exclaimed. "He asked me to meet his kids and I bolted."

"That's exactly what I'm talking about. You have this effect on men."

"What effect?"

"You're the type of girl men will uproot their entire life to make happy. Men want you at any cost." I shrugged. "At Rachel's wedding, I figured you were frustrated because for once you didn't get the guy."

"Interesting theory," she mused. "But I would've thought by now, a couple hours into the night, you would've realized the only effect I have on men is for them to completely fuck with me."

"I'm sure you've suffered your share of heartbreak, but I would place a hefty bet that you've rejected many more men than the other way around. The problem is you're used to men falling in love with you that on the rare occasion it doesn't happen, it's shocking."

"You assume that because I'm pretty I can snap my fingers and get whatever I want? It doesn't work that way," Casey argued, shaking her head. "Whatever lust and infatuation my looks stir in men, it quickly dissipates and I'm left on the same playing field as any other woman, trying to keep a man happy and interested with my personality."

I didn't believe her, but without going into specifics of how her entire package brought men to their knees (including me), I wasn't left with much to say. "So I was wrong about you and Haden?"

"That we were having sex?" she scoffed. "Yes, of course."

"Completely platonic?"

Casey narrowed her eyes at me.

I held my hands up, pleading innocence. "You don't have to tell me. I was just curious if my gut reaction was right. It's usually pretty accurate."

"I should've known this was a self-righteous quest," Casey groaned. "When Haden and I lived together, we hooked up two or three times, and only when insanely drunk. It wasn't a big deal and nothing's happened since."

It's funny how back at Haden and Rachel's wedding I would've felt vindicated, but now I wished I could erase the image of Casey and Haden drunkenly groping one another from my mind. Everything I used to find annoyingly scintillating about Casey became mind-numbingly attractive tonight. She sat before me—legs crossed, one arm on the bar, a strip of toned stomach visible above her jeans and cleavage peeking out from her vest—casually sexy and utterly alluring.

"Go ahead," Casey said. "Say, I told you so."

"Not necessary."

A beat of silence passed, wherein I would have paid handsomely for her thoughts. She looked like she was having fun, but with her dazzling smile and carefree laugh, Casey had the ability to make a funeral look entertaining. I could only hope she felt the same brewing attraction.

"I assume the public defender's office worked out since you're still there?" Casey asked.

"The term *worked out* is relative. It's been up and down," I explained, purposefully vague. My brief experience leaving the public defender's office for private practice was probably only interesting to attorneys in the midst of a career crisis. "I enjoy helping people who started out life on the wrong foot. Sometimes—not often enough—I feel like I've made a difference."

"But don't you miss drawing? Don't you crave it in your bones? If I go two days without designing I get antsy."

"I still draw," I assured her. "It's provided an escape from some of the hardest times in my life. I don't know anything else as cathartic."

"You should try pot," Casey quipped.

I barked out a nervous laugh. There was nothing like a beautiful woman to bring back old insecurities of not being cool enough.

"Ignore me," she said. "You were saying?"

"Drawing's more of a hobby now. I've finally let go of the dream of one day having my own gallery opening."

"That's sad. I mean, I don't know if you have any talent"—I laughed at the ease with which she fired off such brutally honest statements—"but don't you ever wonder how different things could've been?"

"Not really. I'm far too pragmatic to live an artist's life anyways."

"Huh," she mused. "That's been my hobby since turning thirty. Like, if there was a magic pill that would let me go back, what would I change? I've accepted that making mistakes in my twenties was inevitable, but what if I made different mistakes? In your case, what if you told your parents to fuck off and went to art school?"

Usually whenever someone raised the topic of my art, I immediately changed the subject. Which begged the question: why was I talking about it with Casey? Why did I share with her the arguments I had with my parents and the internal struggles I battled with going to law school? Maybe the liquor had opened up the flood gates. Maybe on some level I knew that Casey, as a fellow artist, would understand. Or maybe Casey's openness about her past made me more willing to share my own regrets.

"Okay. Let's play your game. Let's say I told my parents to screw off and went to art school." She nodded along, accepting the challenge. "My parents disown me, I'd be paying off my school loans until I retire and, worst of all, I still might not have enough talent to work as an artist."

Casey pumped her fist in triumph. "That's my point! No matter what decision you made it would've been full of harsh consequences. That's your twenties. Are you better off as a bored attorney with overbearing parents or a poor orphan that wakes up each day excited to draw? Only you can answer that."

"Honestly," I said, "it seems like a pointless game. One of those grass is always greener schemes."

"But it's not pointless. If you really love something it's never too late. I changed careers and went to design school at twenty-five with a bunch of teenagers. I felt ancient, but it was worth it."

"You were a bartender," I retorted. "I'd hardly call that a career." She snaked back from me. "Ouch."

"I meant that going to fashion school was a step up for you. But for me to leave the law for art school...well, it wouldn't make much sense, would it?"

"That's not for me to decide," she answered ominously, as if she was an oracle. "Besides, I didn't mean that you should quit your job. Everyone explores their passions differently. In your case, you could probably find some night classes—see whether you have talent or whether it's something you've built up to console yourself when you feel unhappy in your job."

Night classes. The solution was so obvious that it made me question whether it was fear of finding out I had no talent that kept me from pursuing art seriously.

"What do you like to draw?" Casey asked.

Her question caught me off-guard. No one ever cared enough to ask. My parents ignored my interest completely—they didn't want their questions to be interpreted as encouragement. And Amanda only ever asked when I would be done. Spending time with Casey tonight cemented my resolve that I wouldn't date someone unless they supported my passions.

"Abstract mainly. I like mixing colors to express an emotion or idea. Sometimes I muddle people or places into the background."

"I'd really like to see some of your work," Casey said. "I'm toying with the idea of a possible collaboration...if you're interested."

"What's that?"

"As part of my new collection I'm making some distressed t-shirts. I have the design idea up here"—she tapped her head—"but my sketching leaves something to be desired. I need an artist to translate my vision onto the prints. I've tried doing it myself, but it looks elementary."

I didn't know the first thing about designing clothes, nor had I ever tried to draw something from someone else's imagination. Most of my drawings came from an event or emotion that I'd been dwelling over for days. Was I capable of giving Casey what she wanted? I was afraid if I tried, she would end up thinking it was amateur hour.

"So maybe next week, you could come to my studio?"

"Uh," I hedged, panic burning a path from my stomach to my throat. "I can try, but don't expect much. I don't often show people my work. And by often, I mean pretty much never since my college."

"Don't worry. If I can use it great and if not, I'm sure it will still be fun." She squeezed my hand, assuaging my fears. Worst case scenario, I'd spend more time with Casey. Not exactly a bad proposition. "By the way, what happened with you and Sophie?"

"Not much," I said. "She moved to L.A. shortly after the wedding and joined some eastern medicine group. She's a massage therapist."

"Didn't want to do the long distance thing?"

"Uh, no. Besides, I'm not sure Rachel would've been cool with us dating."

"Shut up!" she exclaimed. "You guys never told her? But why would she care?"

"Too much cross over. Rachel likes everything in her life organized, including her relationships."

"Funny, she had no problem setting us up."

"It's because she doesn't like you," I said soberly. Truth be told, Rachel was adamantly against us hanging out. I begged her for this date, but I wasn't going to share that with Casey. "I'm kidding. It's probably because you're more Haden's friend. So if it doesn't work out, she won't be hearing about it from both ends."

"You're probably right," she mused. "Hey, imagine if Rachel would've found out you guys had sex in her limo. I would've paid money to see her flip out." We both laughed thinking about the scene Rachel would've created. "I didn't think you had it in you."

"Really? I think most guys would've jumped at the opportunity."

"True. But you seem like the type of guy who plays by the rules."

"I spent the better part of twenty-three years playing by my parents' rules," I said. "That spring was the beginning of the end. I finally took control of my own life."

"In what way?"

"Working at the public defender's office is the most obvious example. More recently, however, I broke up with Amanda even though both she and my parents wanted us to get married."

"Your parents liked her?"

"My parents *loved* her," I corrected. "She was like a daughter to them. I spent a good month making excuses about why she was never around before I finally told them we broke up."

"Did they get mad? Threaten to ground you?"

"You don't take anything seriously, do you?" I teased. Casey's sense of humor toed the line between bitchy and witty. Given that I couldn't stop smiling, I think it was safe to say which way I leaned.

"Imagining my parents telling me who I should date is on par with the President calling to advise me on my romantic life."

"It's hard for me to imagine my parents not trying to monopolize my life. But maybe that's changing." We had a big fight about the breakup where they pleaded with me to reconsider. I refused and they haven't called since. If I had any idea how easy it was to stop the onslaught of phone calls, I would've introduced them to my girlfriends years ago. "They don't appear very interested in my life right now."

"Do you care, or is it a relief?"

I shrugged. "They bought stock in the idea of Amanda and me—us getting married, having kids, the whole shebang. I was getting pressured on both ends and instead of caving, I got out. I was sick of people telling me what was best for me."

Casey tipped her shot glass towards me before taking a sip. "Take it from me, parental involvement never leads anywhere good."

"It's certainly easier to avoid meeting the parents when you date married men," I teased. Casey could handle a little gentle ribbing. She might even like it.

"I'm done dating married men," she declared. "Nothing good comes of that either."

"Was this a moral awakening? Or did you just get sick of being jerked around?"

Her eyes grew three sizes. "As a matter of fact, it could qualify as a moral awakening. I like that idea!"

"How does it qualify?"

"It boils down to karma," she explained. "On the off chance I get married, I'd like to believe that he would resist the temptation to cheat with some pretty young thing just because he can."

"Something tells me there's more to this story than simply waking up one day and adopting some Buddhist, first-grade principle of not doing onto others as you wouldn't want done to yourself."

She cupped her heart with both hands, as if trying to rediscover something that had betrayed her in the past. "With Ryan I was already in love with him by the time I found out he was married. I couldn't stay away."

"So what changed your mind?"

"I saw his crippled marriage firsthand and realized he wanted to save it more than he wanted me," Casey explained breezily, her tone betraying the significance of her words. "It was too much to go through ever again."

"Story time?"

"No way. You'd end up hating me."

"You're a different person now," I argued. "And if this relationship was the catalyst for change, it can't be all bad, right?"

The question hung in the air. I wasn't sure why I was pushing hard but my gut told me hearing this was important.

"Fine," she sighed. "But you have to do something for me first."

"What's that?"

She propped her elbow on the bar and rested her head in her hand. She peered up at me, her brown eyes glowing in the dim light. "Kiss me."

Blood raced to my face and my cock. I felt like I was sitting in a sauna. I discretely wiped my brow with my thumb, which thankfully was devoid of sweat. Now if only the other half of me would camouflage its excitement.

"Is that a no?" She gazed at me—beautiful, confident, alluring—probably wondering why she felt attracted to a man that couldn't even answer a simple question.

"It's a yes."

She leaned in, stopping about an inch from my face, and looked into my eyes. My pulse raced like a sumo wrestler climbing Mount Everest. The sweet smell of tequila on her breath tickled my lips. "I had to know what it would feel like to kiss you; just in case you change your mind about me after hearing this story."

"Not necessary," I whispered back.

I combed my hands through her long hair, caressing the silky, soft strands with my fingertips. I cupped her chin in my hands and kissed her mouth with a gentle persistence. She kissed me back, letting her tongue skirt the edges of my lips, tantalizing all my senses.

She pulled away but held my gaze like a hypnotist. "Now I know."

I laughed huskily, disappointed only at the brevity of the kiss. "Tell me anything you want. It won't change how I feel."

Chapter 12

Casey – October 18, 2007

The bar was slow for a Thursday night. Granted, it wasn't even half past ten, but only a few small groups lingered over cocktails at the tables abutting the windows. I suppressed a yawn, silently wishing I was at home tailoring the pants I ambitiously made today that ended up drooping three inches in the ass. Fashion school proved the old adage true: do what you love and you'll never work a day in your life. When I wasn't in class or the studio, I spent my time creating new designs. I was obsessed.

Instead, I was working, making a measly few bucks to pay my bills since financial aid barely covered the ungodly expensive tuition for the Art Institute.

A high-pitched, tittering giggle interrupted my thoughts. My stomach recoiled in response before my brain made the association. I turned around, hoping it was the onset of schizophrenia and I was hearing voices, and saw Rachel had in fact walked into the bar. Two men, smartly dressed in designer suits, flanked her on each side. Rachel was dressed in a black skirt suit, which hid her (admittedly enviable) curves and aged her ten years.

Rachel froze like a deer in headlights when she saw me behind the bar. She waved quickly, barely moving her hand, and inched towards the high-top tables. But one of the suits she was with slid onto a bar stool.

"I'm sure she could use some customers," he said, smiling at me.

Both men were in their mid-thirties, well-groomed and evidently had money to spare based on their designer duds. But the one that smiled at me was jaw-dropping gorgeous. He stood a smidge over six-foot with cropped brown hair, deep blue eyes and a strong, square jaw. His tie was loosened around his neck suggesting a playfulness that came about after office hours. As if he couldn't get any sexier, he took off his jacket and rolled the cuffs of his shirt up to his elbows, revealing toned forearms.

The other guy, however, looked like the first guy's disheveled older brother. He featured the same brown hair, blue-eyed combination, but he had a doughy face and a gut that spilled over his pants from too many late nights at the office.

"Rachel, who are your friends?"

Rachel looked like a Stepford wife with her frozen smile. "This is Patrick." She gestured towards the dumpy man on her left. "And this is Ryan."

Both men shook my hand, but Ryan's hand squeezed mine tighter than necessary, causing goosebumps to run up my arm. He was a strong, confident man who looked capable of handling anything with ease—including me. I wanted him to throw me up against the bar, strip off my clothes and paint my body with his tongue.

"They're partners at the Jesse Law Group," Rachel explained. "I interviewed there today for a job when I graduate."

Over the next thirty minutes Patrick talked to Rachel about the firm, while Ryan kept trying to pull me into the conversation.

"You're bored," Ryan asserted after I excused myself the third time. I wasn't bored but I did enjoy testing his interest.

"I don't want to interrupt. It sounds like serious business."

"You're being polite. Even I'm bored." He turned towards Rachel and Patrick. "Guys, let's cut the shop talk. Rachel looks close to passing out."

Rachel shook her head vehemently. "Talking to you guys and hearing about the firm has been fascinating."

Ryan smirked. "She's required by the laws of interviewing to enthuse about how much she loves us."

"We should call it a night," Patrick agreed. "I'm sure my wife's waiting up for me."

Patrick and Rachel stood up but Ryan remained seated. "I'm going to stay for another drink."

Rachel's alarm was palpable. Her eyes exploded to the size of two apples as they darted between Ryan and me. "Okay! But remember Casey, Ryan might be my future boss, so keep your stories G-rated."

She emitted a high pitched laugh and the men joined in. Only I understood, however, her panic. She was probably regretting every mean word she ever uttered about me.

I felt like jumping up on the bar and singing Justin Timberlake's "What Goes Around, Comes Around." The endless twists and turns of life never ceased to amaze me. Earlier this evening I was so bored I was picking lint off my skirt. Now the hours until bar time stretched before me like a luxurious sunset. I wanted to savor every minute with this delicious man. Even better, this very act struck the fear of God in Rachel. Sometimes life was too good.

"So what do you do when not bartending?" Ryan asked as I refreshed his drink.

I rested my forearms on the bar, giving him a glimpse of the cleavage hidden inside my black lacy bra. He leaned forward, closing the distance between our faces. His lips were wet and shiny. I wanted to taste him.

"I'm going to school to be a clothing designer."

"A creative soul." He grinned. Little crinkles appeared on the outside of his eyes when he smiled. Since when did I find age lines sexy? But on him, it added to his appeal. "What type of clothes do you design?"

"Women's wear. Urban, boho chic."

"No men's clothes?"

"Menswear is so boring. There's very little you can do. Take you for example." Without my asking, he stood up and slowly turned in a circle, as if posing at the end of a runway. "Outside of changing the colors or the pattern, there's nothing I can add to your suit."

"I agree. That's why I only wear suits while working."

"What do you wear when not working?"

"Is this a boxers or briefs type of question?" Ryan asked. He had a dimple on his left cheek that flexed in and out when he talked. I was mesmerized.

"Maybe."

"Jeans, t-shirt and a baseball cap."

"Wow," I deadpanned. "A middle-aged frat boy."

"Ahh!" He threw his hands in the air. "What's the right answer?"

"There is no right answer." I walked away to help another customer. "That goes for everything in life."

We talked for the next hour. Ryan was thirty-four, the youngest of six children in a strict Irish-Catholic family, golfed obsessively and worked constantly. The hefty paycheck was nice, he admitted with a wide grin, but the real reason he stayed was his ego. He was very, very good at his job.

"I was the youngest person to make partner in my firm at thirty. In the last four years I've generated more than half our income."

His ego alone normally would have soured my libido, but his cockiness only related to work. He was self-effacing and quick to criticize himself in other areas. The combination of wanting to slap that hand-in-the-cookie-jar smile off his face and then hug him when he showed his vulnerable side was intoxicating. I wondered whether his bedroom prowess would inch more towards cocky or unassuming. I hoped the former applied.

But just as I was debating whether we would head to his place or mine, he left. I was sure he wanted me, but if he could walk away, I certainly could do the same.

A few minutes later, I picked up his glass to wash it and found a hundred dollar bill—well in excess of his tab. Beneath the money, however, he left his business card. On the back he scrawled: *I need to see you again. Tomorrow night, 9 p.m. @ The Little Easy.*

I felt both vindicated and excited. He wanted me. I wanted him. Game on.

I STOOD IN FRONT OF the mirror the next night, clad in a lacy black thong and matching camisole. I threw on my favorite pair of jeans, black Mary Jane stilettos, a low-cut bronze jersey tank-top that accentuated my cleavage and looped a sheer black scarf around my neck. One-by-one I pulled the curlers out of my hair and let the loose waves fall across my chest. I kept the makeup minimal: mascara, dark eyeliner, a hint of blush and nude lip gloss. The ensemble wasn't over-the-top sexy, but it highlighted and teased in all the right places.

It's funny; I've entertained a few one-night-stands, but I've never set out on the first date with sex as my mission. But my craving for Ryan felt visceral. I spent the day fantasizing about the roughness of his hands, the taste of his lips, the persistence of his tongue and the soft curve of his ass as I pulled him deep inside me. This was happening tonight.

I walked inside The Little Easy, a house converted into a restaurant. The room was small and heavily populated, with a bar to the right and tiny, congested tables to the left. Ryan was sitting in the corner playing with his phone and drinking a glass of wine. Once again, he wore a button down shirt with a loose tie wrapped around his neck. His face was decorated with exhaustion, but that was quickly replaced with a smile when he saw me.

He stood up and enveloped me in a hug. My face locked into the crook of his neck like a puzzle piece. He was the perfect height.

"I thought about you all day," Ryan said as he poured me a glass of wine.

I tried, unsuccessfully, to hide my delight. "I hope you still got some work done."

Like hell I did.

"The day was a waste." He talked at a lightning pace as he detailed a two-hour conference call he had with opposing counsel and the court debating discovery violations. It was sexy to see him get so passionate over something so trivial.

"I need a vacation," he concluded.

"Any chance of that happening?"

"I have a conference in Vegas next month," he said. "At least I'll get out of the office for a few days."

"Maybe you'll even win a bit of money."

"Do you gamble?"

"Mainly with my life, but sometimes I play a little black jack," I joked. He laughed, displaying two rows of glistening white teeth. I half expected a dinging star to appear at the corner of his mouth.

The server set down our food, but we ignored her and continued to grin at each other like two overeager and under-experienced teenagers.

"It's good to gamble with your life," he said, barreling his eyes into mine. "Sometimes you need to take a risk to remember what it feels like to live."

"No reward without the risk, right?"

Ryan leaned over, traced his hands down the nape of my neck and kissed me. The world around me evaporated and life constituted only us: lips parted, tongues explored, legs flirted and hands massaged. Every nerve in my body begged for direct stimulation. I forgot we were in a restaurant until the server nosily set down our check.

A short drive later, Ryan's hand was on the small of my back as he guided me towards my apartment building. Once inside the stairwell, he wrapped my hair into a ponytail and held it in his hand while he kissed down the back of my neck. I was panting with excitement by the time I fumbled the key into my lock.

Ryan emitted a disgruntled sigh like a kid finding coal in his stocking. "I have to go."

"Seriously?" *Was he fucking kidding me? Did he want me to beg?*

"You're mad."

"Nope," I said. "A little confused, but it doesn't matter."

"It's..."—he rubbed both hands on his temples as if trying to stave off a migraine—"complicated. Too complicated to involve you."

I laughed. Everyone said women were queens of manipulation, but men held a monopoly. Men lived in the grey, viewing life as simple or complicated depending on how it suited them. "Not really. You either want me or you don't."

"I want you." Ryan pressed me up against the door, drawing open my mouth and kissing me. We pawed at each other, tasting, smelling and licking. But just as suddenly, he pulled back. "I'll be in touch."

I watched him disappear down the stairs before going inside. I was seething. I walked into the bedroom, peeled off my clothes and threw on shorts, a sports bra and an old t-shirt. A midnight run was the perfect antidote to burn off my sexual frustration.

Lo and behold, I opened the door to the hallway and found Ryan standing there. Neither of us said a word. Instead he picked me up and carried me into the bedroom. He threw me onto the bed like a pillow and tore off my clothes. I returned the favor, unbuttoning his shirt and kicking off his pants. He held my hands above my head and plowed into me, grabbing my ass for leverage.

Was the sex extra passionate because I was pissed off at his attempt to mind fuck me? Whatever the reason, I surrendered. I inhaled his breath as if it was my life force. At one point the pleasure became so exquisite that I levitated above and watched us move in slow motion. When it was over, I felt numb from the waist down and wasn't altogether sure I would ever walk again.

"We're pretty good at that," he commented as he got dressed.

"You've had practice."

"I'd like some more."

"Now?"

Ryan crawled on top of me, leaving an inch or so between our mouths. We stared into each other's eyes but did not kiss. "Soon."

I lay still for an hour after he left, mentally retracing his touch, knowing he wasn't coming back that night but hoping for an encore soon.

I TRIED TO CONVINCE myself that it didn't matter whether Ryan called, but each day of silence became more excruciating. By Wednesday I was in a foul mood, stuck in a vicious circle of sleeplessness, sexual frustration and anger. I came home that night, ready to write Ryan off completely. But as I turned down the hallway towards my apartment, I saw a large box wrapped in scarlet paper propped up against my door.

Inside the box a card was taped to the tissue paper with a ticket inside. *Casey, There's a benefit for ArtWorks this Friday at the Museum. I'll look for you in this dress. Ryan*

I pulled back the tissue paper and drew out a black silk chiffon halter dress with two straps that crisscrossed across the collarbone. It was tight through the bust and flowed freely from my hips to my knees.

Five days without a word and now he demands (he didn't even ask!) to see me Friday. What if I was busy? I wasn't the type of girl to be at someone's beck and call—regardless of how gorgeous and good in bed.

My pissed off inner-self, however, lost out to the romantic girl I thought I quashed long ago. Ryan sent an expensive gift, two days in advance, with a ticket to meet him at a charity event. Put like that, it sounded like he was trying to sweep me off my feet rather than being lazy and purposefully unavailable.

Honoring my inner Cinderella, I made a promise: if the dress fit, I would go.

"Damn him," I muttered. It fit perfectly. It was even tailored properly for my height to hit right above my knee. That *never* happens! I stood in front of the mirror, perhaps waiting for it to talk to me. But I didn't need another fairy tale reference to aid my decision; there was nothing that would keep me home on Friday night.

INSIDE THE MUSEUM, a distinguished crowd of Milwaukee's elite talked, laughed and schmoozed with ease. Ryan stood out from the pack, oozing sex appeal in a pair of charcoal pants, grey button down shirt with narrow purple lines and his trademark loosened tie. For a moment, I hated him. Everything came too easy: his looks, money, success, style and now, even me. But along with hate, came an intense bout of lust and possibly...love? I wanted him to be mine. I wanted him to love me, to need me, to claim me.

"It's official," he said, sliding up next to me. His voice sounded like liquefied sex and my insides quivered. "I've conducted extensive research, and hands down, you're the most beautiful woman here."

"I hope the research wasn't too extensive."

"Do you like the dress?"

"Yes. I'd ask you the same question but I assume you approve."

"It looks better on you than on the hanger," he teased.

"How did you know my size?"

"I drew a picture for the sales lady."

I laughed. "You have a great memory."

He covertly traced the inseam of my left breast down to my hip with his thumb. His long eyelashes drifted closed. "Let's go."

I shook my head. "I just got here."

"Was there someone else you were meeting tonight?"

"No."

"Good. I don't like to share."

Maybe I manufactured it in my head, but I swore people turned to look at us as we strutted out of the room. We were *that* couple. I could taste the envy. It was better than sticking around for dinner.

"SOMEONE'S HUNGRY," Ryan said. His head rested against my stomach, which sounded like a thunderstorm inside. "What can I make you?"

"You cook?"

"There's very little I don't do." He was beyond conceited. But it was rather difficult to engender anything but love towards the man that gave me three mind-numbing orgasms only moments ago.

He walked out of the room, parading his naked, toned body. He returned a minute later, throwing on his clothes. "You have no food!"

He was out the door before I could answer. I burrowed my head in the sheets. It smelled like desire. I was never the girl that borrowed a t-shirt to sleep in and conveniently forgot to return it, but I didn't want to ever wash these sheets. Maybe I wanted to hold onto something because he kept disappearing. There was no guarantee I would see him again. It was both terrifying and freeing. All I could do was enjoy what I was given.

Thankfully, Ryan returned a half-hour later with three bags. I sat on the counter, watching him unpack the groceries. Another surprising emotion popped up as I realized I loved that he wanted to take care of me.

"Do you need any help?"

"From you?" he smirked. "Just sit pretty and admire a genius at work." Ryan cracked a few eggs in one pan and poured pancake batter into another. "You have nice cooking equipment for someone lacking food."

"I studied to be a pastry chef in another life."

He raised his eyebrows. "Byrne, you are one surprise after another. Tell me about it."

I told him about my torturous internships, how my professors hated me and my parents barely believed in me. But I left out the heavier family baggage about their decision to skip my graduation, their refusal to give me a single dollar since and how they reacted with skepticism when I told them I was going to design school. It was too early on to share that dysfunction.

"Does fashion school feel different?"

"Definitely. I've loved fashion and making clothes ever since I was a little girl. It hit me one day that I could make a career out of this." I thought it best to leave out any mention of John. "Going to fashion school was the natural step."

Ryan carried our plates into the living room.

"This is delicious," I said, devouring my eggs. He laughed and covered my mouth with a syrupy kiss.

"You're brave. Most people have no idea what they want to do, but they go to college and get a job just so they don't fall behind." He took a large bite of his triple stacked pancakes. "I think it's great that you tried something, hated it, and then took time off to figure out what you wanted."

"I was having fun. It wasn't a well-concocted plan to figure out my life's passion."

"That's where you're wrong. You understand the need to enjoy life. It's the rest of us in this rat race that are insane." Ryan's voice was tinged with regret. "I want the ability to let go of all my obligations and just say fuck it and have fun."

"I think you're romanticizing the idea of working shit jobs, living in bug-infested apartments and eating easy mac several nights a week."

"I like macaroni and cheese," he said and handed me his plate. "Eat the rest. You'll need your energy."

"For what?" I set the plate aside and crawled onto his lap, straddling him. Like two magnets, our eyes locked onto one another's gaze. He ran his hands slowly over my breasts, stomach and then inside my panties. His slow and deliberate pace only enhanced the sensation. I closed my eyes and rolled my neck back, lost in the pleasure of the moment.

OVER THE NEXT MONTH we got into a pattern of spending abbreviated Monday, Wednesday and Friday nights together. I say abbreviated because Ryan came over at eight and left around four in the morning—*every single time*. He lived by a strict schedule: trainer at five; work by seven; home by seven-thirty.

Thus, I jumped at the opportunity to join him in Las Vegas for a legal conference. Ryan was like a virus with no cure; the withdrawal symptoms could only be managed by spending time together. Three days together was heaven.

Ryan held my hand as we entered ediBOL on our last night. The restaurant décor was modern. The tables had sleek straight edges surrounded by plush U-shaped brown couches. Lifeless trees towered between each table, while red florescent square lights hung from the ceiling. The red accents combined with the dead trees made me wonder if the designer was inspired by a sadistic version of *Little Red Riding Hood*. I felt like I was walking into an enchanted forest, but that something ominous was lurking.

"I feel rather covered up compared to everyone else," I confessed to Ryan once we sat down. All the women wore skimpy dresses that made it impossible to sit without ass exposure or bend over without a nip-slip.

I felt extra sensitive because I designed my dress. It was a short, lilac colored dress made mainly out of modal—my first time working with that fabric!—and a touch of spandex. The front had a modest V-cut, whereas the V-cut on my back plunged to the middle of my spine. Modal was a rather deceptive fabric because it hung loose but showed every flaw because the fabric was so thin.

Ryan traced the V from my collarbone to my breasts. "You're beautiful."

"I feel like I walked into an ad for plastic surgery."

"I have no idea what you're talking about."

I rolled my eyes. "Whatever. So tell me about your day, darling."

I tried to listen. But as he talked about class actions and some new medical device causing problems in heart patients, I got lost in his blue eyes, dimpled cheek and lush lips.

"Oh no," he said, eyes wide.

"What?"

"You have that dazed look my associates get when I talk too much."

I giggled and teasingly strummed his lower lip. "It's hard to concentrate when I haven't seen you all day."

"Just think of this little outing as foreplay." Maybe he wanted to say more but our server interrupted us. She looked like a Perfect Ten model who was serving to pass the time until she either met her rich husband or got discovered. (I doubt she had a preference.) She openly flirted with Ryan, but then threw me for a loop by deliberating grazing my breast while reaching for my wine glass.

"She likes you," Ryan declared with a smile.

"I think she likes both of us. How very eighties of her. Maybe we could get a vile of coke and have a threesome after dinner."

"You have a dealer here?" he asked with a straight face. "And you've waited this long to hook us up?"

"Trust me, what I have planned for you tonight is better than a drug-fueled threesome."

"Those are fighting words, babe."

There was an underlying sexual energy to our conversation tonight, as if we were playing a game of cat and mouse to see who could hold out the longest. It was unprecedented this early to read Ryan's thoughts, but when it came to sex, a fiery glaze overtook his eyes and his desire became palpable.

Ryan ordered a flourless chocolate cake just as I was about to cave. As much as I thought I craved going on traditional dates, it turned out sex and pillow talk was what I actually needed.

"Patience young lady," he teased.

I leaned in for a kiss and started stroking him over his pants.

"Counselor."

I looked up to find an older bearded man and his female companion standing before our table. Ryan subtly adjusted himself before standing up to shake the man's hand. He kissed the woman on the cheek.

"Ryan, how are you?" She smiled but the frostiness in her eyes remained.

"Great. You guys here on vacation?"

"Depositions," the man answered. "Sharon decided to tag along for some sun."

Sharon glared at me. "And who are you?"

"Casey," I said and stood up. Sharon limply shook my hand as if I had a communicable disease, while her husband nodded in my direction.

Maybe fifteen seconds of silence passed, but each second felt like I was getting a cavity filled.

"It was nice seeing you guys," Ryan finally said.

"You'll tell Claire I said hello?" Sharon pressed, locking onto Ryan's arm like a tigress.

"Of course."

We sat down and stared at the untouched chocolate cake. My mind spun a web of scenarios to explain away the mention of Claire—a coworker, his sister, a hairstylist—while my stomach contracted painfully at the thought of Ryan with another woman. Logically, I knew we had only dated a month and were free to see other people, but emotionally, I felt gutted. Never mind the intense sexual chemistry; I was in love with Ryan. It never occurred to me that Ryan's feelings had not accelerated at the same rate.

"Kevin was a partner at my firm when I started but he left a few years ago," Ryan explained. I waited for him to continue, but he filled out the credit card slip instead. "Ready?"

I cocked my head to the side. "Are you kidding? Who's Claire?"

He reached for my hand and led me out of the restaurant. "This isn't the place to have this type of conversation."

"What type of conversation is this?"

"A private one," he grunted, depositing us in a cab.

We didn't talk. Maybe he was preparing his remarks or giving me time to cool down. Either way, when the taxi dropped us back at our hotel, I felt a kinship with prisoners grasping their last few breaths of freedom before serving a life sentence.

Ryan walked into the room and proceeded to tear at the knot in his tie as if it was strangling him. "I've wracked my brain trying to think of what to say, but everything sounds cliché."

"What cliché applies here?"

Ryan paced back and forth in front of the windows. "I'm not happy. She doesn't understand me. We got married too young. I don't love her. Pick whichever one you want," he added miserably.

I collapsed on the couch. Each word worked as a bullet, zapping all my strength. The *she* he was talking about was Claire—his *wife*. Ryan was married.

"Why did you ask me out?" I whispered.

"This wasn't some calculated plan." He paused, searching my eyes. "I never thought I'd be the kind of guy to cheat on his wife. Sneaking around, lying, pretending—that's not me! But when I met you, I felt things I hadn't felt in a long time, if ever. I thought if I spent time with you, this, this infatuation would go away. But then I fell in love." Ryan looked tired. The worry lines on his forehead deepened and the bags underneath his eyes hallowed out his face. "I wanted to tell you. It's been killing me, lying to you."

"Am I supposed to feel bad for you?"

"I don't expect anything," he muttered.

"Are you still married? Separated?"

"We're married, but..."

"But what? She doesn't fuck you anymore?" His head snapped back as if I slapped him. *Yeah, I can be a bitch too*, I wanted to say. *Your wife and I have something in common.*

"If you must know, we rarely have sex and only at the scheduled time."

Scheduled sex? Christ, no wonder he's in love with me.

"Where does your wife think you are when you're with me?" I asked.

"Home," Ryan shrugged. "She's an ER nurse; works three nights a week. We mainly see each other on weekends. It's always been that way, always will, unless...never mind."

"Unless what?" I asked, giving into my sick curiosity to know about his marriage.

"Unless"—he looked directly into my eyes—"we had children. We agreed to work less if children came."

I felt worn out. My anger should have kept me awake, but I felt my eyes droop and the sweet whisper of sleep beckon me. Ignoring Ryan, I crawled into bed, pulled the covers over my head and fell into a dreamless sleep.

FOR THE FIRST FEW DAYS after flying home, I stayed strong and worked hard, ignoring the feelings of sadness, betrayal and loss. *It's good you found out early,* Cadie said. I murmured my agreement, but really, what does that mean? Anyone who's been slapped to the ground ass-backwards by a lethal combination of love and lust knows it doesn't matter whether it happens on day one or day three thousand. You were fucked either way.

Ryan called numerous times. I refused to answer, buoyed by my righteousness. I could see my campaign slogan: *Casey Byrne: Upholding today's moral standards for a better tomorrow!* But I saved his messages in case one day in the distant future, when I was blissfully happy, I wanted to listen.

My resolve lasted one week.

Saturday night, fueled by several shots of Jaeger, I listened to his messages. *Casey,* Ryan said, and already I was in tears. I missed his raspy voice; his inflection; every little hesitation as he mulled over how to convey his feelings. Regret was the theme of his messages. He ended every call with the same words: *I'm sorry. I love you. Please forgive me.* I fell asleep on the couch clutching the phone to my heart.

I woke up clearheaded and resolute in my decision to forgive Ryan. (Assuming, of course, one is ever thinking clearly when deciding to engage in an affair.) I didn't know where Ryan lived—why had I never asked him before?—but I did know he would be at the gym until nine on a Sunday. I showered, threw on a pair of jeans, a t-shirt and another one of my designs, a knitted pale grey cardigan with oversized metallic buttons down the front. I finished the look off with motorcycle boots and a maroon pageboy cap.

In all great Hollywood love stories, people locked eyes across a crowded room and knew they were meant to be together. That's not what happened here. I sat shivering on a bench outside the 411 building next to a couple of anorexic trees and waited. Ryan finally exited the revolving doors and strode right by me. I ran after him, yelling his name, but the wind swirled up my voice and spat it back in my face. I ran through a red light—narrowly avoiding a car and a future as a paraplegic—and was within an arm's length when Ryan suddenly turned around, causing me to knock him onto the sidewalk with a sickening thud. I toppled over, banging my knees painfully into the frozen cement. Nothing about this scenario was romantic or funny, as it would have been in a movie.

I crawled over to where he lay on the ground sputtering tiny breaths. "Are you okay?"

"I think"—gasp, gasp—"you knocked the"—gasp, gasp—"wind out of me."

"I was waiting for you outside the gym, but you didn't see me, so I ran after you."

"And then ran into me," he finished. Ryan held out his hand and we stood up together. "You came back to me."

It was a statement, not a question. "I'm stupidly and hopelessly in love with you."

Ryan took me into his arms, nuzzling his head in my neck. "I missed your smell. I missed your voice. I missed your touch. I missed you."

Those words worked as a balm to my broken heart.

I didn't ask any questions as we walked to my apartment. Maybe I should have. But as I said, who's thinking clearly when embarking upon an affair?

THE BRAIN IS AN AMAZING organ. It allows you to rationalize any behavior, including cheating, as long as it makes you happy. My top three reasons included: one, Claire and Ryan were not happily married; two, Claire might also be having an affair (I watched enough *Grey's Anatomy* to know the on-call room was used for more than naps); and three, it's impossible to steal a person. I wasn't making Ryan do anything he didn't want to do.

"Don't you worry someone will see us?" I asked at dinner one night. There was still no fall out from running into Kevin and Sharon in Vegas. We went out to eat, saw movies and took long walks—three nights a week.

"Lots of people can see us." He smiled smugly, basking in his obtuse answer. I stared back, unwilling to let him charm his way out of answering me. "I'd worry more if we went out on the North Shore. No one knows me here."

"Oh." So our freedom was due to geography. *How romantic.*

"Besides, it's late. Everyone I know is already in bed."

His answer made me anxious and I had no idea why. *You want to get caught,* my subconscious retorted. *You want him all to yourself, like a normal, boring couple.* The thought startled me. Was I striving for a suburban-eat-dinner-together-talk-about-our-days relationship?

If this was true, then I had major problems. First and foremost, Ryan sought me out because he was bored and unfulfilled in his marriage. I doubted he was up for a second ride. Second, Ryan never said he was ready to leave Claire.

It was my fault. I made the decision, with open eyes, that a married Ryan in my life was better than no Ryan. I was so happy that I didn't pressure him for any further explanations about his marriage or us. But it was getting hard to keep my feelings in check when I wasn't sure whether they would ever be fully realized.

I WAS GOING CRAZY. I hadn't seen Ryan in almost a week and I wasn't sure whether I would see him tonight. I sat at my desk, picking up and discarding pieces of fabric. I should have left. But the thought of spending another night alone in my apartment was too much to bear.

My phone sat on the table, dull and silent. Half of me wanted Ryan to call simply so I could yell at him. He couldn't cancel on me twice in a week without any consequences. I had a life too! But the other half of me missed him so much that I feared I'd take whatever scraps he threw at me.

It was time to face the truth: I wanted Ryan to myself. I didn't want to share. (Don't think I didn't notice the irony, as the other woman, complaining about sharing.) Could I ask Ryan to leave his wife? What if he said no? Was I willing to risk losing him?

"Are you okay?" Ryan asked a couple days ago when I silently accepted the news that he was cancelling our evening, *again*. His wife was sick and he had to go home.

"No, I'm not okay, *Ryan*." I spat each word. I hated that he chose Claire over me. "I feel rather fucked up. Fucked and fucked up, that describes us, right?"

"I hear what you're saying and I understand why you're upset." His voice abruptly changed from sincere into his placating, smooth-talking lawyer persona. Someone had obviously come into his office, hence the flood of corporate clichés. "How about we touch base tomorrow?"

"Sorry Ryan, that won't work. I'll be busy fucking a guy that isn't married, won't lie and doesn't stand me up."

Ryan hasn't called since my tantrum. I had no idea whether he was going to show for our regular date tonight. I left the studio around nine, equally exhilarated and terrified as to what I might find at my apartment. But it was all wasted emotional energy. There were no flowers waiting or apology note slipped underneath the door. I went to bed, distraught that Ryan and I might really be over.

A loud banging awoke me. I felt groggy and unsure of what the sound was and how to stop it. I grabbed the plunger from the bathroom (the best weapon I could find on short notice and little brain power) and crept into the living room. The noise was coming from the door. I looked through the peephole and saw Ryan's face.

I opened the door and started to walk away, but Ryan pulled me back, wrapping his arms around my waist and kissing me.

"Stop it!" I yelled, pushing him away. "I'm pissed off at you."

"Because...?"

I tugged at my hair, willing myself to be honest with him. "I hate knowing that when you're not here you're with your wife."

"I hardly see my wife and when I do it's nothing like how it is with us." He laughed. "Well, except for now. Arguing is an area Claire and I excel in."

I threw a pillow at him. "Generally, when someone makes themselves vulnerable the other person reciprocates with their feelings instead of making jokes."

"How do I feel?" He spoke deliberately, never removing his eyes from mine. "I'm frustrated. I feel like you don't trust me."

"I guess I find you hard to trust given your behavior. You didn't tell me you were married, you obviously have no problem lying to your wife and you disappeared the past couple of days without even a phone call."

"Why would I call?" he argued. "You made it quite clear that I was replaceable."

"You knew I didn't mean that!"

"What is it that you want, Casey?"

I bit my lip. "You."

"For how long? The next week, year, forever? Are you ready to build a life together?"

It was impossible to argue with a lawyer. By the time I was ready to respond to one question he moved onto another. "Ryan, those aren't fair questions. I love you but nothing is guaranteed in life."

"Precisely," he said with smug satisfaction. "You don't know what you want but you're more than willing to ask me to walk out on eleven years of marriage for something you might decide next month no longer interests you."

"I wouldn't think walking out on a marriage that makes you miserable would be such an issue."

"You don't know the first thing about marriage," he snapped. "Just because I'm no longer in love with Claire doesn't mean I don't care about her. We have a history. I'm not ready to put her through the pain of a divorce when you've shown an inclination to change your mind about us every two seconds or throw a fit like a child when you don't get your way."

Someone could have driven a knife though my heart and it wouldn't have hurt as bad as hearing Ryan defend his marriage to me as if I was a naïve child. "So you want a commitment from me and yet you're unwilling to make one yourself?"

"I just think we need to get to know each other better before doing anything drastic."

"How convenient," I muttered. "You stay married and I see you three days a week. This could go on forever."

"I wouldn't let that happen," he reassured me. "You have to trust me. For a long time I thought being miserable was normal, but then I found you. And you've given me hope that the type of relationship, the woman I dreamed of, exists. But I can't rush this. I can't make a mistake twice." Ryan quickly rubbed away the tears in his eyes, but his voice remained broken. "I used to think Claire was my soul mate. But after we got married our lives revolved around having a child. We've poured ridiculous amounts of time and money into having a baby, but despite being completely healthy, nothing has worked. Claire's become a miserable, bitter person that I don't even recognize."

"I'm sorry." I felt horrible. I loved this man. I loved that he acted strong one minute and vulnerable the next. I walked over and sat in his lap, wrapping my arms around his neck. "Are you guys still trying?"

"She no longer stalks me to have sex when she's ovulating or drags me to endless doctor appointments. But," he hesitated, and the knot in my stomach tightened. "On the rare occasion we have sex, we don't use protection."

I squeezed my eyes shut to erase the image of Ryan and Claire fucking inside their gorgeous house.

"Listen to me," Ryan whispered as he stroked my jaw line. "I love you. But I want to make sure you're sure."

"Promise me you won't cancel any more dates at the last minute."

"I promise."

"And call me back, even when you know I'm pissed off."

"Promise." He leaned forward to kiss me, but I gently pushed him away.

"And stop having sex with your wife."

"I'll do my best." Ryan sighed. "Anything else?"

"Take me to bed."

"No." Ryan pushed me back against the couch. "I want you right here."

LIKE ANY MISTRESS WANTING to believe her relationship had taken a turn for the better, the next few months proceeded blissfully. I finally felt able to be me: sexy, goofy, emotional and even bitchy. I opened up, insecurities and all. I confessed the full extent of my strained relationship with my parents and how it caused me to feel unlovable—a failure that was little more than a pretty face.

In turn Ryan talked about his strict Catholic upbringing, where a strong work ethic and a strict moral code ruled the household. As the youngest of six kids, there was never enough of anything—money, love or attention. He feared that no matter how successful he became, it would never be enough.

But in all those conversations, he never talked of his wife and I never asked. I no longer wanted to know. I pretended she did not exist until a snowy night in March made that impossible.

Haden and I went for a drink after a long day spent house hunting for his upcoming move. I confessed to seeing a married man, but Haden cut our night short before I drank enough to give incriminating details.

"Not even married a year and you already have to run home to her," I commented when he explained that Rachel wanted him back early.

"Come summer we'll be living in Milwaukee and we'll get pissed together every night. It will be just like old times."

"It will never be the same." A frigid gust of wind with tiny snowflakes assaulted us as we stepped outside. "She wouldn't even let you sleepover on a cold, snowy night."

"Rachel misses me," he said with a wry smile.

"More like she didn't want you spending time with me."

Haden went into a half-hearted defense of Rachel, but I stopped listening when a couple in the window of Plated caught my attention. Ryan was tucked inside the same side of a cozy booth with another woman. The woman sat with her back to the window, partially blocking Ryan's face, but I knew it was him. I spent hours memorizing every inch of his body.

They clinked glasses and kissed. It was a short kiss but definitely not platonic. I felt dizzy. I wanted to collapse and let the snow slowly numb my pain.

Instead I hugged Haden goodbye and walked into Plated. The hostess sat me at a booth about ten feet away from Ryan's. I held the menu just below my eyes and covertly watched them. Ryan's back faced me. His broomstick posture and grip on his wineglass told me he was stressed out.

Claire was even prettier than I imagined with pale blonde hair and clear, piercing sky blue eyes. She had sharp cheekbones, flawless ivory skin and the type of pink pouty lips that immediately made men crave a blow job. Her off-the-shoulder dress showed delicate collarbones and small but perky breasts. She looked sophisticated and yet sad.

Ryan got up from the table. In an act of bravery, insanity or desperation (take your pick!), I followed. I was acting on emotion. The logical part of my brain was on strike.

By the time I got to the small corridor by the restrooms, Ryan was already coming out.

"Casey!" He glanced down the hallway before ushering me behind the wall that led to the men's bathroom. "What are you doing here?"

"I met a friend for dinner and saw you. I wanted to say hi." I sounded much calmer than I felt.

"I'm with Claire," he said hastily. The dimple on his left cheek twitched in and out with each word, like a clock ticking away the seconds of freedom he had left.

I knew he had to leave, but I couldn't let go. I felt tears on standby. My lack of self-control was growing more appalling by the second. I put my fingers through his buckle loops in an attempt to pull him closer to me and further away from her. "What are you guys talking about?"

"Why?"

"It looks serious."

"It's complicated," he whispered and rested his forehead against mine.

"Of course," I mocked and pushed him away from me. Nothing good ever came from his use of that word.

"Don't be like this."

My mom always warned that I made life tougher on myself than necessary. I disagreed, but if tonight was any indication, perhaps she was right. "Just tell me what you guys are talking about and then I'll go."

He peeked around the corner again. "She wants to adopt."

"A baby?" I screeched.

He put his hand over my mouth. "Yes, a baby," he hissed.

"Obviously you told her no."

Ryan's shoulders crumpled. A part of me felt bad for this man that I loved so much as he tried to navigate his way between a wife he cared about but did not love, and a girlfriend he loved but couldn't be with without hurting so many people. But the other part of me wanted him to grow a pair and leave her already!

"I don't know what to do."

His answer knocked the wind out of me. I leaned against the wall and closed my eyes. I opened them to find Claire standing beside Ryan.

"Is everything alright?" Claire asked, touching his forearm.

Was I dreaming? I zeroed in on her touch. It demonstrated both concern and protection of her property.

Ryan cleared his throat. "Claire, this is Casey Byrne. The firm helped her out on some legal work."

Claire's steely blue gaze appraised me. I felt naked, like she knew all my secrets, including the numerous times and positions I'd fucked her husband.

"What type of legal work did Ryan do for you?" Claire asked.

"Sexual harassment," I blurted, thinking of my old boss when I interned as a pastry chef. He was number one on my list of people to sue.

"How odd," Claire mused. "Ryan specializes in class actions."

"I didn't take the case myself," Ryan interjected. "Rob helped her out. I just met her at the office a couple times."

"And you stayed in touch?" Claire asked.

My heart beat like a tribal drum, but Claire's voice remained as unemotional as her unlined face.

"Of course not," Ryan said with a forced laugh. He pushed Claire's hair behind her ear and pulled her chin up so that their eyes met. It was a gesture he often did with me. "We just ran into each other tonight."

I nodded along like a good puppet, but inside I was reeling. How dare he touch her with such intimacy in front of me? Wasn't anything sacred?

"I'm ready to leave," Claire said.

"Right. Casey, it was nice to see you."

"Oh no," Claire laughed and I saw how beautiful she truly would look if she were happy on any level. "Please stay and converse with your delightful friend. I'd *hate* to interrupt."

Claire glared at me before swiftly walking back into the dining room.

"I have to go after her," Ryan sighed.

"It's clear that's what you want to do."

Ryan grabbed my hands and implored me with his eyes to forgive him. But seeing firsthand how he interacted with Claire sobered me. He would never leave her.

"I'll come over tomorrow," he promised. But it was too little, too late. I stepped outside of our cocoon and saw with clarity that there was no future for us. This was the end. I could no longer bleed for this man when he chose to live a handicapped life with another woman.

"Don't." I let go of his hands and walked away. My body worked on autopilot. Before I knew it, I was back at my car and could almost convince myself I never went inside. Except that everything I knew, felt and hoped for an hour ago was gone.

Chapter 13

Casey – September 21, 2012

"So, be honest, on a scale of one to ten, how much do you hate me?"

Joshua rolled his eyes. "I don't think *hate* is the right word."

"Alright; how about disgusted, turned off or disappointed?"

"I still like you," he said. "Which I think is what you're really asking. Nothing's changed on my end."

"Why?" I felt baffled. Either he lacked some serious moral guideposts or he was a hell of a lot more understanding than me.

"Hmm…why don't I care?" Joshua rubbed the stubble on the bottom of his chin. I wondered whether it was a natural thinking gesture or one he concocted over the years because he liked the look. Perhaps Joshua was a tinge vain? "First, it happened four years ago. I'm not the same person I was four years ago, so I'm going to assume you're not either. Second, you said you're done dating married men. Obviously you learned something and aren't some serial adulteress, despite what Rachel likes to tell me." He winked at me, which I didn't find nearly as juvenile as a couple hours ago. "Third, people make mistakes. Nobody's perfect."

"I think the brief account of my history tonight should assure you I'm nowhere near perfect."

"I always thought you had this perfect life. You acted so happy."

I laughed. I had to. Men complimented me on my willingness to have fun almost as much as my looks. But it was all a carefully concocted charade, a game I started playing at such a young age that the line between make-believe and reality permanently blurred. That is, until I met Dr. Kate. We've spent the last few years untangling my insecurities and discovering what I actually enjoyed. The results still surprised me. Tonight was a prime example; I thought attending church would prove more exciting than drinking with Joshua.

"I learned from watching my parents that no one wants to be around someone that's always complaining," I said. "Happiness is a choice and I made sure everyone saw me as fun and happy."

"You're smart. You realized early on that life is all about perception, showing others what you want them to see. As a kid, I didn't get that. I felt like my every flaw and insecurity was on display." Joshua laughed. "Then again, it didn't help that I had glasses, braces, looked anorexic and didn't hit a growth spurt until college."

"But you're cute now," I whispered, more to myself.

Where had this chemistry originated? Maybe it resulted from sharing intimate details of our pasts when first date protocol usually called for little more than funny anecdotes and occasional sexual bantering. Joshua was an interesting paradox: down to earth, confident and passionate and yet surprised that I found him attractive. I'd been through enough men that backed up their confidence with selfishness, insensitivity and arrogance that maybe I was finally able to recognize and appreciate a quality man.

Or maybe it was the tequila.

"You know, I saw you and Ryan together," Joshua said. "When you were dating...or whatever."

"Really?" I wracked my memory. We didn't spend time with either of our friends for obvious reasons. The secrecy only intensified the relationship; it felt special, rare and ours alone.

"Yeah," Joshua said, rubbing the scruff on his chin. *Oh no!* I was starting to find his gestures endearing. "Rachel and I came to Milwaukee for a mock trial competition and stayed at the Pfister. We were way too keyed up to sleep so we went to Sky Bar. Ryan was there talking to you."

"You're right!" I forgot about that night. Snap-shots and conversational bits rapidly flashed through my mind as I resurrected this hidden gem. But the razor-like pain in my gut reminded me that although I was happy that night, the story didn't end well.

"I see that night in a very different light having heard your history with Ryan."

"Tell me."

"I remember Rachel froze when we walked into the bar and immediately said she wanted to leave. I thought it was due to seeing you. You guys weren't close back then," he joked. I rolled my eyes at the understatement of the year. "You and Ryan were huddled together, talking and laughing."

"He was telling me about how he had to sit through an entire day of depositions while his co-counsel hit on him," I said. "He gently explained that he was married. For some reason we thought this was hilarious, likely because he was dating me."

I felt so loved at the time. He wouldn't cheat with just anyone. He chose me. God, I was smug in my naivety.

"Rachel was so freaked out about seeing her future boss that she didn't even notice the intimacy between you guys. I thought it was odd," he said and shrugged, "but dismissed it as you being you. You were always flirting."

"I'm not sure whether that's a compliment or an insult considering I was up to something a lot worse."

Joshua grinned. "Take it any way you want. You will anyways."

"So tell me, what was your impression of Ryan?"

"Wow, umm..." Joshua scrunched up his eyebrows. "You're really testing my memory."

"Ryan was also at that New Year's Eve party Rachel and Haden threw." I shuddered as I recalled that horrible night. "Remember that night?"

"How could I forget the pleasure of giving you a ride home?"

"Love the sarcasm," I quipped. "You can thank Rachel for that. She bullied you into giving me a ride because she didn't want me to leave with Ryan. I have no idea whether she knew about us or was afraid I'd throw up in his car, but either way, you got babysitting duty."

"She should've worried more about you getting a nose bleed."

"Hilarious," I said. "So do you remember Ryan or not?"

"Vaguely. Amanda and I talked briefly to Ryan and his wife."

"What did you think of Claire?"

"These are hard questions."

"I thought you liked a challenge," I teased.

Joshua hesitated. "She was pretty."

It shouldn't have hurt. She was beautiful. Pretty was about as tame of an adjective he could've used. But still...I hated hearing it.

"And what about Ryan?" Why Joshua's opinion mattered was beyond me, but I'd come to respect it. He was logical and yet emotionally intuitive. I knew he would answer honestly but delicately.

"He was confident and friendly, but it was hard to tell whether his kindness was genuine or an act." He shrugged. "A bit of a fast-talker as my mom would say."

My heart seized. I had hundreds of memories that supported Joshua's characterization—Ryan was both cocky and a coward—but I didn't want to dwell on that storyline. I loved Ryan despite his flaws.

"You know," I said, feeling brazen from the liquor, "I haven't told you the whole story."

"Oh?" Joshua's eyebrows shot up.

"Only Dr. Kate knows."

I took a deep breath. I was choosing to let Joshua in with the hope that maybe if I told someone the entire story, someone I wasn't paying to listen to me, that the tiny, fractured grip Ryan still had over my heart would loosen and fade entirely.

There were so many nights when I wanted to confess to Cadie or Haden, but fear took the words away. But Joshua's track record tonight in listening to my crazy past with empathy told me he would keep my secret safe. Maybe he wouldn't want to date me, but he wouldn't betray my confidence.

"That night at Plated wasn't the end of our relationship, per se." I sipped my tequila, allowing the alcohol to boil my taste buds before swallowing. It seemed we had come to an unspoken mutual agreement to slow down our drinking before we passed out on the floor, but I still needed an extra boost of courage. "Ryan showed up the next morning at my apartment. I'd never seen him so upset. He looked ill at the idea of never seeing me."

"Forgive me for not feeling bad," he said dryly. "He had a choice."

"He said he would worry about me if I refused to see him."

"This guy is unbelievable," Joshua scoffed. "Even for a lawyer, he's incredibly egotistical."

"That's not it," I protested. "Ryan loved me—I truly believe that—but he felt obligated to support Claire through the adoption process. When he realized I was serious about ending it he didn't want to leave me without anything."

"Sure," he laughed. "So what happened?"

I shifted in my seat, uncrossing and re-crossing my legs. "He said he wanted to invest in me..."

Joshua cocked his head to the side. "Invest in you?"

"He offered to pay for school," I explained. "At first I told him to fuck off. It felt like a consolation prize. But Ryan argued that by allowing him to pay, I would know he cared about me, regardless of whether we could be together. He believed in my talent and wanted to give me my first big break."

I knew Joshua didn't understand. Like most people, Joshua saw only the surface of Ryan: a cocky lawyer with too much money, good looks and charisma. But I knew the real Ryan: cocky, yes, but also sensitive and deeply caring. I saw the pain on his face when he understood we were over and his future lay with his wife.

"How did this 'investment'"—Joshua used air quotes—"work?"

"He paid off the loan I took out for my first year and after that, whenever a tuition bill came, he paid it."

"That's it? He wrote out checks and said, 'Thanks for stopping by!'" Joshua spoke with an exuberant customer service voice, while miming writing out a check.

Joshua's impression wasn't intended to be an accurate portrayal of Ryan, but it was at such odds that I couldn't stop laughing. "We met for lunch about once a month to talk."

At first, the lunches were unbearable. Is anything worse than sitting across from the person you love, talking and laughing, all the while knowing they will never be yours? We carefully avoided the topic of us, but by the end we usually faltered. (*Are you happy? Do you miss me?*) It was a torturous game that thankfully we grew out of over time.

"You can judge if you want to," I continued, "but Ryan's the reason I'm even remotely successful today. His money allowed me to take an internship with Kipp Lerner. Kipp mentored me, developed my talent and gave me my big break by selling my clothes in his store. Best of all, I graduated without any debt. Without Ryan, I never would've had the money to start my own line."

Joshua placed his hand gently over my mouth and I stopped talking. "I'm not judging you. My parents paid for everything until I turned twenty-five."

"Yeah, but you paid heavily in terms of compromise."

"Yes! That's *exactly* what I'm hung up on." Joshua slapped the table, as if I found the missing murder weapon in one of his cases.

"You said the affair was over, right, so what did Ryan get out of this arrangement?"

I felt it was best not to mention the numerous times a hug lingered or a kiss on the cheek turned into a kiss on the lips which turned into a groping session. But we never had sex. You would think that would be the hardest part but it really wasn't. The worst part was the knowledge that he chose his wife over me despite his misery.

"I'm not sure," I said. "I just don't think he was capable of saying goodbye."

"Do you still see him?"

"Rarely." I thought back to the lunch when he told me he was leaving with Claire that weekend to adopt a little girl in Ethiopia. Until that point, I believed Ryan and I would one day be together. I hoped his insistence on meeting for lunch, paying for school and calling was his way of buying time until he could leave Claire. Hearing that Ryan and Claire finalized the adoption was the finishing blow in a series of punches that should have knocked sense into me a long time ago. "They adopted a baby last year and I took that pretty hard. I finally listened to Dr. Kate and stopped seeing him."

"So you've never told anybody about...his financial investment?"

"Only Dr. Kate."

"And you wanted to tell me?" He wore an endearingly sweet smile.

"Oddly, I find you very easy to talk to."

"Oddly?"

"You're different from what I thought when I first met you," I admitted.

He held up his straw and shook it playfully at me like a gavel. "The flaw in your argument, Ms. Byrne, is that we've talked on numerous occasions. So you can't really blame your inaccurate assumptions on a false first impression."

"My first impression of you bled into every other interaction," I insisted. "But, you're right, I probably would've realized I was wrong before tonight if I put some effort into getting to know you."

"Better late than never." Joshua held my gaze. We were both thinking the same thing: tonight had gone much better than expected.

"So any confessions you want to make? Any skeletons in your closet? Best to lay it all out," I ventured, letting the possibility of more hang in the air.

"Nothing that would scare you away."

"It doesn't have to be anything big like an affair with a married man."

"Well if I had an affair with a married man," Joshua said with a devilish grin, "I doubt I'd be out with you."

"It's always a relief to find out that my date isn't gay."

"Well," he hesitated, pulling off his glasses and cleaning them with his shirt. We had a Clark Kent/Superman situation here. I couldn't get over the difference. Sexy both ways, but the first guy belonged in a library, while the second could star in a Calvin Klein ad. "There is this one thing."

"Spill."

"On one condition."

I raised my eyebrows. "What's that?"

"You have to kiss me first." His confidence was understated, but it was definitely alive and ticking.

"Oh yeah?"

"Yeah," he grinned. "Just in case you hate me afterwards."

I knotted my hands through his curly hair, pressing soft kisses as I navigated my way along his jaw line. When I reached his mouth, his lips parted slightly to accept mine.

His hands gripped my hips and pulled me in closer. My mind fogged up with pleasure and I had to force myself to pull away first.

I took a deep breath to still my nerves and settle the blood flowing through my veins.

"Story time Mr. Shaw."

Chapter 14

Joshua – May 17, 2008

"This is one of the biggest days of your life and you look like you spent the night consuming a fifth of whiskey and sleeping on the streets," Rachel said, grinning up at me beneath her black graduation cap as she tried fruitlessly to smooth down my unruly curls.

In stark contrast to my disheveled appearance—I woke up a half-hour ago and barely had time to brush my teeth—Rachel looked immaculate. Each piece of hair was perfectly coifed underneath her cap, her makeup was flawless and her manicured nails sparkled like diamonds. She looked ready for a photo shoot, not a graduation ceremony.

"Trust me," I snorted. "You'll be so bored in five minutes you'll be begging me to leave."

"You can joke because you took it for granted that you would graduate. But I can't tell you how many nights I spent the past three years wondering if I would ever make it here."

I put my arm around her as we crept our way towards the auditorium doors. "The fact that you're graduating *cum laude* shows how much you worry unnecessarily."

She tugged on the yellow ropes that hung loosely around my neck. "Yes, but I'm not *magna*."

The accolade meant very little to me, but my parents acted like I earned a Purple Heart. They ignored my protests and continued to proudly (and obnoxiously) display all my degrees, trophies and certificates on a bookcase in their dining room.

As I stepped into the auditorium the music of Fanfare bled into my ears. Flashbulbs shot off in every direction making it look like a meteor shower. Family and friends gazed towards us with pasted smiles. I felt relieved when we finally got to our seats until I saw that Rachel was crying.

"You've got to be kidding me."

"It's the song," she protested, while retrieving a tissue beneath her robe.

I blanked out for the speeches but when the Dean Forsett began handing out diplomas, I really tried to feel something. I was waiting for the magnitude of the moment to descend upon me when he called my name.

The walk across the stage didn't strike an emotional cord. *I'm a lawyer now*, I repeated in my head, gauging the sound and fit. Why didn't this mean more? Was Rachel right? Was I simply underwhelmed because I never questioned the outcome? As a kid, I envisioned freedom when school ended. Today, the day I truly transitioned into adulthood, I felt only relief at never having to take another exam. Excitement wasn't even within my arsenal of emotions.

When the ceremony ended, Rachel and I walked up to the roof with our classmates to take pictures and meet up with family and friends. The wind whipped us, threatening to blow off our caps, but the view was breathtaking. I leaned against the railing and looked out towards the inlet of Lake Monona. A pang of sadness hit me as I realized it was all over. My three years evaporated, snapped up into a photo album of memories that would fade over the years until law school became little more than a stopover in my life.

MY PARENTS AND I ATE at Uno's on State Street. They thought the city was run by hippies and thus didn't trust the cleanliness of any of the local restaurants. *We're safe with a chain*, my dad announced, as if we were in Istanbul and all the local restaurants had undetected health code violations.

"We're very proud of you," my dad said, fishing a crisp white envelope out of his breast pocket. "We know you had some doubts about law school"—biggest understatement ever—"but we always knew you would pull through."

I pulled out a white card with blue balloons on the front. *Congrats Grad!* The inside read: *Best luck in the future!* My parents signed and dated the card. I stifled a laugh. They were so well-intentioned and yet so clueless. The artificial emotion made it perfect for a distant relative, not a parent.

I was stunned into silence, however, when I saw the five thousand dollar check inside. I shook my head. "You guys, this is too much."

"This is just to start you off on the right foot," my mother insisted, her brown eyes pleading with me to allow her to care for me a little bit longer.

An internal battle waged: half of me wanted to take the money as a cushion, while the other half wanted to reject it and put an end to the twenty-five years of the Shaw regime. I had to stop taking before I could truly stand on my own two feet.

"It's a gift. The polite thing to say is thank you," my dad grunted. He tipped his glass back and finished off his beer.

"Thank you."

"Plus, on your salary, I wouldn't exactly be turning away money."

Both of my parents had their reasons for wanting me to take the money and it boiled down to control. My mom wanted to ensure her only son always needed her, while my dad wanted a say in my life. Neither would ever change.

"Despite my meager salary,"—I looked pointedly at my father—"I think I'll be able to manage just fine from here on."

My father sighed, resigned that his only son—a lawyer!!—would work as a public defender. "I suppose we'll see whether you can manage it. Life gets expensive. Maybe down the line you'll be more amendable to taking my advice."

"I'll always *listen* to your advice, Dad."

He stared at me for a moment but then let it drop.

After paying the bill we walked back to my apartment. For the past three years I lived on the top floor of a three-flat house on Dayton Street. It was old and run down, but the rent was reasonable and it gave me the luxury of having both a bedroom and an office. My parents, per usual, hated it and begged me to move into one of new high rise apartments on Johnson Street. With all the shiny new buildings, Johnson Street was starting to look like Park Avenue. It lacked character. I hated it.

I held the screen door open for my parents and followed them upstairs. As I made the turn for the third floor, my mother squealed. I thought she saw a spider, but then I heard my dad say, "Can we help you?"

I turned to see Leah sitting on the top step. Five steps and two confused parents separated us, but I could tell something was wrong. She wore sunglasses, but the rest of her face was red and blotchy.

"Mom, Dad, this is my friend Leah," I said.

Both heads swiveled in tandem from me to Leah and back to me again. My father was the first to recover his manners.

"Nice to meet you," he said, stretching out his hand. "I'm Robert and this is my wife Catherine."

Leah stood up and shook their hands. I saw my mother's eyes immediately assess the cropped top that exposed Leah's belly button and the jean shorts that provided little more coverage than underwear. The scene would have been comical—four adults stuffed into a narrow and winding hallway—if I wasn't so perplexed by Leah's presence.

Leah and I ran into each other earlier this semester and resumed the same friends with benefits relationship we had before she left for Rome last year. She didn't expect anything, but she didn't really give a lot either.

"Could I have some water?" Leah asked, breaking the silence.

I unlocked the door and everyone shuffled inside. My parents took a seat on the couch, while Leah and I went into the kitchen.

Leah turned on the tap and said the phrase most dreaded by men in the English language: "We need to talk."

"Now?" I whispered back, watching my parents try (and fail) to conceal their interest a mere ten feet away.

She drank the entire glass of water before answering me. "That would be nice." She pulled my tie towards her. "And why are you so dressed up?"

"Graduation," I smirked. "Too busy to attend yours?" I teasingly flicked her sunglasses onto the top of her head, but instead of being met with her usual mischievous eyes, I saw a pair of puffy, red-rimmed eyes. "You've been crying."

"It's nothing." She quickly pushed her sunglasses back down as some stray tears escaped. "Maybe your parents could go get some coffee."

"They'll think I'm kicking them out."

"So?" she challenged.

I was baffled as to what was upsetting her. It couldn't be about us; we weren't serious enough for our demise to necessitate any tears. With anyone else I would've thought maybe it was fear of graduation. But not Leah. She planned to travel, write and work odd jobs to pay her way. She couldn't wait to leave Madison.

"I'll talk to them." My parents watched me as I walked back into the living room, wide-eyed and nervous, as if I was the President about to give the State of the Union address.

"I know this is a lot to ask," I said, "but would you mind walking back to State Street and grabbing some coffee?"

"Who is this girl?" my dad demanded, looking put out. But then again, he'd pout if the Packer game started even a minute late. He was a man who liked a schedule.

My relationship with my dad was like riding a rollercoaster. I made him proud one second—graduating law school—and disappointed the next—kicking him out of my apartment. It was impossible to always please him. Merely living my life ensured ups and downs.

"We'll be back in an hour or so," my mom interrupted, pulling my dad up to leave.

I felt a rush of gratitude for the woman who stood up for me on the most random of occasions—as if pulling cards out of a hat.

"What's wrong?" I asked Leah when the door closed. "You're acting very strange."

Leah took off her sunglasses, put her head in her hands and laughed bitterly. "I've felt strange for the past few weeks. I hardly recognize myself."

"Well, you have a lot going on," I said, going off on a tangent about the pressures of graduation.

"You're really not getting it."

"I think I get it," I said tentatively. "I've been through it myself."

She shook her head and looked up at the ceiling as fresh tears streamed down her face. I wiped each one away with my thumb.

"I'm pregnant," she whispered. My hand froze on her cheek and fell limply into my lap like a bird shot dead out of the sky. "It's yours."

I haven't spent a lot of time (any if I'm being honest), imagining the moment I would hear those words. But if I had, it probably would've included a Hallmark moment wherein my wife woke me up by jumping on the bed, holding the victorious pregnancy test in her hand. I would take her in my arms, feeling both overjoyed at what was to come and proud that I, Joshua Shaw, had created a baby.

I never envisioned this script.

"Do you have any idea how?"

Leah threw her hands up in the air. "Your guess is as good as mine. It's a marvel that a baby can function with my lifestyle."

Oh shit. The baby might already be damaged. We drank together and Leah often showed up stoned, but what else did she do when I wasn't around? She might be shooting up heroin or using Adderall to study. But it was way too late to ask those questions.

"You're sure you're pregnant?"

"Three positive pregnancy tests in three days seem to think so."

"That's a lot," I agreed.

I was going to be a father. It seemed a cruel twist of fate that only an hour ago I dismissed my father's lecture on how life gets unexpectedly expensive. My salary as a public defender suddenly felt paltry. I couldn't support a baby. They needed all sorts of stuff: food, clothes, diapers, toys. Hell, they devoted an entire section to babies at Target!

But an even worse thought struck me. Where was Leah planning on raising the baby? She didn't have family in Milwaukee. Would I have to move? Apply for a new job before I started working? How would I explain that to potential employers? *Hi, I'm Joshua, My sperm is so powerful that it blew through a condom to knock up my fuck buddy. So now I have to help raise a child I never planned on having. But don't worry, I'm very responsible and will be a great asset to your team!* I saw my career plummet before it even started.

"Are you okay?" Leah asked. "You're sweating…a lot. I'm going to get you some water."

She walked to the kitchen but kept her eyes on me the entire time, probably wanting to make sure I wasn't going to run out the door and never come back. My options were limited, but that one was still available.

Leah handed me a glass of ice water, which I immediately held to my forehead. Amazingly, my first thought was that she was going to make a great mother. A few minutes ago that thought would never have occurred to me. But it was true. I saw from her passion about travelling and writing that she had the capacity to care a great deal. Our relationship, however, never fell into that category.

"I'm being an asshole," I said. I tried to smile but it was a struggle. I probably looked more like a stroke victim than someone genuinely happy about his impending fatherhood. "This must be so much worse for you. I mean, not worse, but more of a shock. God, I'll stop talking."

Leah giggled and rested her head on my shoulder. What a refreshingly familiar sound. "I've never seen you like this before."

"I've never felt like this before," I admitted.

"How do you feel?"

I let out a deep breath. "It sounds stupid, but I never thought you'd get pregnant. We wore condoms! Yet I'm sitting here wondering how it happened like some fifteen-year-old jock that knocked up his cheerleader girlfriend."

"Trust me, I've spent the past three days wondering the same thing."

I sighed. "So what do we do now?"

"Schedule the appointment, I guess." Leah paused to steady her breathing. "I have a good six weeks to work with, but I'd rather get it over with now."

I often think I'm listening, but don't realize I'm off in my own little world until something the other person says snaps me back into reality. Such was the case here. Leah looked at me expectantly. But only when I repeated her words did I catch the significance.

"Wait. What do you mean, get it over with?"

Tears spilled over her eyelids. She bit down hard on her lower lip.

"Seriously?" she croaked. "We can discuss this, but we're not ready to be parents. More importantly, neither of us *wants* to be parents."

Leah hunched over and sobbed. She looked broken. She lived with this information for three days. Three terror-filled days. Did she want me to convince her to keep the baby? Was this a test as to whether I wanted the baby? That seemed too manipulative for Leah. She was a straight shooter. But was she even thinking clearly? I've heard all sorts of crazy stories involving pregnancy hormones. Maybe she'd feel differently tomorrow.

There were so many questions. Most important was whether I wanted the baby. This was my chance to live my life as planned. I would be free to move to Milwaukee, work at the public defender's office and date. I might have a child one day, but that day wouldn't come in eight months or so.

But my gut told me the answer wasn't as open and shut as the facts led me to believe. Feelings couldn't be quantified and categorized like my life. The idea of Leah having an abortion made me feel sad and uncomfortable. But I also felt sick about the idea of having a baby. Either way, whatever decision we made, I knew there was no way to erase this situation completely.

"You should do whatever you think is best," I said.

"Best for whom? Me? You? This baby? Which life takes precedence?" Leah screeched each word, losing what remaining bit of emotional control she had. "Most of the time I think the best thing is to get the abortion, but then there's this little annoying voice telling me that I'm just being selfish. We could raise this baby. I mean, give me a fucking break, teenagers in the ghetto with no money and no education raise children. We're middle-class, white and educated. Aren't we essentially doing this because it's not convenient? We're spoiled fuck-ups."

Anger radiated off of her like heat from a flame. She sat rigid, eyes narrowed, with her fists clenched.

"We don't have to make a decision today," I offered up impotently. Nothing prepared me for this moment and I was failing miserably. "We have time."

She shook her head. "No. I want it out of me."

She skipped from one emotion to the next—sadness, confusion, anger—culminating with blind conviction in her decision.

"Okay," I said. "Where do we go? I mean, I've never…"

"There's a Planned Parenthood on the east side that does it." She took a deep breath and met my eyes. "I'll call on Monday."

A heavy clamping sound became louder as someone climbed the old wooden stairs outside my apartment. I reentered my pre-baby life and remembered that my parents were in town. I wished I had sent them home. But how was I to know Leah was about to drop an atomic bomb?

"My parents are back," I muttered. "I'll get rid of them."

"No. Don't. Sitting around here cursing the condom companies isn't going to help."

She smiled half-heartedly at me and put her sunglasses back on before nearly knocking my parents over in her rush to leave.

I was left with two parents that wanted answers. Correction: parents that *thought* they wanted answers. Grandparents to a baby whose mother they met only today? The truth would cause immediate cardiac arrest. I smiled and took a vow of silence.

THE MORNING OF THE abortion I drove around Madison hoping for clarity, or at the very least a distraction, but I remained a hostage to my thoughts. I remembered sitting at graduation nine days ago, still blissfully naïve as to the hell Leah was going through, and sulking over the predictability of my future. Marriage, kids and a good retirement account. I should've known that the fragility of life is never tested faster than when you complain while surrounded by so many blessings. Nothing in life was guaranteed.

Even dumber was the thought that merely getting my degree made me an adult. How does studying for three years confer adulthood? Earning money, paying bills and no longer financially relying on my parents was just the tip of the iceberg. But at least that part of adulthood was utterly clear: you needed money to live.

This week I parsed through the bullshit and hit the realities of adulthood head-on. It's about making the best decision when only terrible outcomes exist. It's accepting responsibility when the easiest answer is to blame someone else or walk away. It requires you to support the decisions of the people you love even when you disagree. Being an adult is hard work with little reward.

Leah and I talked daily, mainly because we made the joint decision not to tell anyone about the pregnancy. Consequently, I took on a dual role of confused, angry and sad father/fuck buddy, as well as Leah's conscience and friend. We spent hours arguing about whether we were doing the right thing and then commiserating about the unfairness of this situation.

Yesterday got particularly tense, however, after Leah accepted a position teaching English in Beijing. Up to that point, I still thought she'd call off the abortion.

"Say something," she begged when I greeted the news of her job announcement with silence.

"I can't."

"You can."

"I have this nagging feeling that we're making the wrong decision."

She started crying—small, wracking sobs that made her entire body convulse. "You're not the one who has to give up everything for this baby. I'm twenty-two. If I have a baby now, what's left for me?"

The lawyer in me saw several ways to attack her argument. My life would never be the same either. I wouldn't carry the baby, but I'd move, change my job, and stop dating. I'd be a father. Was there any bigger life-changing event?

But I quickly backed down. I couldn't argue passionately when I wasn't sure either. Keeping the baby was only a gut feeling. Why torture her with pointless mental exercises?

I pulled up outside Leah's apartment building now. She was waiting for me on the cement steps.

"Hey," she said, lowering herself into my car.

"How are you feeling okay?"

"Nervous."

"That's probably normal." I felt nervous and a bit nauseous myself.

Leah pulled her knees up to her chest, wrapped her arms around her legs and rested her head between her thighs. "I'm sorry," she said, turning to look at me. "This wasn't exactly what you bargained for in this arrangement."

Considering our arrangement didn't have any formal terms, I didn't have any standing to make a challenge. "Neither of us bargained for this."

I PULLED INTO THE PARKING lot of a flat, non-descript two-floor office building. It could have housed any business except that the stark white paint and hooded windows gave it a clinical feel.

The sight only aided my dueling emotions: the building appeared menacing while full of absolution. We would walk out of here with a second chance. But at what cost?

Leah held my hand as we crossed the parking lot. It felt funny. We had sex countless times, but I never held her hand. I squeezed it tightly a few times to let her know that we were in this together, for better or worse.

The walk inside was uneventful. I worried that the building would be overrun with protestors, but a lone security guard sat inside the front doors. He took our names and buzzed us through, but that was the only real sign that this was anything other than an ordinary doctor's office.

Leah checked in and we sat in the corner of the waiting room while she filled out forms. Leah didn't ask for any help and I didn't volunteer. If this experience taught me anything it was that I really didn't know her all that well. Sex was a façade. I knew how she smelled and tasted and what parts on her body to stimulate, but those had little to do with her essence. The essence came over time: spending nights laughing until you cried; making the other person feel special amidst the daily grind of life; and surviving arguments even when you're convinced the other person was a direct descendent of Satan. Leah and I hadn't even peeled back the first layer when we were thrown into this mess. We hadn't wanted to.

Leah walked sluggishly up to the front desk, holding the clipboard away from her body, as if it was a piping hot urine sample. The same girl who used to hold impromptu dance parties appeared to find walking too much of an ordeal. It was another reason to keep quiet. It was torture watching the joy of life drain, pint by pint, from Leah's frail frame.

A woman in purple scrubs called Leah's name. We followed her through another set of security locked doors into a standard patient's room with a single lounge chair, a sink with different medical supplies and gadgets adorning it and two plastic chairs. Leah took a seat. The nurse set Leah's arm on a foam contraption, wrapped an elastic band around her forearm, found a vein and rubbed some alcohol on it.

I turned away. I learned at a young age that I simply didn't have the stomach for medicine when I fell off my bike, splitting my shin open to the point where I could see the bone through the gushing blood. I nearly died of shock. Since then, the sight of blood, even from a paper cut, caused heart palpations.

"You okay?" Leah asked, tugging on the back pocket of my jeans.

"Is it over?"

"Yes."

I bent down next to her chair and gently rubbed her arm where the nurse had taped a piece of cloth. "I told you I wouldn't be any help. You're going through hell and I can't even handle watching you get blood drawn."

"You're going to have a hell of a time if you two ever decide to have a child," the nurse interjected with a laugh. "There's lots of blood involved."

We both stared at her. The comment felt so crass. She had to know this was a traumatic experience and not the best time to bust out her inner Jerry Seinfeld.

The nurse pulled off her gloves, completely oblivious to our shock, and handed Leah a floral cotton gown. "Take off everything, including your undergarments." She then turned to me. "I'll give you a minute to talk and then you need to wait outside during the procedure."

The nurse left and Leah began to remove her clothes. There was a line of freckles that ran from her left shoulder blade down to her butt that I never noticed in my darkened bedroom.

She craned her neck around and looked at me. "Tie me up?"

I made a loose knot. "I never noticed that line of freckles on your back before. It's like a happy trail leading to your butt."

A tiny smile played on the corners of her mouth. "Please tell me you're not thinking of sex at a time like this."

"Trust me, that's the last thing on my mind."

"Nothing ruins your libido like a good abortion," she muttered and rested her head against my chest. "Sorry, lame joke."

"Not any worse than the nurse's comment while taking your blood."

Her head bolted up. "I know! Common sense dictates not talking about future children to a patient in the process of getting rid of one."

"Do you want me to find her supervisor and complain?"

"No," she said and relaxed back into me. "I just want to bitch about something dumb because I can't complain about what's really bothering me."

"You can still change your mind," I whispered.

She shook her head.

The nurse knocked and poked her head in the doorway. "We're ready to get started."

We stood frozen, hugging, not ready to let go. I turned to leave, but Leah tugged on my shirt.

"We're doing the right thing," she vowed.

I nodded. Because, really, what else was there to say? From this point forward, we had no other choice but to believe we made the right decision.

AN HOUR DRAGGED BY and still there was no sign of Leah. What were they doing? Leah said the procedure lasted about ten minutes and then she would spend time in the recovery room. But this seemed excessive. The woman at the front desk typed on her computer and occasionally answered the phone, betraying no sign that anything was wrong. But I'd seen enough *Grey's Anatomy* to know that extra time spent in the waiting room was rarely good news.

I felt the familiar rise of frustration from being utterly powerless. Leah and I were in this together, but not as equal partners. Leah was pregnant and thus the final decision rested with her. I was a secondary player, little more than a spectator watching this moment pass by.

But my frustration was secondary to the guilt. Sadly, it wasn't even the right kind of guilt. It was selfish guilt: my life would be easier, most likely happier, without a baby. I could bury the last ten days in the recesses of my mind and get on with my life.

I didn't feel guilty for aborting the baby—the fetus was a pinprick of cells at this point—but I did wonder at the potential that life could have brought to the world. We could've had the next Mozart, Einstein or Jordan. Then again, maybe the kid would've been incredibly fucked up—creating a meth lab in our basement or running a teenage prostitution ring—because it felt neglected and resented by his or her parents. That seemed likelier at this point.

The same nurse that drew Leah's blood stood before me. "She's waiting for you in the recovery room."

I followed her through the secured door once again. She led me down a different hallway and into a double room with a curtain pulled between the beds. Leah lay on the right, pale and subdued, looking out the window.

I sat down on the edge of her bed. "How are you feeling?"

"Okay." The sun shone through the window and we both averted our eyes. "Maybe it's a sign we made the right choice. It was cloudy before and now it's sunny. A new day and all that stuff positive people always say."

I smiled. "I always thought you were one of those positive people."

"Not anymore," she sniped. "I'm too jaded. If you watch *Oprah*, every woman in the world that wants a baby can't get pregnant and yet we get pregnant while using a condom. Nobody gets what they want."

"We're getting what we want, just not how we expected it. You'll go to Beijing, end up having the time of your life, which you'll detail in a yet-to-be-named bestselling novel. Meanwhile, I'll work in Milwaukee as a modern day Atticus Finch, defending the wrongly accused."

"And then we'll see each other one day in the future," Leah injected, picking up on my story line. "Maybe in a restaurant or an airport, but we won't say anything. We'll just nod, safe in the knowledge that we went to hell and back together and survived."

I took her hand in mine. "We'll finally understand that we weren't bad people, but rather the world had a better plan for us."

"I like that ending," she said as a few tears melted from her eyes.

"It can be our story. Although, I'd be pissed if you didn't say hello. To be honest, you sound like an asshole in the future."

"It's romantic!" Leah insisted. "There's nothing left to say."

Even now, it was true: there was nothing left to say. The decision had been made, for better or worse. Maybe it was because I wasn't the one that underwent the procedure, but I felt relieved. Relieved that Leah was okay; that I wouldn't have to spend hours agonizing about whether this was the right decision; and that I was free to move on with my life.

I hoped Leah felt the same, but I didn't ask. She needed to cry on someone else's shoulder. The foundation of our relationship simply wasn't built to outlast more than one crisis. It would crumble and we would end up blaming each other for any feelings of regret in the aftermath. It was best to part with the knowledge that we did what was best under the circumstances.

When I dropped Leah off that afternoon, she walked towards her apartment building with renewed grace and energy, as if she couldn't wait to start the next chapter of her life. She didn't need to tell me that we did the right thing. I could see it in the way that she moved.

Chapter 15

Joshua – September 21, 2012

"I'm pretty much the last person in the world that would ever judge you," Casey assured me. "But do you feel better having talked about it?"

I shrugged. "It wasn't like I was waiting years to finally unburden myself of this deep, dark secret. I accepted the decision and moved on."

Casey looked dubious. "So why tell me when you never told Amanda? I mean, you guys dated, what, a couple years, and it never came up?"

These topics flowed easily with Casey, but with Amanda...well, every aspect of our relationship felt fraught with tension—particularly anything having to do with marriage and children. I fell victim to the old bait and switch: Amanda convinced me that living together didn't mean we had to get married. But as soon as her bags were unpacked, marriage and children became a daily topic. I quickly learned that she saw moving in together as a short hop, skip and a jump from a proposal.

"There wasn't any point. It would've made things worse."

"Why's that?"

"I didn't trust her," I confessed, something I only admitted to myself on especially dark days. Hearing the truth of those four words made me realize how dysfunctional our relationship was by the end. "She really wanted kids. And the longer we dated, the more she pressed the issue. I was afraid that if she knew I got someone pregnant without even trying, she might take advantage of the information and stop taking her birth control. I couldn't deal with that situation again. It would have undone me."

"Wow," Casey said. "That's quite an accusation."

"I could be wrong," I admitted, although I didn't think I was. Living with Amanda at times felt like lining up in front of a firing squad. She'd shoot until she got the desired result. "But her obsession with getting married and having kids only exacerbated my fears."

"I can't imagine trapping a man like that. Babies make relationships *worse* for the first few years, not better. If he didn't want you before the baby, he won't want you after."

"You never thought about getting pregnant with Ryan? Force his hand?"

"No-o-o," Casey said, shaking her head adamantly. "I had enough close calls to know I wasn't ready for a baby—even if a baby would've given me Ryan."

"Close calls?" I asked, intrigued. As a victim of an accidental pregnancy, I couldn't help but notice that it struck with the same randomness as cancer. Plenty of people had unprotected sex and yet only a small number ended up pregnant. Why did it happen to Leah and me when we used protection? Even today it was hard to shake the feeling that it should have happened to someone else, someone less responsible, someone more culpable.

"In case you haven't noticed by now," she mocked me, "but I'm pretty disorganized. I usually don't notice that I'm late until I'm *really, really* late. But there was one time that I truly thought I was pregnant and even bought a pregnancy test."

"Really? When?" How the hell did we end up talking about periods on a first date? This only happened to me.

"Not long after Ryan. Similar to Leah, it was beyond my comprehension that I could even get pregnant. I worked constantly, slept little, ate even less and partied hard. In short, I wasn't mommy material."

"So what happened with the test?"

"Oh," Casey laughed. "I hid it underneath my bathroom sink, hoping the situation would take care of itself. Thankfully it did."

"You're one of the lucky ones," I muttered.

"Can I ask you something? And feel free to tell me to fuck off if it's none of my business, okay?"

"Unlikely, but okay."

"Have you seen those pro-life commercials where they have some woman staring pensively out the window? Then she turns to the camera and says she will never forgive herself for getting an abortion because today would've been her child's sixth birthday or whatever." I nodded, sensing her question. "Do you ever have those thoughts? Is there a void in your life?"

My first instinct was to tell her no. I found those commercials misleading, manipulative and offensive. It's normal to feel a sense of loss right after, but I had difficulty believing most people lived the rest of their life with regret. It wasn't a choice anyone made flippantly. Those groups wanted to guarantee a life for the child while the mother was pregnant but didn't give a damn about the baby once it was born. Every single day in my job I saw the results of such propaganda: parents turned towards crime to provide for children they could never afford to have, or worse, drugs because they couldn't handle the responsibility.

But Casey wanted an emotional answer, not a forensics debate.

"Occasionally I'll think about what my life would be like if we had the baby," I admitted. "But I quickly move on because it's so unimaginable. I found out Leah was pregnant and ten days later she wasn't. I didn't have enough time to grow attached to the baby or even the idea of raising it. So it's not something I've done since."

"That makes sense," Casey said slowly. "So do you ever want kids?"

"You mean why didn't I want to have a child with either of them?" I retorted. Casey had a way to cutting through the bullshit and homing in on my insecurities, but instead of feeling exposed I felt like someone was finally trying to understand me. "Nothing felt right with Leah. We were young, we weren't in love, we had other dreams. The fact that we could manage it if forced wasn't a good enough reason."

"And with Amanda?"

I sighed. "I just couldn't see being happy with her in the long run."

Casey tapped her chin as if she was a psychologist in the midst of giving an analysis. "So you're not opposed to having children, but you haven't found the right person yet?"

"I hope so," I said. The men I knew that were fathers reveled in their role, but I still felt skeptical that I would ever get there. It was a nice thought that maybe I wasn't dysfunctional or scared but rather I hadn't found the right person yet. "Perhaps you could help me convince my mom."

"Ha! After Amanda I'm probably the last person she'd want to show up with her son."

"Why do you say that?"

"Obviously I don't know Amanda all that well, but she seemed"—she hesitated, searching for the right word—"Plastic."

"Meaning?"

"You're obviously not a *Mean Girls* fan," Casey teased. "Meaning, she says the right things, constantly smiles, acts overly helpful, all the while lying to your face. She's one thing in public and another behind closed doors."

She was right about the last part. Amanda insisted on a show of happiness whenever we went out. Oddly, she didn't have any qualms complaining about our problems (i.e. me) to her family and friends. They were just never allowed to see them firsthand.

"Oh my God!" Casey gasped. "You know who she reminds me of? Rachel."

"They have their similarities," I grunted, shaking my head. Casey figured out something in one night that took me a couple of years to latch onto. Why were men so oblivious while women could assess the core of another woman in roughly fifteen seconds?

"So was Amanda another one of Rachel's setups?"

"Yes," I admitted. The night I met Amanda I didn't fall prey to any love clichés: time didn't stand still, my heart didn't skip a beat and I wasn't particularly tongue-tied. But she was cute and nice and I had fun. "We met at one of Rachel's dinner parties. We were the only single people invited, so Rachel's plan was kind of obvious."

"I'm a bit offended. It sounds like Rachel has been pimping you out for years and only now does she ask me to go out with you."

I blushed, but stayed quiet. I hoped if it ever came to light that tonight was my idea, and not Rachel's, Casey found it romantic and not pathetic to pine over someone for years without acting on it.

"I'm probably Rachel's last single friend," Casey continued, making air quotes around the word *friend*. "She probably falls asleep at night, smug in her domestic bliss, only to wake in a panic when she remembers that I'm single. Then you and Amanda broke up and the clouds parted—salvation might still be possible for Casey!"

With most girls I would've assumed there were a few grains of truth to such a diatribe, but I could tell Casey found Rachel's meddling ridiculous. Casey joked about being left behind in the dating game, but I doubted she spent Saturday nights at home, watching *Sleepless in Seattle* for the millionth time and wondering where her life went wrong.

Besides, as much as I'm sure she'd like to forget some of the harder times, it grounded her. In the past her confidence intimidated me: she acted like she knew everything, everyone, exactly where she was going and didn't have time for detours. The Casey I saw tonight, however, was vulnerable from her mistakes and yet confident in her future. This Casey didn't act supercilious or like she was doing me a favor by having a drink. Having spent years in awe of her beauty and confused by her personality, it was the openness tonight that kept my interest.

"I doubt Rachel was at home plotting out our date," I said.

"Why's that?"

"She was firmly in the camp of people mad at me for ending it with Amanda." Amanda ran right to Rachel with every last detail. Rachel in turn was furious at me for lying, not trying hard enough and, as she put it, *refusing to grow up*. "Besides, Rachel doesn't like you enough to spend sleepless nights thinking about how to save your life."

"Touché," she said with a wide smile.

"Seriously though, you were joking about being upset that you're still single, right?"

Casey looked towards a couple groping one another at a nearby table. "It sounds odd, but I never thought about getting married and having kids. I was too busy having fun and fucking around with all the wrong guys."

"Too many girls underestimate the importance of fun in making a relationship last," I interjected.

"Shocking. Guys always rate fun and pleasure high on the compatibility scale," she quipped. "But guess what? Passion fades. People get annoying. Life gets hard. There has to be a solid friendship beyond great sex and crazy nights out otherwise the relationship will crumble upon the first sign of adversity."

"Maybe that's why I'm still single," I agreed. "I haven't been able to find a relationship with both passion and friendship."

"It's the secret to happiness: find a friend to laugh and cry with that you also want to jump."

"Do you think it's possible?" Perhaps I naively assumed I would one day meet someone who would make marriage and kids appealing. But what if I never felt ready to make that leap? I could make the argument at twenty-five that I wasn't in love with Leah and not ready to be a father, at thirty that the relationship with Amanda was far too toxic, but what would the argument be at forty? How many relationships had to fail before I questioned whether the problem was me?

"Sure," she shrugged. "But, in the meantime, I'm not losing sleep over it. My career is finally taking off and that's all I really care about. If someone comes along, great, but I'm not making the mistake of putting my dreams second to a guy ever again."

"So there's no one in the picture right now?" Ten years ago I would've been too nervous to ask such a direct question. (Let's be honest, ten years ago my geeky ass wouldn't have been a position to ask Casey this question.) But I've learned there is little downside to the direct approach.

"Right now?" She tilted her head to the side, teasing me with a flirtatious smile.

I leaned forward, lacing her fingers through mine, and whispered in her ear. "Is there anyone not in this bar that's in the picture?"

Her chocolate brown eyes glistened in the dim light, mesmerizing and mysterious. Her eyes alone could make a man walk unarmed into battle. "Not really."

Vague; but it would do. "You're so different tonight."

"From when?"

"I don't know...pretty much every time I've met you."

"Well you never really seemed very interested in getting to know me," Casey retorted.

"I was intimidated by you," I confessed. "You're too beautiful."

"Or too stupid to participate in your 'intellectual conversations' with Rachel?"

"That's not it."

"Forget it," she waved me off. "I'm happier partying with Haden."

I couldn't tell whether she was hurt that I hadn't made more of an effort in the past to get to know her or whether she could've gone ten more years being virtual strangers without a care in the world. Every time I thought I made progress inside her head, the door closed and I had to look for a window to unlock. How could I convince her that I dreamed of more but lacked the confidence to make that a reality? I wanted to tell her that she was never completely out of my thoughts, but somehow that just made me sound like a stalker.

"What happened at Rachel's New Year's Eve party a few years ago?" It was a long shot, but maybe she would remember it was the one night that I made the move to understand her better. That perhaps tonight wasn't an aberration but rather finally some progress on a stalled train.

"You *know* what happened," Casey stressed. "You were privileged enough to take me home when I was in the midst of a wicked downward spiral."

"Yeah, but fill in the gaps. When I dropped you off, it felt like a lot more than a bad hit."

"Every story I tell you makes me look worse," she laughed.

"In for a penny, in for a pound?" I suggested with a wink.

She winced. "Ugh. You're a winker and you talk in clichés."

"Have another drink. Maybe then my idiosyncrasies will become attractive."

"At this rate, I need to keep drinking so that I'll forget everything regrettable that I've shared tonight."

"I'm hoping you won't forget everything."

Our eyes locked. I pulled her wrist up to my mouth and kissed the inside of it. She smelled sultry and sweet, like a juicy, freshly picked strawberry that you wanted to sink your teeth into.

As she began to talk, I realized it wasn't her beauty, confidence or charisma that turned men into pubescent boys. Without a doubt, these parts worked in tandem to make her absolutely magnetic. Rather, it was her effortless ability to leave men craving more that made her irresistible. I settled in to listen, giving in to her gravitational pull—as if I stood a chance to resist.

Chapter 16

Casey – December 31, 2009

Jayden's sapphire eyes stared up at me, memorizing my every feature, as she enthusiastically suckled milk from the bottle. There was such sweet adoration on her face that she was impossible not to love. Perhaps she even loved me too—she was too young to know better.

Jayden finished her bottle and cooed in delight, proudly displaying her gummy smile. She was rather adorable when not screaming at a decibel that would make Steven Tyler jealous (as she had for the first fifteen minutes after Cadie and Chris left).

I paged through a photo album, hoping to keep Jayden entertained. It was stuffed with snapshots of domestic bliss: Cadie and Chris on their wedding day, honeymoon and finally holding precious Jayden. With their deliriously happy faces, their album felt like Kodak's wet dream.

Jayden reached out one of her saliva-filled hands and streaked it across one picture. "You miss Mommy and Daddy?"

She squealed. What a happy baby. At what point would that change? At what stage do we understand that the world doesn't revolve around our every need and desire? When do we realize that everything we do isn't really unique, clever or special? At only five-months-old, I already dreaded Jayden's loss of innocence.

My phone beeped. It was a text from Dan Latos. *Pick u up at 8.*

My feelings for Dan changed daily. He was unreliable, conceited and immature. He was also hold-onto-the-handrails handsome—chiseled jaw line, juicy lips, grey eyes and cropped brown hair made him look like Jude Law's taller, full-head-of-hair brother—rich (by default) and always game to party.

I met Dan while working at his parents' house for their annual end of the summer Labor Day bash. (I use the word *house* flexibly as it was actually a gated mansion on Lake Michigan.) After a long night offering guests glasses of champagne, miniature crab cakes, bacon wrapped scallops and *figs* in a blanket (because pigs were low brow), Dan approached me as I was loading up the van. I had little patience for men—even more so when I noticed that he looked airbrushed up close—until he uttered three magic words: *Let's get high.*

Outside of designing, getting drunk and high helped pass the lonely hours without Ryan. Pot provided so much relief at such little cost. I didn't have the will power to say no, even when the offer was made by a stranger. We got high in his car, thereby starting some sort of mutual use relationship.

While spending time with Dan had its benefits, he was as unreliable as a restaurant reservation. He disappeared for days, insisting he was getting into character for an upcoming play. (His "struggle" as an actor involved showing up for auditions.) In reality, he took spontaneous vacations to Vegas to gamble or Vail to snowboard or merely decided to drink until he was unconscious. He would eventually resurface, usually when I had a mini-collection due, ready to party and expect me to drop everything.

Our entire relationship consisted of partying. This sometimes included sex, but one of us usually passed out before the desire hit. I didn't care. The section of my brain that controlled emotions such as love and lust died along with my relationship with Ryan. It was a relief to spend time with someone that needed less than I was able to give.

"Good, she's sleeping." Cadie's voice surprised me. I must have fallen asleep with Jayden and didn't hear them come in. I eased Jayden into Cadie's arms. "How was she?"

"Angelic," I sighed, as we walked to the door.

"So what are you doing tonight?"

"Haden's having a party, so we'll go there," I said. I reached down and pulled on my boots, already dreading the slippery drive home in the snow.

The casualness of my relationship with Dan—fucking and getting fucked up—probably offended Cadie, but she hid it. Perhaps she finally accepted her sister was incapable of a normal, healthy relationship. Or maybe the exhaustion of motherhood tempered her puritan opinions. Either way, she ragged on me less these days.

"We should all go out sometime," she said.

I laughed. I appreciated my sister more than ever, but I wasn't ready to integrate her and Chris into my social life. It would be like bringing a priest to a strip club. The night would be hilarious, of course, but at my sister's expense. I no longer found that as thrilling as I used to.

"Yeah," I said. "Maybe we could go out to a nice dinner at the Olive Garden and then hit up the multiplex."

She rolled her eyes and pushed me out the door. "Be careful tonight."

"When am I not?" Since the dawn of time, no one has ever said those words without later regretting them. I was no exception.

"YOU LOOK SMOKIN'!" Dan bellowed as his eyes leisurely roved over my body in the bathroom mirror.

I loved my latest creation: a long black, silk dress with a deep plunging V in the back that came together at the vertex to hug my butt perfectly. Most of my back was covered with my wavy hair, but tantalizing snippets of skin appeared as I walked. It looked like a modest black dress from the front with a straight line cut atop my collarbones, but the open back gave it a pop of sexy. The silk charmeuse proved almost impossible to tailor without snagging or popping the fabric but the extra time spent in the studio was worth it. I felt like a seductive princess ready for the ball.

"I love how it gives the appearance that you're naked underneath."

"That's because I am." I spent hours manipulating the fluidity of the fabric to make it look like there wasn't a single seam in the dress. Even a G-string would ruin the clean line.

Dan grabbed my hips and pushed his pelvis against me, pinning me to the sink. I heard his breath catch and felt his excitement build, but I pushed him away. I wasn't wrinkling this dress before the night started.

"Tease," Dan muttered before leaving the bathroom.

I glanced once more in the mirror. The breakup with Ryan caused catastrophic damage to my self-esteem. The after-shocks—the constant questioning of what was wrong with me and why he didn't want me—still haunted me. I spent so much time ensuring I was exactly what Ryan wanted that I eviscerated the confident, sassy girl he fell for. But she slowly trickled back and tonight felt like a homecoming.

I threw on my heels and walked into the living room. Dan kneeled before the coffee table, measuring out two lines of coke with his oft-used platinum Visa credit card. Dan had many faults, but generosity was not one of them. His outlook on life was that everything, including drugs, was better when shared.

Dan looked up at me, eyebrows dancing mischievously. He proudly spread his hands out over the table as if presenting me with a seven course meal that he spent hours preparing instead of two lines of coke. "Let's start this night off right, hey?"

Outside of pot, I wasn't an avid drug user. It was expensive and I could usually have fun without it. But tonight, New Year's Eve, felt like the perfect occasion to add that little something extra to enhance the party.

"Gentlemen first," I said.

Dan snorted the coke in one long swoop. I followed suit. It felt like hot coals crackling in my throat and filled my mouth with the taste of chalk. I loathed the burning sensation. But it was a small price to pay for the resulting feeling of freedom and energy.

I walked towards the mirror to ensure that any remnants of the coke had disappeared. Nothing to worry about—I looked amazing.

HALF-HOUR LATER WE arrived at Haden and Rachel's house in Shorewood. The house was too old, big and suburban for two people in their twenties without children, but Rachel insisted on buying it...and then gutting it down to the studs for a massive makeover. Haden hoped the renovations would divert Rachel's attentions away from having a baby.

The living room—with fresh slate grey paint and white crown molding—was crowded. Music played in the background, but it was hard to hear over the din of conversation. A fire burned in the fireplace on the opposite wall which, Rachel announced with a pompous air on numerous occasions, gave the room a nineteenth century charm. The party, like the fire, felt hot and stuffy.

Dan grabbed my hand and led me into the newly renovated kitchen. They knocked the back wall down and put up an addition so that what was once a small, cozy kitchen had transformed into a gallery fit for a chef.

The bar was set up on the island with every type of hard liquor one could desire, as well as two large, silver buckets filled with champagne, wine and beer on ice. Holiday themed glasses with gingerbread men, candy canes and snowmen were stacked nearby.

Dan spotted the array of liquor and his eyes lit up. Other than the occasional acting gig, Dan partied his days away. By the excitement on his face, however, you would've thought he spent the last year living at an ashram in India.

"What would you like?"

"Tequila. Straight."

"Well if it's not the lovely Casey Byrne!" a voice boomed behind me.

Ross Richardson, one of the bartenders at the hideout, the martini bar Haden managed, stood beside me. Ross was always friendly, but there was something lascivious behind his banter, as if he was waiting for the day I'd come into the bar wanting more than a drink. His marriage, however, was first on a long list of reasons why that would never happen. I vowed to never date a married man again and Ross, who cheated with any girl smaller than a size eight with squeezable tits, could never tempt me to break that promise.

"How did I know I'd see you here?" His smarmy grin and the slow-motion once over he gave me suggested I organized this party as a rouse to spend New Year's with him.

I shrugged. "Haden's my best friend so it was a pretty good guess."

Dan handed me my drink, while I made introductions.

"You're Casey's boyfriend?" Ross asked, holding Dan's hand in a vice grip.

"I doubt anyone could tame Casey enough to make her commit," Dan laughed.

Oh, if only he knew.

"That sounds like the Casey I know." Ross licked his lips and winked at me—actually winked!—as if we just had a quick fuck outside.

I saw Haden nibbling food in the dining room and ran, literally, into the safety of his arms. Haden twirled me around like a ballroom dancer.

"I'm being stalked by Ross Richardson," I whispered.

"He's a git," Haden agreed.

"He makes me feel icky...down below." We both cracked up, recalling the numerous times we used this phrase in Key West to describe a rich, nasty vacationer who thought fucking the bartender was part of the all-inclusive package.

Rachel walked over to us, looking visibly annoyed, per usual.

"Hi Rachel! You look beautiful!" The coke was kicking in, which in turn made me generous with compliments. She did look pretty—if you preferred women that looked like life-sized Barbie dolls.

"Thanks," she muttered with a venomous smile. "I assume there's a story behind your off-color comment?"

Haden and I looked at each other and laughed even harder. *Off-color comment.* She talked as if she was in a 1950s sitcom.

"Long story, babe," Haden soothed. "Probably not good for a laugh on the second go around."

"Who are all these people?" I asked.

"The sober wankers are Rachel's work mates." Rachel hit him in the stomach. "Ouch. And anyone who looks mildly interesting I met at the Hideout."

Rachel shook her head and continued to scan the crowd like a queen on her throne.

"Are we boring you?" I asked.

"You are many things Casey," Rachel taunted, "but boring is not one of them."

Haden wrapped his arms around both of us. "Ah, my two favorites birds."

Dan stole me away shortly thereafter, thereby eliminating the tension. We went into the living room where we danced to classic 1980s hair bands, old school hip-hop music and a little top forty pop mixed in.

The music coursed through my veins, making my limbs fluid. I danced with everyone, creating a dance floor full of love, sweat and hormones. I took swigs of whatever liquor was around. My stomach was soon filled with a mixture of unknown spirits, dancing together to a familiar beat.

I'd been this girl countless times—carefree and wild—but never without the awareness that I was playing a role. But tonight I lived in the moment, intoxicated with dancing, men and liquor in equal measures.

At some point Dan dragged me into a room upstairs. Bright colors flashed like fireworks inside my head until he flipped on the light. We were in a bathroom. A claw tub sat against the far wall, a toilet between and a vanity stood next to the door. Gaudy gold finishings sparkled on each appliance. I laughed thinking about how this 1980s inspired bathroom probably caused Rachel nightmares.

Dan sat down on the toilet and wiped the sink clean with a tissue. Inside his shirt pocket he procured his tiny bag of coke and began constructing four even lines.

I leaned over the sink and looked at myself in the mirror. My pupils were a bit dilated, but other than that, I looked fabulous.

"Hey, be careful!" Dan pushed me away from the sink and I went flying into the door. I saw the crash in the mirror but didn't feel any pain.

The door busted open behind me and nudged me forward. Joshua's eyes made a bee line from mine to Dan's to the coke before settling back on mine.

"Sorry," Joshua muttered before quickly closing the door.

"Great!" I slapped the wall. "He'll run right to Rachel and tattle on us."

"Re-lax," Dan replied lazily, drawing out the *re* and the *lax* into two words. He obviously didn't care if Rachel knew. Why would he? These weren't his friends. "He's not going to tell her. And if he does, we'll leave."

There was a knock at the door. Dan and I froze. If this was a movie, we would've immediately flushed the coke down the toilet. But, of course, it wasn't and the coke stayed put on the sink.

Dan cracked open the door. "Hey man."

Haden walked inside and I breathed a sigh of relief. As co-host of this party, Haden's participation legitimized our activities. Any thoughts of Rachel and the wrath she might bring down immediately dissipated.

Haden rubbed his hands together greedily. "Let's stop mucking about and get on this!"

A wave of nostalgia flooded through me as I remembered all the great times Haden and I had before Rachel came into his life and, as she says, *cleaned up his act.* I liked his act better before.

Dan did the first line, followed by Haden and then me. For some reason the second time never burned as much and it always hit me faster. I was toeing the line between feeling invincible and out of control, but I wasn't there yet. I was fine. Super, in fact. Well on my way to an excellent evening.

Dan pointed at me. "She's worried about your wife finding out."

"'Bout what exactly?" Haden asked. "Casey would prefer my wife not know anything about her."

"Hardly. She's the one that has no interest in getting to know me." Haden sat down on the edge of the claw tub. "Sod it. Let me enjoy my first high in months."

"You should come out more."

"You should invite me out more," he retorted.

"Too bad your wife won't let you out."

"You guys fight like brother and sister," Dan said. He gestured towards the coke. I shook my head, while Haden dismissed him with a wave. Dan did the final line and wiped the sink clean. "Let's join the party."

THE NIGHT PASSED BY in a blur of dancing, drinking and laughing. Midnight, and the end of 2009, came quickly. Rachel passed out blow horns and silver, pointy hats with 2010 written across it in bubbled, red letters. Dan, tapping into his non-existent gangster side, wore his hat to the side so that it covered his left ear.

Dan stood behind me with his arms wrapped around my waist as we counted down the last ten seconds of 2009. At midnight I blew the blow horn for a few seconds before Dan turned me around, plucked the blow horn out of my mouth and dipped me backwards for a luscious Hollywood kiss.

Dan resumed dancing, but a pit of anxiety took hold of me. Each beat of the song pulsated loudly in my ears. The dancers moved too fast. I felt claustrophobic and dizzy. I had to get out.

I went back upstairs, found an empty bedroom and crawled into bed. For some reason the ending of last year and the start of this one set off an alarm bell. An intense bout of anxiety percolated in my stomach. *But why was I anxious?* School was on break. I didn't work tomorrow. I was free. But instead of calming me, these thoughts amplified my sadness. *No one needed me. I had nothing to do, nowhere to go. Nothing. Nothing. Nothing.*

My life was a disaster and about to get worse when I graduated. I wasn't ready to enter the competitive design world. I saw Kipp struggle to compete with the other boutiques, as well as the chains.

What if I never sold my designs? What if I was stuck bartending for the rest of my life?

I felt like I was living life wrapped up in a straightjacket. I kept repeating the same behaviors, expecting a different result. There was a certain ebb and flow to it. The highs were easy to live with, but the lows, like tonight, brought painful clarity. I needed to make some changes. Otherwise, ten years would pass and I'd end up drunk and coked out, mulling my wasted life, in a perfectly decorated bedroom of one of Rachel and Haden's kids.

A bit later—had I passed out or was I just deep in thought?—the door opened. Impulsively, I dove under a heap of throw pillows. Maybe the person would be too drunk to notice me.

"Casey?" Someone shook my leg. I froze in the hope that whoever it was would assume I was sleeping and leave. But this person was persistent, pulling off each pillow one by one, as if they were a paleontologist digging for fossils.

Mixing coke and liquor has never caused me to hallucinate, but when I opened my eyes, I hoped that was the case. Rachel, Ryan and Claire stood above me, looking annoyed, worried and curious (in that order).

"Are you okay?" Rachel asked.

Stupid wasn't a broad enough term to describe how I felt. Embarrassed, mortified, idiotic and humiliated also came to mind. Combine all of those and you'll still fall short of my state of mind.

"I'm fine," I said with my most dazzling smile. (It no longer felt dazzling. Tears had dried on my face, making it feel like I wore a clay facial mask.) "Just tired."

Ryan sat next to me on the edge of the bed. I refused to make eye contact. I wanted to scream at him to go away. He was the only person I ever loved and he abandoned me, regulating me to a financial investment in his life. *I hated him.*

"This is Ryan, a partner at my firm, and his wife, Claire," Rachel said, introducing us as if I hadn't met Ryan before. Had Rachel forgot that we met? Was it possible that Rachel didn't know we had an affair? Haden knew. I confessed the sordid details one drunken night well after it was over. But maybe Haden never deemed it important enough to tell Rachel. More likely, it wasn't worth the drama. She'd blow the whole thing out of proportion, making Haden endure every "what if" scenario about how her young career could have been tarnished by my lack of morals. "I was giving them a tour of the house."

The only positive was that Claire had yet to remember me. Her face was still in concentration, like she was rereading a book she read a long time ago but couldn't remember the ending.

"Don't let me stop you," I said. "I was just resting."

Rachel narrowed her eyes at me, knowing I never rested during a party. But Ryan stepped in before she could speak. "Why don't you guys head downstairs? I'll get Casey a glass of water and make sure she feels alright."

"Maybe I should look at her," Claire offered.

Ah, yes, Claire, the perfect nurse. Perfect wife. Perfect everything. I gave Ryan a stern look that said: *I'll kill you if you let her touch me.*

"She's fine. Probably just drank too much." I perked up, trying to look half-way sober. "A little water and she'll be as good as gold."

"Okay," Rachel hesitated. She didn't want to leave us alone, but didn't feel right contradicting her boss—even in her own house. Rachel gave me a scathing look before closing the door. Maybe she did know.

"Just go," I complained, hugging a pillow to my body.

"I'm not leaving." Ryan's face was set in a grim line. "You don't look great, in fact—"

"That's perfect!" I interrupted, striking the first blow. "I run into you and your wife, who looks gorgeous, *of course*, and you immediately tell me I look like shit. Thanks!"

"I'm worried about you," he replied, ignoring my rant. Ryan excelled at ignoring things he didn't want to hear. "Did you drink too much?"

Ryan's blue eyes peered down at me. When he spoke, the dimple on his left cheek flexed in and out causing tiny, sharp needles to puncture my heart. If I was stronger, sober, or a little less in love, I would've walked out. But I felt needy and lonely and he satisfied the gaping hole better than anyone. I wanted Ryan next to me, touching, talking and fretting over me. I wanted to pretend for a few minutes that we were still together.

"Maybe." I pretended to recall how much I drank, all the while knowing liquor had little to do with my downward spiral. I should've taken the extra line Dan offered. At least then I would've avoided this nasty comedown until I was in the privacy of my own bed. "I'm not really sure how much I had."

"Do you feel sick?" Ryan reached up and pushed some hair off my face that was virtually glued to my lip gloss. The picture I had of myself earlier tonight as a sex goddess vanished. It was replaced by a poster in our high school hung to scare us away from drugs. The girl was a meth addict with stringy hair, black bags under her eyes, hallowed out cheekbones and a sad, flaky mouth. I probably looked like her older sister.

"I just want to sleep," I mumbled.

Ryan lay down next to me on the bed, resting his hand on my hip. His face was mere inches from mine. I could almost taste the minty coolness of his breath, feel the slight stubble of his five o'clock shadow against my lips and hear the thoughts of desire roaming in his head. Tears sprang to my eyes as I digested, for the millionth time, that his lips, smile, essence, would never belong to me. I could kiss him, but the pain would be too great knowing that nothing had changed and he would return to Claire.

"Did you take anything besides alcohol?" Ryan whispered.

Drugs caused the only fight in our relationship that wasn't about his marriage. I got coked out one night and left a message on his cell phone accusing him of not really loving me and crying about how I would spend the rest of my life alone, pining after him. (Foreshadowing anyone?) Terrified, Ryan left Claire in the middle of the night to see if I was okay. After a dirty fight (and even dirtier makeup sex), he made me promise I wouldn't do coke again. And I didn't—until we broke up. If he could break promises then so could I.

"You don't get a say in my decisions anymore."

"Of course I do," he said. "I care about you. My feelings for you didn't vanish just because we broke up."

"I know," I said, suddenly feeling guilty. Ryan was never deliberately mean or said hurtful things to provoke a reaction. He was a man caught loving two women and I never once tried to understand. "I just hate you seeing me like this. I want to leave."

"So let's get you home."

I threw a pillow over my head. Was he dumb or just that conceited that he thought he would never get caught? "Ryan. Your wife is downstairs."

"She doesn't remember you."

"Trust me, she will. Women always do," I stressed. "Besides Dan is somewhere around here. He can take me home."

Ryan's brow furrowed. "Who's Dan?"

"No one."

"I can't even ask you a simple question?"

"It's not simple. It's never simple with us and you know that."

"Fine," he huffed. "Then I'll have to assume the worst."

Even when I tried to stay on the sidelines, he somehow dragged me into the match. "And what's that?"

Ryan voice was low and controlled but his eye contact was menacing. "That he's your boyfriend. That you love him. That you'll marry him one day."

"He's not my boyfriend," I retorted. There was no way to win this game. Ryan and I couldn't be together because he had some twisted loyalty to his wife, but he still got angry when I dated other men. No wonder I was so miserable.

"But you're having sex with him," Dan said.

The passion between us was palpable. Wasn't that a sign of real love? I buried my head in my hands. This was a disaster. We quickly regressed into embattled exes when not guided by the strict confines of our lunch meetings.

"You have no right to ask me that." I sat up, fueled by a burst of angry energy. "I don't ask you how often you fuck your wife. I don't ask whether you regret staying with her. I don't ask how often you think of me. These are questions I don't ask not only because I have no right, but because it would kill me to hear the answers. I suggest you do the same."

I jumped up off the bed, feeling both dizzy and weak, and fled downstairs. The place was deserted. I went into the kitchen, but found that empty too. It was almost two in the morning. *Where was Dan?*

I turned around and ran into my favorite trio: Haden, Rachel and Claire. "Have you guys seen Dan?"

Claire's face remained impassive. I couldn't help but marvel at her beauty. She was truly an ice princess: blonde hair, blue eyes, pink lips. Not a single wrinkle adorned her porcelain face. Ryan once told me that he would come up with outrageous stories just to see if she would register any emotional response on her face. But she only ran on one gear. In essence, she was my opposite in both looks and personality. My dark hair, dark eyes, olive skin and soon-to-be lined face from too much smiling and partying were probably her biggest WASPy nightmare—other than not having kids.

Haden's face was a picture of confusion. "Dan left an hour ago."

Impossible. But then again, knowing Dan, it was very possible. He was the most unreliable, piece-of-shit friend. I wasn't a big resolution person but I decided to set one for 2010: only date men that cared about my well-being. It was time to clean house emotionally.

It was only when Ryan joined the group and was brought up to speed on my little predicament that I truly wanted to fall to the floor, start digging for China and never, ever come back.

"We can take you home," Ryan said. I saw Rachel glance at Haden in alarm.

"Or you could crash here," Haden offered, causing Rachel to have a small seizure. She wanted me gone, but on her terms.

"Joshua," Rachel called out. We all turned to see Joshua walk into the kitchen, holding a pile of dirty plates in each hand. Like a good samaritan, he started cleaning up the party. "Would you mind taking Casey home? She lives in the Third Ward, so it's on your way."

Joshua's eyes flicked towards me. He looked conflicted. Only a few short hours ago he saw me snorting coke in the bathroom. For a boy scout like him, this was not an easy favor to grant. A few beats of silence passed.

"Don't worry," I assured him. "I'll sleep here and Haden will take me home in the morning."

As much as I wanted to be in my own bed, I couldn't stand here and have everyone treat me like I was the last kid left to be picked in a game of dodgeball.

"It's not a problem," Joshua answered with a tiny smile. His good nature apparently won out over his concerns.

After saying our goodbyes, I walked outside into the frigid night with Joshua and his girlfriend Amanda. My teeth chattered as I crawled into the backseat of his car.

"The car's new so the heat works pretty fast," Joshua said. He adjusted the vents in the backseat so that they faced me directly.

Amanda smiled at Joshua and gave his arm a gentle squeeze. "Thanks for driving tonight so I could have a glass of champagne."

A glass of champagne? One, single, uno? And she needed a designated driver? I felt like I was in an episode of the *Brady Bunch*, listening to a night out between Mike and Carol. I looked around the car, half-expecting the laugh track to kick in or to hear a collective *aww* from the audience because those two were just so damn cute.

Amanda turned around. "You're not going to be sick, are you?"

"I hope not. I only drank a bottle of champagne." I saw Joshua bite his lip to stifle a laugh in the rearview mirror. "That's well below my limit."

"Wow!" Amanda started as if I had slapped her. "Drinking all the sugar is horrible for your skin. It dries it out. That's why I like to stick to red wine, but tonight was a special occasion. You know, when in Rome!"

"Don't let Amanda fool you," Joshua piped in. "I've seen her down a bottle of red on more than one occasion."

The atmosphere in the car suddenly felt as icy as the temperature outside.

"Yes," Amanda answered through gritted teeth, "but red wine is very different than champagne. It helps nourish your skin. It also prevents heart disease and certain kinds of cancers. Any doctor will tell you that red wine is good for you."

"But will they say a *bottle* of red wine is good for you?" I asked with the sickening sweetness of maple syrup.

"I rarely do that," she snapped. She ignored me for the remainder of the ride.

Joshua pulled up outside my building and parked in the loading zone. Unsurprisingly, given his polite nature, Joshua chivalrously volunteered to walk me to my door.

"Can I come in for a minute?" Joshua asked, catching me off guard.

"Sure." I opened the door. What was I supposed to do? His girlfriend was waiting in the car. Surely he didn't plan on staying long.

"Nice apartment," Joshua commented. "How long have you been here?"

"Almost three years," I said as I hung up my jacket in the closet. As I turned around I caught Joshua staring at me. I couldn't read the emotion—lust, wonder, concern?—on his face, confusing matters further. "I moved here before I started at the Art Institute."

"So I"—Joshua's voice cracked and he stopped to clear his throat—"I wanted to make sure you're okay."

I could've acted like I didn't know what he was talking about but that would have only extended the conversation. I already felt like the entire night was an after school special and I wanted to get the credits rolling.

"I'm fine," I promised, shielding my heart with my right hand for good measure. "Honestly, I'm just tired."

"Really?"

"Yeah, it's been a long night. Long year, actually."

Having shed my heels, we were approximately the same height. Since I was tall, I gravitated towards tall men and was used to looking up at them when speaking. It was oddly intimate to look directly into a man's eyes.

"Okay," Joshua hesitated, unsure if he should believe me. "Well I'll let you get to bed then."

For the split-second that we held each other's eyes, I thought there was something else underlying his actions. His concern didn't add up. We hardly knew each other. I had good friends that wouldn't go to these lengths to ensure I was alright. Plus, I'm sure Rachel insinuated I was out drinking and doing drugs nightly. *Rachel.* Had Rachel made him promise that he would get me home safe? That must be it. No one was this vigilant with someone they weren't obligated to care about.

"You looked beautiful tonight," he said before leaving.

What a random comment! Was he trying to make me feel better since I looked like a train wreck?

I was too exhausted to care. I threw my dress on the bedroom floor—yes, the same one that took me hours to design, create and tailor—like an old magazine and flopped into bed without washing up. It was only then, when the silence of my apartment began suffocating me, that I realized I wouldn't be able to sleep. My mind was running sprints, evaluating the events of not only tonight but another disaster of a year.

MY FIRST THOUGHT UPON waking was that I had gone blind. Numerous layers of dried mascara crusted my eyes shut. It took several failed rubbing attempts to wash away the grit before I could finally open my eyes.

My head pounded. My stomach growled. My throat felt like sandpaper. My heart ached. Was happiness even possible on January first? But I knew my state had little to do with New Year's Eve. Too often I woke up feeling depressed and in pain. Scrapes and bruises, missing or stained clothes, a stiff neck or an acidic mouth from puking—it was quite normal for me.

Then there was the mental ordeal as I endured the inevitable reconstruction of the night's events. Reconstruction was always troubling because the events played like scraps of a film. The scenes would jump ahead or backward without warning. Some mornings I could laugh, but more often lately, I woke with regret. I didn't understand why some nights stayed carefree and others caused a cataclysmic breakdown, like last night.

I remembered lying in bed with Ryan. Sweet, infuriatingly addictive, love-of-my-life Ryan. Why was he there? Did he hope to see me? *Fuck, fuck, fuck.* Such useless questions!

I gingerly walked to the bathroom where I drank three glasses of water. I brushed my teeth and stared mercilessly at myself in the mirror. I looked like a whore. Dark eyeliner, charcoal eye shadow and mascara were caked around my eyes, but the twelve-hour blush was still holding strong. (At least some people kept their promises.) Basically, I was a contender for wife-of-the-year on *Cops*.

I jumped into the shower and let the warm water wash away the dirt from last night. If only it could cleanse my mind.

My phone rang as I crawled back into bed. It was Ryan. Curiosity held my good judgment hostage...again.

"Hi," I croaked. I knew my throat hurt, but I didn't realize until trying to speak that I had basically lost my voice.

"You sound horrible," Ryan (a.k.a. Captain Obvious) pointed out. "I've been up all night wondering if you're okay."

"I told you, I'm not yours to worry about anymore."

"I can't stop worrying just because you want me to. It's not like a light switch that I can flip on and off."

True, but it wasn't my problem. Ryan forfeited the right to tell me how much he cared. It was far too dangerous for me to engage with his emotions.

"Well, neither can I, but I don't call you to talk about it," I retorted. Arguing had become a song and dance to us, where we blindly repeated the same feelings with different words knowing the outcome stayed the same. "You choose Claire, remember? Go be with her and leave me alone."

I sounded tough, but my gut seized in fear imagining a life without Ryan—even the abbreviated one we had now. I preferred to rip the Band-Aid off in slow motion.

"So last night, I should've said, *Casey's fucked out of her mind. Thank God she's not my problem anymore.*"

"What were you doing there anyways?" I asked, ignoring his sarcasm.

"Rachel invited us. We had a party downtown and stopped by on the way home."

"Did you know I was going to be there?"

"Casey, I never know where you're going to be," Ryan drawled. "You excel at being utterly unpredictable."

My stomach clenched up before I even formed the question. My body had an uncanny way of sensing danger before my mind registered it. "Were you hoping I'd be there?"

"Part of me hopes to see you everywhere." Ryan paused. "But I'm not calling to rehash us. I'm worried about you."

"I'm *fine*," I wailed.

"Does getting drunk and coked out seem fine to you? Does passing out in the middle of a party seem fine to you? Does staying in bed all day seem fine to you?" He adopted his lawyer persona in both tone and rhetoric—cold, cutting and confident—which meant that nothing I said would matter. "You need to get some help."

"Fine. I'll get some help," I deadpanned, knowing my careless tone would infuriate him, which in turn gave me a small amount of pleasure.

"I'm serious. You keep everything bottled up and instead of talking to someone about it, *like me*, you go out and get drunk—"

"I do enjoy your ability to abdicate all responsibility for this situation and then say, with a straight face, that I need help."

"How long are you going to use our breakup as an excuse?" Ryan asked. "Whatever issues you have going on inside your head that make you act like you did last night were there long before me."

He was right, of course. The need to fake happiness and be the life of the party to earn the adoration of others had been there for as long as I could remember. The only time I really knew it was me was when I woke up feeling depressed, isolated and unlovable. It was a dull, throbbing ache throughout my whole body that would not leave until I distracted myself with work, sleep, alcohol or drugs.

But no one wanted to feel unlovable. People self-medicated in all sorts of ways to cope with feeling depressed. My coping mechanisms hadn't proved to be a problem. Didn't AA espouse that the first sign of a problem was that you couldn't live your daily life without the substance? Well, that certainty didn't describe me. Between work and school, I really didn't even have time to party more than a few days a week. So what if I woke up hung over, lonely and depressed? Was it really that abnormal for a single girl in her twenties? Anyone who wasn't middle-aged, living in his McMansion in suburbia with his filler-injected wife could appreciate the difference.

But even through all my bravado, there was a nagging sensation that things could be better. I didn't want to hang around guys like Dan that felt entitled to use and discard me. I didn't want to hold out hope that Ryan would decide I was the missing piece in his life. I was trudging through life, functioning, but definitely not thriving. As much as I enjoyed getting high, the comedown seemed worse each time. Whatever reprieve it gave me from my thoughts immediately assaulted me when the high was over.

"You're right," I finally responded. "Maybe I should talk to someone."

"Thatta girl!" Ryan whooped. "I have someone in mind too."

I put my hand up to stop him from talking, even though he couldn't see me. "No. I'll find someone on my own."

"Make sure to find someone covered under your health insurance."

"That would be helpful if I had health insurance," I quipped.

"C-a-a-a-s-e-e-e-y," Ryan strung out the vowels in my name through gritted teeth. "Do you know how dangerous it is to live without health insurance? What if—"

"Stop!" I almost chucked my phone across the room. "You only get one lecture per day."

"Fine," Ryan conceded. "Keep me posted."

An hour later I devoured a pepperoni pizza while searching the internet for therapists. It was hard, however, to find the right therapist when I couldn't identify my problem. Did I want a specialist in depression? Drug and alcohol abuse? Relationship issues? I felt like I had a problem that could fit into each section of psychiatric medicine. (*How scary was that!?!*)

I was about to give up when the mouse moved by itself, as if my laptop was an Ouija board, and hovered over Dr. Kate Baylor. She had long dark hair, ebony skin, a wide, friendly smile and trusting eyes. But what really caught my attention was the Diane von Furstenberg wrap dress she wore. I felt an instant kinship. Anyone with style was my type of therapist.

I called her office and left my name and number. But when it came to explaining my problem, I faltered.

"...I'm not sure I need a therapist, but my ex suggested it because he thinks I party too much. But he just worries because he can't take care of me anymore. He went back to his wife. That's a *long* story. Anyways, I'm not a drug addict or an alcoholic, although I do dabble. And sometimes I feel depressed. Generally when hungover or I see Ryan. It's not like my life is one of those Prozac ads. God, I'm babbling...anyways, you have my number..."

Despite the cringe-worthy message, I felt pleased. Without getting out of bed, I made the first step towards the new me. At the very least, it eliminated the dull, throbbing pain in my gut. I didn't even have to take a shot or light up a joint—if that wasn't progress than I didn't know what was.

Chapter 17

Casey – September 22, 2012

"It's so weird hearing you talk about that night, because I never would've guessed you were dealing with"—Joshua's hands made a small windmill gesture—"all that. You were always laughing and goofing around. I assumed drugs and drinking was all part of the fun for you."

"It was. And in some ways still is," I amended, pointing towards the tequila in my hand. "But it's good to hear that I appeared happy. At least my public persona wasn't tarnished."

"I remember you were very quiet on the ride home, but I assumed it was because you didn't want a ride home from us."

"I didn't," I admitted. "I felt bad that Rachel forced you to take care of me. No one wants to take care of the drunk girl—especially when you hardly know the drunk girl."

"To be fair, I wasn't worried about you being drunk. I'd dealt with enough of my drug addicted clients the morning after their arrest to know what a bad come down looks like."

"I'm not an addict," I argued, cringing inwardly that Joshua's first thought was to compare me to his clients. If we ended up dating and I went out one night and didn't come home, I'm sure he'd immediately assume I was coked out. Would our relationship be like a ticking time bomb: him waiting for me to fuck up?

"I know," he said softly and clasped his hand atop of mine. "But a bad comedown can be brutal whether you're an addict or not."

"I guess."

"I can't believe you thought I was going to tell Rachel," Joshua said, eagerly switching to more lighthearted matters. "I ran out of the bathroom because I felt like an idiot."

"You're Rachel's best friend. I assumed you hated me too."

He cocked his head to the left and laughed. "It's actually a relief to find out that you were dismissive of me merely because I hung out with Rachel and not because you saw a fatal flaw in my personality."

I held my right hand up as if I was under oath. "I can say in complete honesty that your only real flaw was being friends with Rachel. The rest I incorrectly assumed as a result."

"You're horrible to her," he admonished, shaking his head.

"It comes out more when I drink," I admitted, gamely taking another swig of tequila. "Did you ever tell Amanda about the coke?"

Joshua's eyes widened behind his glasses. "Ah, no. Definitely not. Amanda would've freaked out if drugs were in the house."

"*Drugs?* It was a small vile, not a pound."

He grinned sheepishly. "You'd think as a guidance counselor she'd be used to dealing with drugs, but at the Jewish Day School the kids are all privileged and shielded, like her, from reality. It was another one of the reasons why she hated that I worked as a public defender. She couldn't shut her eyes to the crime that happened in Milwaukee."

"Hmm...remind me, what did you guys have in common?" I teased him.

"Not enough," he said. "So where did Dan disappear to that night?"

"I don't know."

"What do you mean?"

I scratched my head as I struggled to recall the exact turn of events. "He called a week after New Years and I didn't call him back. He called a few weeks later and I never called him back. The end."

"He didn't call the next day to make sure you got home alright?" Joshua looked shocked. I guess if you were Joshua—the type of guy who would take a random drunk girl home in the freezing cold to make sure she was safe—not calling the next day was sacrilegious.

"No way. I'm sure he was still bingeing. A week later, when he finally sobered up, he remembered me."

"At least you were smart enough to ditch him."

"The credit for that goes to my therapist," I admitted with a laugh.

"Ah, yes. The esteemed Dr. Kate. I can't believe she took you on after hearing your rambling mess of a message."

"Dr. Kate adores me." I swatted my hand playfully against his thigh. "I'm pretty much her favorite patient."

"I'm sure," he answered with false pity.

"Well, maybe not her favorite," I conceded, "but she's stuck by me the past few years. Of course, I pay her..."

After Dr. Kate diagnosed the immediate reason I felt depressed—I drank excessively, did drugs and had causal sex to mask my feelings for Ryan—she gave me a few things to work on. First, I wasn't supposed to drink or get high when I felt sad, stressed or angry. (An equation I dubbed: no alcohol plus no drugs equals no fun.) She wanted me to feel my emotions, get to know the real me, regardless of how uncomfortable it seemed at first.

Second, I wasn't allowed to talk to Ryan. Dr. Kate viewed the relationship as toxic. The affair was both forgivable and understandable, but the breakup had morphed into an emotionally manipulative power game where he held all the cards. It needed to end.

My relationship with Ryan was so consuming that it felt like I was nothing before him. I was born, bloomed and died via Ryan's hands. Dr. Kate guided me through a "rebirth" of sorts, where she helped me rediscover my essence and believe that I could be happy without him.

Third, no more one-night stands. She wanted to help *reframe my views* on sex (her words, not mine). Thus, sex was only on the table when there was a potential for a healthy relationship.

I broke these rules...repeatedly. They were harder to follow than I anticipated, especially not talking to Ryan. But I soon learned talking with Ryan was a slippery slope. Even when discussing mundane topics, I left depressed and ended up drinking or hooking up with a random guy to dull the pain. I eventually learned that the key to my emotional stability (and following the rules) was keeping Ryan at bay.

"Are you completely honest with her?" Joshua asked.

"Usually," I hedged. There were times when I didn't want to tell her the truth: when I slipped up and got high; had sex with a guy because I wanted to feel wanted; or called Ryan just to hear his voice and ended up crying for an hour while he listened. I struggled with wanting to sugarcoat my life at the beginning, but I quickly realized that I had to tell her the ugly truth if I really wanted to get better. "It became impossible to ignore my bad decisions when I had to sit face-to-face with Dr. Kate and admit what happened and then spend an hour discussing why I did it. Reflection is a bitch, but for me, it's led to better decisions."

"Smart and beautiful?" Joshua shook his head. "It's almost unfair."

"Hardly," I replied. "I've become a total new age, crunchy granola, Pilates devotee, can't-live-without-my-therapist-type-of-girl. It doesn't exactly make men swoon. What about you? Do you have a therapist?"

"Nope," he laughed. "It's not really my thing."

I learned by now that men wanted to fix their own problems—not talk to a stranger about them. But given what he told me tonight about his overbearing parents, the baby with Leah and his high pressure relationship with Amanda, a little therapy would go a long way.

I shrugged. "I never thought it would be my thing until I tried."

"Well, I'm glad you did."

I held out the inside of my left forearm where I had an ampersand tattooed in thick blue ink. It was two inches wide and two inches long. "I got this tattoo shortly after starting therapy. It's there to remind me to have faith in the process of life: there's a before and after to everything. If I can just get through this part, regardless of how insufferable it might feel, I'll be better afterwards for having gone through it."

He softly traced the curve of the ampersand with his thumb. "Does it work?"

I looked down at my first and only tattoo. Against all odds, it worked exactly as I envisioned: it calmed me. "I know it sounds stupid, but when I get stressed, I trace it, like you're doing right now, and I relax a bit knowing that whatever is bothering me is just one moment in time."

"That's a better reason than most," Joshua muttered.

"I take it you don't have any tattoos?"

Joshua met my question with an indulgent smile. "Of course not."

"Why?"

"If I said I was scared of the pain, would that completely ruin everything else I have going for me tonight?"

I pretended to mull over the question. "Absolutely. I'd have to revoke your man card and have the bartender escort you out."

"Good to know. Truth is, nothing has ever been meaningful enough for me to have it permanently inked into my skin with a needle."

"It's not that bad." I grabbed his forearm and rhythmically pricked my nail into his skin.

"Yeah, I'd probably pass out just from the sight of it." He clasped his hand over mine to stop the tapping. I grinned at him, thinking about the possibilities his sensitive skin held. "So did this therapy of yours work?"

"Meaning?"

"Well," he hesitated before firing questions like a machine gun. "Are you happy now? Do you still do drugs? Are you still in love with Ryan?"

I froze. Essentially he wanted to know: Are you worth investing my time or will you break my heart when you go on another binge, fuck a random guy or dump me because I don't match up to Ryan?

"Well, I'll answer from the easiest to the hardest," I said. "I haven't done coke for almost two years."

"Because it makes you sad?"

"Pretty much. The comedown exaggerated everything I didn't like about myself."

"I've never done coke, or really any drug," Joshua admitted. "But from what my clients tell me, that's pretty normal. Although instead of dealing with those negative feelings, my clients opt to use more drugs to prevent the comedown. It never works, of course. I mean, you either comedown or die, but I guess they're not really thinking clearly."

"It's hard to understand if you've never done it. I've yet to figure out if the comedown is really that bad or if it feels unbearable because the high was so good."

Joshua laughed. "Sounds like you miss it."

"I'm just saying that if it wasn't fun people wouldn't do it. Sometimes it's worth putting up with all the bullshit afterwards."

He gasped. "What would Dr. Kate think if she heard you say that?"

"What can I say? I'm a bad girl, turned good, with more than a little bit of bad left over."

"A little bit of bad can be very sexy."

Joshua locked his knees around the outside of mine so that I couldn't move. His slight frame was deceiving. Although his muscles weren't large, they were clearly defined through his thin t-shirt. The curve of his biceps and the tension in his forearms, combined with this little exercise of power right now with his legs, showed he could easily hold me down or tie me up. Very surprising and very hot from the quiet, mild-mannered boy I assumed him to be all these years.

I leaned over and teasingly kissed his scruffy jaw line, feeling the tickle of his whiskers against my lips, as I made my way up towards his ear. "What was the second question?"

He sighed softly. "You were going to tell me about Ryan or whether you were happy."

"I told you, Ryan and I stopped seeing each other as much when I started therapy and even less once I graduated and he adopted a baby."

"I remember you stopped seeing him, but I'm wondering when you moved on?" He quickly amended his statement. "I'm wondering *if* you've moved on."

Ryan consumed a miniscule fraction of my thoughts each day, but he still rented space. I doubted my ability to ever evict him. I automatically compared any guy I dated to Ryan in terms of personality, support, looks and most importantly, my feelings. According to Dr. Kate, I idealized Ryan to the point that he took on a mythical quality no man could ever meet. We've debated this issue tirelessly and have yet to reach a consensus.

But these were not thoughts to share on a first date, let alone with a man to whom I felt a connection. I had no idea what to say. We both opened up tonight, raw and without agenda, about some of the most excruciating and momentous events in our lives. Yet I found myself toeing the line between honesty and my feelings for Joshua, carefully choosing my words.

"Ryan will always hold a place in my heart. He was the first man I truly loved. He—"

"What about John?" Joshua interrupted.

I shook my head. "I thought I loved John, but looking back now, I idolized him more than anything. I never let him get to know me because I was afraid he was too good for me. That's not love."

"Alright." Joshua held out his hand, inviting me to continue.

"Right, Ryan," I said, collecting my thoughts. "I finally admitted to myself, maybe a year ago, that Ryan and I weren't soul mates. He wasn't *the one*. We loved each other, but we never had a future. Plain and simple: it was a bad affair."

"Do you still believe *the one* exists?"

"Who knows?" I muttered. "I was convinced Ryan was the one and look how that turned out. All I can do is trust my gut and take a chance."

"What does your gut tell you about me?"

Despite the loud music and background conversations, I could hear the soft strum of Joshua's breath as he waited in anticipation for my answer.

"It's on red alert," I admitted. "I spent years thinking you were someone else. And yet tonight, well, you've surprised me. I'm curious as to what else I'll find out."

He stretched his arms out wide, as if preparing for a giant hug. "I'm an open book. Ask me anything."

"Hmm..." I tapped my lips with my index finger.

"But first you have to answer my final question. Are you happy?"

"I'm happy *tonight*."

He waited, clearly not satisfied with my glib answer.

"In short, when I pay attention to what makes me happy—designing clothes, my friends, my sister and niece—I'm fine.

But it gets hard at times because everyone else promotes these ridiculous societal rules: married by twenty-five, two children, a six-figure salary and a house in the suburbs. It's all bullshit but completely pervasive. I'm constantly reminding myself that's not what I need or want to be happy—it's all just noise."

"Everyone talks about how times are so different than fifty years ago, but little has changed," Joshua agreed. "Anyone single in their thirties or who expresses any skepticism about marriage and kids is questioned at best and treated as a social pariah at worst."

"Social pariah?"

"Well, maybe that's a bit dramatic," he conceded. "But I just felt such immense pressure to propose to Amanda."

"From who?"

"Amanda, our friends, my coworkers, her Rabbi"—he cracked a smile—"my parents, of course."

"I was fifteen when my parents gave me their one and only piece of advice regarding boys: *Don't get pregnant*."

"At least you listened."

"They're very proud," I enthused, wiping away a fake tear. Whereas Cadie acceded to my parents' authority, I questioned and defied every rule I was given—curfew, dating, drinking, school. When I turned eighteen they threw their hands up in defeat. To this day, the relationship remains chilly with no happy ending in sight.

"My parents think there's one way to live and they don't like to be contradicted." Joshua rubbed his face with both hands. It felt refreshingly odd to spend time with a man that wasn't hiding his emotions. "It's exhausting."

"My parents ignore me to let me know they disapprove."

"You think it's that simple?"

"The simplest explanation is usually the correct one, right?"

"Nothing is simple when it comes to my parents," Joshua grumbled. "Never mind. The last thing I want to do is turn tonight into family therapy."

"Agreed." I twisted a long strand of hair around my finger until it was wound in a tight spiral close to my ear. "I'd much rather hear why you broke up with Amanda. You don't seem like a commitment-phobe or the kind of guy to string a girl along, so what changed?"

Joshua blinked rapidly a few times and his jaw locked. "Honestly, I feel weird talking about it; like I'm being disloyal."

"Disloyal?" I repeated. It seemed odd that Amanda would cause him to clam up after everything he revealed tonight. "I don't think it's disloyal to talk about what went wrong. You own the experience as much she does."

"True..."

"But no worries if you feel weird. It's sheer curiosity on my part; nothing more, nothing less."

He grinned. "Sheer curiosity, huh?"

"I'd like to hear about the last woman to win your heart."

"Looking for some pointers?"

I laughed. "From the woman that didn't make the cut? Unlikely."

"Nah, you're right. It's better you figure out those things on your own." Joshua winked at me from underneath his glasses. Again with the winking! "Plus, you don't strike me as someone that needs a lot of pointers."

"Even if I did, I wouldn't admit it."

He threw his hands up in the air. "Alright, you win. But let me warn you, you'll probably end up bored. For better or worse, I've avoided most of the drama that's infiltrated your relationships."

"Stop stalling and start talking," I teased.

"I won't be offended if you take a nap in your tequila."

"Trust me." I leaned forward so that I was only a couple inches from his face. "I haven't been bored since the moment I walked in the door."

Chapter 18

Joshua – June 28, 2010

Bzzzzzzzzzzzzzz! *Bzzzzzzzzzz!*

I groggily pulled the pillow over my head, trying to block out the alarm and the bright sunshine. Regardless of how often I stayed at Amanda's apartment, I always woke disorientated and exhausted. Amanda had blinds but, when I asked if we could use them, she laughed like I made a joke and said they were for *decoration*. Thus, I never slept heavily or consistently once dawn hit and the rising sun transformed the room into a sauna.

I shut off the alarm and peered around Amanda's clinically white bedroom. White furniture, white sheets, white picture frames with black and white photos, white walls. The first time I saw her bedroom I made a joke that white must be her favorite color. She looked around the room, her eyebrows furrowed. *The chase is eggshell and the bed and dresser are vanilla*, she explained. *Only the walls are white.* I nodded, unsure of the difference.

Amanda appeared in the doorway wearing nothing but a white V-neck t-shirt that crept just below her butt. Her nipples poked through the sheer fabric and my body stirred awake. She sashayed towards the bed and handed me a cup of coffee.

"Thanks," I said, still unaccustomed to having someone anticipate my every need. But Amanda insisted she enjoyed getting me coffee in the morning, making dinner or reminding me to bring my umbrella because it was going to rain. "Why did you set the alarm? It's Sunday."

"You forgot," she jokingly chastised me. She pulled her knees up to her chest, stretched her t-shirt over her legs and wrapped her arms around her knees. "We have brunch with Eric and Amelia at eleven."

Amelia, Rachel and Amanda were sorority sisters in college. But Amanda and Amelia were roommates, which has led to a lifetime rivalry as cutthroat as the Packers-Bears. Brunch would be filled with conversational tennis as they volleyed their latest accomplishments back and forth, each trying to score a winner. Today would be particularly brutal because Eric and Amelia just announced their engagement.

I set the coffee on the table and pushed Amanda down onto the bed. I climbed on top and started kissing her neck. Perhaps I could entice her to cancel brunch.

"We're going to be late," she giggled.

I kissed down her chest towards her stomach. Her legs sprung open like a Jack-in-the-Box, forgetting whatever concerns she had about time. Amanda had become much more sexual lately. She claimed summer always put her in the mood, but I think three magic words sparked the change. Ever since I told her I loved her, she fulfilled my every sexual craving. It was so simple that I almost, *almost*, questioned why I waited.

Falling in love surprised me. When we started dating last October, I thought Amanda was cute and fun, but I didn't think much about the future. I was forced to confront my feelings, however, in early May when Amanda left town to help care for her ailing grandma. I missed her. I missed waking up with her, hearing her incessant commentary while watching TV and the numerous ways she said *oy* depending on whether she was surprised, pained or angry. I knew I liked her, but a week without her made me realize I loved her.

I told her the second she returned home. She crawled on top of me and covered my mouth with a hungry kiss, as if she spent forty days lost in the desert and I finally offered her food, water and a ride home. We spent the night cuddling, whispering those magical words to one another, looking to any outsider like the ending of some chick flick where everyone's haphazard life ends up tied in a neat bow. I didn't know a relationship could get this good. Famous last words, right?

"I was thinking," she said now, roughly two minutes after we finished having sex. Her head rested against my chest, listening to my deaccelerating heartbeat. "When my lease expires at the end of July we should move in together."

If I was looking for something to stop my heart cold then, once again, Amanda supplied the perfect antidote. She must have noticed that my body tensed, I stopped breathing or had some other unconscious reaction because she jumped out of my arms and pulled the sheet around her body. Her bronze tan glowed against the crisp white sheet and her icy blonde hair.

"Do you think moving in together is a bad idea?" The question was rhetorical. Based on her tone she may have well asked: *Do you think that the Holocaust was a good idea?* No one in their right mind would answer yes.

"It's not a bad idea," I hedged, entirely caught off guard. We just had sex. My brain barely worked. "But I think we should talk about it."

"Beyond the practicalities of saving money and time, I really want to live with you." She squeezed my hands. "It sounds cliché, but I want to go to bed with you each night. Go grocery shopping. Buy furniture together. Have a party at *our house*. You know, build a life with you."

My concern rose exponentially. She wanted to buy furniture together? But my house was already furnished. What more could she want to buy?

"What are you thinking?" She smiled serenely, lost in her daydream of buying furniture and groceries.

"I don't know. Lots of things."

"Like what?"

"Umm, where would we put your stuff?" I owned a duplex and lived in the upper unit. It had two spacious bedrooms, but there wasn't room to implant her entire one-bedroom apartment into mine.

"We'll combine everything," she replied, as if she already took mental measurements and organized our belongings. She ran her fingers leisurely through the trail of hairs on my stomach like I was her prize winning pup. "What else worries you?"

What if we breakup? I wanted to scream. But I knew better than to ask. "I just need time to think. Okay?"

"Sure." She bounced off the bed, letting the sheet drop to the floor. Was that intentional? As she walked into the closet I couldn't take my eyes off her firm, perfect ass. Seeing her naked on a daily basis would be a bonus. "We're late, anyways."

I brushed my teeth while thoughts swirled through my mind like a tornado. I loved her. But did that mean we were ready to live together? After only eight months of dating? We needed to have a discussion when I wasn't incapacitated by sex. She caught me off guard today, but next time, I would be ready with an arsenal of arguments.

AMANDA MOVED IN AT the end of a July on a muggy, one-hundred degree day. I spent the first few weeks tiptoeing around her, unsure of how this arrangement would work. *Were you going to take a shower?* she asked as I stripped naked in the bathroom. I let her shower first. *Did you finish the milk?* she asked, holding up the empty carton as evidence. I ran out to buy more milk. *Do you always eat with the TV on?* she asked as we ate one of her immaculately prepared meals while the Brewer game blared in the background. I shut off the TV. Was I setting precedents? Every question felt like a test.

We lived together a month, however, before all pretenses fell by the wayside and I lost my temper. It rarely happened, but when it did, I imploded with verbal daggers, my comments working like jabs to the kidney.

I returned home from work on a Friday night to find candles, cloth napkins and four place settings on the dining room table.

"Shabbat dinner," Amanda said, avoiding my question of *who* was coming to dinner.

"Who did you invite?" I repeated. It was a long, hot day. I wanted to take off my suit, throw on a pair of shorts and sit on the porch with some ice cold vodka and savor the last bit of summer.

"Your parents," she admitted with a tentative smile.

"How? Why?" I sputtered. I felt disorientated, as if a pack of wild dogs attacked me.

"Your mom called here this afternoon. She didn't realize I moved in." Amanda had the audacity to sound obtuse, as if she didn't know I lived my life on a need-to-know basis with my parents. "So I invited them to dinner to celebrate!"

"Are you out of your mind?" I spat. "Did it occur to you that maybe there was a reason I hadn't told my parents?"

Amanda took a step backwards, visibly surprised by my venomous tone. But she quickly collected herself. She was a strong woman that never shied from sharing her opinion. "Frankly, I couldn't think of any reason you would want to hide this from them."

"What time are they coming?" I asked through gritted teeth.

She glanced at the ticking clock—ticking time bomb??—on the wall. "Seven."

She walked back into the kitchen where she was cooking a feast. It smelled like brisket and my stomach disloyally growled in response. Like a petulant child, I wanted to take the brisket out of the oven, smash the pan on the floor and leave. Let her deal with my parents. Instead, I showered, changed and sat outside sipping my vodka until I heard the ominous ding of the doorbell.

A few minutes later Amanda appeared at the screen door flanked by my parents. I obligingly kissed my mom and shook hands with my dad, neither of whom acted coldly towards me. Perhaps I was blowing the situation out of proportion. My parents really liked Amanda. Maybe they would be happy for us.

My parents waited to attack until Amanda went into the kitchen to finishing preparing the main course.

"When did Amanda move in?" my father asked.

I chewed my challah bread into miniscule bits. Both sets of eyes stared at me, transfixed, waiting. I swallowed. I sat through enough interrogations to know the less I said the better. "About a month ago."

"When were you planning on telling us?"

"I hadn't given it much thought."

"Don't be a smart ass."

"It's not like I was hiding it from you," I lied.

"It's a big deal, living with someone," my mother jumped in.

I shook my head. "Not really. Everyone does it."

What was Amanda doing? I imagined her in the kitchen, ear glued to the door, straining to hear every last word. I wanted to dropkick the door, expose her cowardice.

"Everyone does it?" my dad repeated with a snort. "Remind me, how old are you?"

"That's not why—" I started, struggling to keep my composure. "Obviously, we love each other."

"Are you planning on marrying this girl?"

"I don't know," I admitted.

"That's not really fair to Amanda," my mom interjected.

"Mom, I didn't say I *wouldn't* marry her, but one step at a time, okay?" I felt like I was making sound arguments but my father's wrinkled forehead and my mother's pout told me something got lost in translation.

I stood up and walked towards the kitchen door, flinging it open. As predicted, Amanda was leaning up against the fridge, listening to the entire exchange. I glared at her. "Care to join us?"

"You're talking with your parents."

"You invited them here to celebrate. So come on, *let's celebrate.*"

Amanda narrowed her eyes at me before entering the dining room with the grace of Audrey Hepburn. She flashed my parents a placating smile.

"Do your parents know that you moved in with Joshua?" my mom asked.

"Of course." She fixed her eyes on me momentarily, letting me know this was my fault. If I was honest with my parents we wouldn't be enduring this uncomfortable conversation in the middle of her immaculately planned dinner. I stared right back, refusing to cede an inch.

"And they're okay with this arrangement?" my father asked.

"Yes. They love Joshua. They're really happy for us."

That was a bit of a stretch. They liked me, but I couldn't help but feel that with every dinner or holiday I attended more of their dream of having Jewish grandchildren was flushed down the toilet. Whenever they prayed, her mother took me aside afterwards and talked very slowly as she explained their religious customs. (It was as if she thought Christianity prevented me from seeing and hearing.) Her mother was very sweet, but, much to her dismay, the chances of me converting to Judaism was a notch below my desire to become a professional cage fighter. Thus, I wondered whether they loved me as much as Amanda said. But, unlike my parents, they were happy if Amanda was happy.

"They're not worried about what it might mean?"

"They trust me to make my own decisions," Amanda answered, a virtual slap in the face. Trust was a completely foreign concept to my parents. They viewed it as the right of parents to impose their will.

"Hmmm..." my parents said in unison.

"But," Amanda continued hurriedly, "I think I can address your concerns. While we don't have a date set"—she had the audacity to pause and look at me, as if she thought I might seize the moment, get down on one knee and propose—"I can assure you we both view marriage as the next step."

I sat there, dumbfounded, staring at the new white rug Amanda put under the table (excuse me *snow colored rug*), as I tried to make sense of her words. We've never spoke of marriage. More specifically, neither one of us has ever said: *When we get married*; *I want to marry you;* or *Getting married is the next step*. She fabricated an entire conversation and lied to my parents about it! My memory wasn't great but I think a few alarm bells might have sounded if she brought up marriage at any point.

"That's good to hear," my dad said, eyeing me steadily.

"I'll say," my mother chimed in, laughing in relief. "It's important to us that things happen the right way."

I was fuming. I didn't trust myself to talk. The only words that would leave my mouth would be insult-laden expletives. Amanda was my mom's new favorite person and no one, not even her only son, could tear her away from asking questions about what Amanda wanted for her, ahem, *our*, wedding.

Five minutes after my parents left, I grabbed my wallet, purposefully forgot my phone, and stormed out of the house. I walked to my favorite dive bar, Shakey's. It was all dark wood, worn leather seats, stained mirrors and cagey customers. Perfect for brooding.

I sat on a stool closest to the open window hoping for a reprieve from the aroma of stale sweat and beer. The bartender, a short, anorexic looking guy with two sleeves of tattoos and a ponytail approached. I grunted a greeting and ordered a double vodka on the rocks.

Tonight's charade was caused by Amanda's lack of respect for my boundaries. She freely shared intimate details of our life—disagreements, sex, money. Nothing was off limits. But I'm woven from a different fabric. I operated on a need-to-know basis—especially with my parents. She knew this and yet didn't respect my decision to keep our living arrangement a secret.

I ordered another drink. I didn't know what to do. She'd pressed my boundaries in the past by divulging personal information to her friends. I believed her when she said it was unintentional, but tonight she acted deliberately. The worst part is I think she felt entitled; like living together bestowed upon her the right to meddle in previously untouchable areas of my life. She certainly didn't look sorry.

And what was up with all the marriage talk? She pushed too damn hard, too fast! We weren't ready to get engaged. Okay, fine, *I* wasn't ready. (I'd be an idiot to not realize what Amanda was gunning for tonight. But she was an idiot to ignore the flames of anger rising from me as she told my parents we'd be married within the year.)

I felt duped. She orchestrated the move merely to propel us towards marriage even after I confessed that I feared it was too serious of a step. *We're just living together*, she assured me a mere two months ago. *It's not a life-long commitment.* Was she lying? Manipulating me from the start?

After another drink the solution crystalized in my mind. Amanda had to make two promises: First, marriage, and any discussion of it, would be put on the back-burner indefinitely. Second, she must respect my boundaries, specifically with my parents.

But first I wanted an apology; a groveling, crying, regretful apology.

I threw down some money and walked home, tripping over my feet the entire way. Everything swirled around me. The streetlights appeared far too bright, cars whizzed by at a break-neck pace and each voice I heard sounded hostile and threatening.

I stumbled up the stairs and into the dark kitchen. I flipped on the lights to see that everything was clean and pristine. I pushed open the door to our bedroom and saw Amanda curled under the sheet sleeping. *No fucking way!* She doesn't get to sleep. She needed to answer for herself.

"Get up!" I yelled, ripping the sheet from her body. "We need to talk."

I took a step backwards, but misjudged the distance to the wall and stumbled into an eight-by-ten picture Amanda hung of us. It fell to the ground and shattered. *I'll take foreshadowing for five hundred, Alex.*

I left to get a broom to sweep up the glass. When I came back the light was on and she was picking up pieces off the floor.

"What's your problem?" Amanda demanded, snatching the broom out of my hands.

"My problem?" I barked. "You, for starters."

Amanda stood with her hands on her hips, all five-foot-one of her slight frame scrutinizing me. I became fixated on the sight of her hard nipples poking through her skimpy grey tank-top. She wore black bikini briefs on the bottom, which left a good two inches of taut stomach showing. I wanted to reach out, pull down her panties and take her right here. I was defenseless to her body.

"Let me get this straight." She held out her left hand, numbering her arguments, starting with her thumb. "You decided not to tell your parents we moved in together. You forced me to defend our decision while you sulked like a child. You went out and got drunk instead of helping me clean up the dinner I cooked." She scoffed. "Yeah, I think you'll be waiting awhile for that apology."

Any willingness I had to forgive her in favor of make-up sex was abruptly forgotten. Turns out she could do something to tame my libido: act like a self-righteous bitch.

"That's a nice story, but let me tell you what really happened. *You* told my parents we were living together knowing it would upset me. *You* invited them over for dinner without asking. *You* promised them we were getting married when we've never talked about it."

"You were never going to tell them that I moved in, were you?" she accused.

"Why do you care?"

She threw her hands up in the air. "They're your parents and yet you keep me from them like I'm a dirty secret. I thought if they knew we lived together you would finally let the four of us have a relationship."

"You don't understand my parents," I grumbled, baffled as to how she managed to spin her mistake as my fault. "If I give them an inch, they want a foot. Trust me, it's better to love them from a distance."

She clasped my hands in hers. "If they know we're serious, they'll learn to respect our decisions and back off."

"You're giving my parents more credit than they deserve," I laughed. I had no idea how she did it. One minute I was livid and the next I felt like we passed the twenty-five mile marker and the finish line was in sight. "I'll try to include you more, but don't complain to me about how overbearing they are. Consider yourself warned."

She giggled and saluted me. "Officially warned."

I pulled her onto my lap and cupped her face in my hands, ensuring she heard me. "But you need to slow down. It's way too soon to think about marriage."

She drew away from me.

"I want to marry you," she insisted. "I wouldn't be here, living with you, if I didn't."

"That makes sense," I conceded, momentarily giving her a pass on her failure to mention these thoughts to me *prior* to moving in. "But you need to stop pushing me. It's not just the marriage issue or inviting my parents over tonight. It's everything. If you think you're right, you keep pushing until I give in. That can't happen. I'll end up resenting you."

"So I can't give you my opinion?"

It felt like a trick question.

"Give me your opinion, *once*, and leave it at that."

"Okay," she hedged, obviously doubting my intellectual capabilities. "But I need to know we want the same things for the future. You see us getting married, right?"

I stifled a groan. She was pushing again, immediately after she promised not to push. There was no easy way to tell her I didn't know without enduring hours of conversation. So I stretched the truth. "I could see that happening...eventually. But you need to let me go at my own pace, okay? Let's live together first and see what happens."

I kissed her before she could ask any more questions. Drunken make-up sex cured most problems, but in this case the anxious ache in my stomach remained. Had I promised to one day marry Amanda?

THE ISSUE OF MARRIAGE fled as quickly as it appeared. Over the next few months, I slaved away as a public defender while she lent a sympathetic ear to spoiled rich kids. We were happy.

At least I thought we were. But slowly—because these things always appear to happen in slow motion—things started to disintegrate. She began drinking a bottle of wine for dinner most nights. The cause of her depression? Her job. It was a daily reminder of everything she wanted—working as a stay-at-home mom, kids attending private school, country club membership, heading up charity drives—but could never have on our combined income. She subtly hinted at her desire for that lifestyle over a period of months. I ignored her comments, assuming it was a pipe dream like the one I had of moving to Bali and working as a street artist. That was my mistake.

Amanda eventually abandoned the subtle hints in favor of a new tactic: all out confrontation. Because she couldn't bully me into proposing, she targeted her desire for me to leave the public defender's office. *You have a much higher earning potential than me,* she argued. *If I could help our future by switching jobs, I would.* The implication was that I was acting both selfish and stupid. I felt like I was back under my parents' domain; everything boiled down to money.

It wasn't all bad, of course. Like a boxing match, she would come out swinging, flinging comments left and right before retiring to her corner for a few peaceful weeks. But it was erratic living with her. I never knew which Amanda I would get.

A perfect storm of events, however, took place when we went to Eric and Amelia's wedding in June. Amanda took to the couch each night the week before the wedding with a bottle of wine. She watched *Father of the Bride, My Best Friend's Wedding, The Wedding Singer, The Wedding Date* and *27 Dresses.* If there was a down-on-her-luck girl who was saved by the proposal of a rich and handsome guy, Amanda was going to watch it. And cry. And shoot me looks like I was the enemy whenever I walked into the room or dared to breathe audibly.

On the morning of the wedding I made the mistake of suggesting we skip the ceremony. Given that Amanda was still pissed that Amelia only asked her three sisters to be bridesmaids, I thought going to the ceremony, seeing Amelia take her vows and kiss her very own Prince Charming would only make her feel worse. Score a couple of points for the sensitive boyfriend? Not even close. *Skipping the ceremony is tacky*, she muttered.

After the ceremony we stood outside the temple and I watched Amanda as she greeted her college friends. She looked beautiful in a pale pink strapless dress. Her blonde hair had grown out and almost touched her shoulders in soft waves. Her face lit up with excitement and I felt transported back to when we first met and she gazed at me with an enchanted smile. I wanted to capture her mood, bottle it and spray her when necessary.

She used to be happy with me, but the only emotions I invoked now were anger, annoyance and resentment. Was the charming girl I saw now, the same girl I met, still alive and yet suppressed by our relationship? I vowed to try harder to make Amanda happier. We both needed her back.

Things began looking up when we got to the reception and saw that Amelia placed us at a table with Rachel and Haden.

"I didn't see you at the ceremony," I said to Haden.

"Yeah, we didn't go. Those things are a bit of a drag."

I nudged Amanda. "Amanda said we had to go because it's tacky to skip."

"I had to work," Rachel interjected. "Otherwise we would've gone."

"Rachel works at a large firm that pays her a lot of money to work Saturdays," Amanda said. Her threatening tone would make Saddam

Hussein cop to the location of his weapons of mass destruction. She turned back to Rachel. "I'm trying to convince Joshua of the benefits of private practice. More money, more opportunities. I mean, you love your job, right?"

Rachel gulped her wine. "Love is a strong word."

"It's a rare weekend when she doesn't get called in," Haden said.

"That's one of the best parts of my job," I said, seizing the opportunity to point out the fault in Amanda's logic. "The pay may not be great, but we get to spend more time together. Imagine if I missed dinner most nights or had to work every weekend."

"We'd manage," Amanda retorted. "The reality is we simply can't afford a house, kids and any sort of life on our salaries."

I chugged the rest of my drink. There are some things that should remain private, even from the closest of friends. I counted our financial stability and future plans regarding marriage and children in that category.

"I need a refill," I announced.

Rachel jumped up. "I'll go with you."

We made our way to the bar, where I ordered a double vodka on the rocks as well as a glass of chardonnay for Rachel. We walked outside and sat on the steps, basking in the early evening sun. It was one of those great summer nights that made you doubt that six months from now these same plush trees and luscious, green grass would become brittle, leafless and covered in snow.

"Nothing I ever do is good enough for her," I muttered.

Rachel stayed silent, probably debating where her loyalties lay. "She's getting impatient. You've lived together almost a year now."

"And? What does that have to do with my job?"

"Don't be glib," Rachel retorted. "Changing jobs is just one way to show her you can provide for a family—"

"She's always ten steps ahead," I grunted, yanking my tie loose. "Why the hell is she worried about providing for our imaginary children when we're not even married?"

"So ask her to marry you."

I downed my drink and chucked the empty plastic cup towards the garbage. It fell short, just like me apparently. "I don't want to. Not yet, anyways."

"I wouldn't have picked you to suffer from a Peter Pan complex."

"I don't have a Peter Pan complex," I mocked her. "But I'm not going to ask someone to marry me unless I'm sure. We're not all that happy right now, in case that fact escaped your attention."

"Everyone has fights," she reasoned.

"It's not the fighting. It's the fact that she shows absolutely no respect for me and, on the most basic level, what makes me happy. She doesn't care that I enjoy my job. She doesn't care that I'm not ready to get married, let alone have kids. She acts like she's the only one in this relationship."

Rachel sighed. "All I can tell you is that she's getting restless. If you're not ready to propose, perhaps getting a new job is one way you can show her that you're serious about your future together."

My head fell into my hands. What a fucking mess. It was a catch-22. I could either quit my job or propose, both of which would make Amanda happy and me miserable. Or I could keep my job and wait on proposing while Amanda inched closer to the door each day.

Despite her selfish tendencies, I really loved Amanda. I wanted to make her happy. But how deep was my love? Enough to leave a job that made me happy? When would the compromise on her side come in?

"It wouldn't hurt to look around, see if any firms interest you."

"In this economy?" I scoffed. "No one's hiring."

"Well," Rachel hesitated. "Baker & Carlson are looking for a new criminal defense associate. It hasn't been posted, but I know the guy who's leaving so I could put in a word if you're interested."

I was not interested. I loved my job. The extra money would be nice, but at what cost? Enduring the daily drudge of the billable hour and firm politics? No thanks.

I stole a drink of Rachel's wine, which went down my throat with the ease of sandpaper. "Fine. Float my name and we'll see what happens. But let's keep this between us."

"Deal."

We walked back inside, wherein Amanda and I spent the night ignoring one another when no one was looking and faking our affection when necessary. We left to a farewell chorus of wedding wishes from her college friends: *You'll be next!*

Amanda squeezed my hand harder with each comment, as if I was both blind and deaf and she was doing me the favor of delivering the message in Morse code.

BY THE END OF JULY I was the newest associate at Baker & Carlson. It happened fast—too fast for me. I interviewed on the Monday after the fourth of July and they brought me back two days later to meet with all eight partners. They salivated like rabid dogs while I explained my trial experience, which was far more than most of the partners at the table.

Like one of the twenty girls on *The Bachelor* vying for the attention of a single man, the firm wanted me at any cost. (I knew Amanda was making me watch far too much reality TV when that was my point of comparison.) I had an offer three hours after I left the second interview, which included a salary almost double my current pay. On the downside I now had a minimum billable hour requirement and likely wouldn't see the inside of a courtroom until Iran became a democracy. But, not to worry, I could still *help* the partners *prepare* for trial. Lucky me.

I kept the interviews a secret from Amanda. I was willing to set aside my job satisfaction for her to feel confident in our future, but first I had to make Amanda understand that taking the job wasn't permission for the future—namely Amanda's vision of the future—to start immediately.

A couple hours later, after Amanda stopped jumping around like on cheerleader on Monday Night Football, I explained my first condition: she needed to keep working. We needed to save the extra money from my paycheck, otherwise the job switch was pointless.

She scrunched up her forehead. "Why would I quit my job?"

"You said you wanted to."

"When?"

"You're always saying how you wish you could be one of those moms that runs the bake sale, takes tennis lessons and makes gourmet meals each night."

"I was talking about when we have kids," Amanda said. "Obviously I'll work until I get pregnant."

I should have felt pleased but instead my throat constricted. I hated it when she talked about having kids as if it was a done deal. As if Tom and Sally were asleep in the second bedroom.

She swallowed audibly. "Anything else?"

This was hard. Marriage was as polarizing of a topic in our house as immigration, sometimes leading to a civil war where we didn't talk for days. I took a cue from my experience delivering bad news to my clients and gave it to her straight.

"Taking this job doesn't mean I'm ready to get married."

She nodded slowly as my words infected every channel in her brain. "I don't get it," Amanda finally said. Tears pooled in her eyes. "Why don't you want to marry me?"

My gut churned. Why did she take everything to the extreme? I didn't say we would *never* get married, I just said not right now. Why couldn't she see the difference?

"Amanda, please, I'm asking you to be patient." I brushed the tears away with the edge of my shirt. "Can't you see how much I love you? How I'm doing everything I can to make you happy?"

"This isn't like some terrible joke to throw me off the trail,"—the strain of hope was evident on her weary face—"is it?"

It took all of two minutes before she resumed her habit of dissecting my words for hidden meaning. "I'm not ready to get married."

"And I'm sick of waiting," Amanda whined. "It's been a year-and-a-half. You're ready. You're just scared."

"Stop it," I warned. I wasn't ready to get married. Having her tell me over and over that I was, like some amateur hypnotist, wasn't going to work. "Before I take the job, I need to know you're on board. No more moping around the house, waiting for a sign that we're heading in the right direction. This is the sign. Right now."

She climbed on top of me, straddling my waist, and kissed me. "Take the job," she purred in my ear.

I looked up at her beautiful, doll-like face, relieved to see her pouty lips turned up into a smile. "All I want is for you to be happy."

"I am."

"But there's one more thing you have to promise me." I threw her back onto the couch, pinning her arms down with my hands. "No more reality TV. My brain can't take it."

She giggled and tried to squirm away. "Never."

I buried my face in her neck, inhaling her sweet floral scent. "Fine. But you have to give me a blow job for every reality show we watch."

She laughed but began kissing me with greater urgency. I drove a hard bargain, but one of the reasons I loved her was that she usually met me half-way. "I'm sure we can reach some sort of agreement."

NEW YEAR'S EVE IN MILWAUKEE was brutally cold. I drove home from work listening to every disc jockey advise listeners to curl up and spend the night inside. That sounded perfect after spending the holiday week working long hours, but Amanda trounced the idea. We had dinner reservations with Haden, Rachel, Amelia and Eric and, despite seeing them most weekends, she insisted on going.

The heat engulfed me like a cocoon as I entered our home. I heard Bon Jovi blasting from the bathroom. I peeked through the slightly ajar door and saw Amanda putting on makeup wearing nothing but a white tank-top and a black, lacy thong, further weakening my desire to go out.

She stood on her tip-toes inches from the mirror and concentrated with the precision of Picasso while putting on her eyeliner. I liked the contrast of her dark lined eyes against her pale skin and icy blonde hair. She looked like an evil seductress.

Ten minutes later she found me in the living room, nursing a beer and watching football. She wore a short, sleeveless black dress, black tights and impossibly tall heels that would topple upon meeting the ice patch outside our back door. "You're going to freeze."

"You could've just said that I looked pretty," she scowled and stormed out of the room.

I could've chased after her, but it wouldn't have mattered. With Amanda I had a three second window to compliment her. After that it wouldn't make an iota of difference if I told her that she was the most beautiful woman on the planet. *You're only saying that because I'm upset*, she'd sneer. Well, yes and no. She always looked beautiful, but yes, at those moments I complimented her merely because she was having a fit. I couldn't win.

Ignoring her outbursts sometimes worked and tonight, thankfully, was one of those nights. She was back in good spirits by the time we got to the restaurant.

Both Rachel and Amelia—similarly dressed in unseasonably short black dresses—jumped up and hugged Amanda. They shrieked in the way that only girls who saw each other a mere two nights ago could manage.

We ordered drinks and the conversation quickly divided down gender lines. The girls gossiped about gifts and parties, while Eric, Haden and I talked about the upcoming bowl games. Haden claimed to find American football boring, but the enthusiasm with which he watched led to a different conclusion. He enjoyed living here despite consistently threatening to kidnap Rachel and bring her back to the U.K. once she got pregnant.

There was a familiarity to tonight that was reassuring in its simplicity and yet surprising. Growing up I never envisioned celebrating New Year's Eve with a beautiful girlfriend and a large group of friends. Back then I spent the night either watching the ball drop with my parents or holed up in my room playing video games.

The disparity between my lonely childhood and the reality of my life still startled me at times. Girlfriend, friends, job, house, money—it seemed too good to be true. I put my arm around Amanda and kissed her on the cheek. "You look beautiful."

She smiled back, glowing from my compliment. She wanted to hear it an hour ago, but I knew it was worth more now. She loved it when I fawned over her in front of Rachel and Amelia—both of whom she felt insecure around because they were light years ahead of her in the game of life. As long as I was willing to play the role of the doting boyfriend her good mood could last for days.

But not tonight. Too many forces worked against us. We drank and ate slowly, ordering more tapas as the mood hit us, eventually hitting a wall. When the server asked if anyone wanted desert, we greeted him with a collective moan of fullness.

"You don't want any dessert?" Amanda asked. It was one of her idiosyncrasies—she felt guilty eating dessert alone so I pretended to eat it with her. But tonight I felt too full to even look at dessert.

"I'm good, but go ahead and order something."

"You seriously don't want anything?"

"Do you want me to order the dessert for you and pretend like it's for me?" I whispered in her ear.

She huffed and pulled away from me like I had a communicable disease. I was about to cut through the bullshit and ask what caused her sudden bitchy mood (in different words, of course), but Eric began tapping on his wineglass with his fork, trying to get the group's attention. Eric and Amelia both had wide grins plastered across their faces like they were auditioning for a toothpaste ad.

"We have news—" Eric started, but Amelia interrupted him.

"We're expecting!" she whooped.

"Oh my God!" Rachel exclaimed. "Congratulations!"

She immediately engulfed Amelia in a hug. We all followed suit, taking turns exchanging hugs with the happy couple like we were square dancing.

After the *congratulations* and *Mozel Tov* dissipated, however, an awkward silence descended on the group. Rachel briefly met my gaze, revealing two shiny eyes ready to spill fresh tears. Haden rubbed her back with one hand while texting with the other. I knew Rachel and Haden had suffered a couple miscarriages, which explained her mixed emotions, but Amanda's pained expression confounded me. She looked like she was in a hotly contested battle with gravity to keep her smile from turning into an angry grimace.

This was the problem with going out with other couples. Amanda took other people's good news as a reflection that something was wrong or missing from our relationship. She lacked the ability to be happy for someone else without it leading to a grand introspection.

"What's the plan now?" I asked after we settled the bill.

Amelia yawned loudly. "We're going home. I'm exhausted."

"Sorry guys," Eric smiled smugly, sounding not at all sorry. "I think we've already entered the lame old parent stage."

"But it's not even midnight," Amanda objected.

"Midnight?" Amelia laughed. "I'm lucky I made it this long!"

Haden pulled out his phone, reading a text. "I told Casey we'd meet her at Murphy's. Want to join us?"

"That's what we're doing?" Rachel grumbled.

"Do you want to go?" I asked Amanda while Rachel and Haden whispered furiously at one another.

"Well, I don't want to go home," she snapped.

Incidentally, Amelia and Eric's good news left Haden and I to deal with two pissed off women. "So, we'll go."

Outside the cold weather used us as a punching bag, jabbing us mercilessly the entire walk to the car. Once inside, we sat hunched over, shivering, while we waited for the car to warm up.

"I'd like to drink tonight," Amanda declared through chattering teeth. "I'd like to get really drunk, actually."

"Fine."

"I drive all the time so you can drink," she reminded me. She was right, of course, but it had less to do with her generosity than with keeping up appearances. The several bottles of wine she consumed weekly at our house was a well-guarded secret. "That's the least you could do for me tonight."

The least I could do? She acted like I knocked up Amelia. "I said fine."

"I didn't like your tone."

The night only got worse.

MURPHY'S WAS AN IRISH bar that spanned two floors of a corner lot in downtown Milwaukee. It was adorned with the traditional Irish fare: dark wood bar, black-and-white snapshots of patrons tacked to the bar, clever signs from the old country on the walls (*Lovely day for a Guinness!*) and a fair amount of green paraphernalia. But it was also very much an American party bar with live music, drink specials, scantily clad women and overeager men.

New Year's was no exception. Every square inch of the bar was hopping with people eager to obliterate their memories of 2011. I felt like I was in the middle of a mosh pit. Music pounded from the speakers, further disorientating me. After ten minutes, I worried we would never find Haden or Rachel.

"Let's get a drink," Amanda yelled. "Maybe they'll find us."

We navigated towards the bar where Amanda ordered a shot of tequila.

"You don't drink tequila."

"Yes I do," she countered. "You don't know everything about me."

I looked on with amusement as she threw back the shot. Things appeared fine for a millisecond until her brain received the message from her taste buds that she ingested something rancid. She coughed uncontrollably, spilling tequila out of both sides of her mouth.

Taste good? I wanted to ask, but swallowed the question.

As we resumed our search for Rachel and Haden, two thoughts came to mind: first, this crowd was young; and second, everyone appeared drunk, single and ready to hook-up. Maybe it was the unofficial dress code requiring the women to wear low-cut dresses that barely covered their asses, or the fact that all the men looked like starved dogs, ready to pounce at the first indication of tender meat. Back in college I would've stood in the corner, sipping my beer, feeling like a fraud. Tonight, however, I simply didn't care. This would never be my scene. I was finally okay with that.

Ironically, this wasn't Amanda's scene either, but she was doing her best to assimilate. She danced as we crossed the bar, jutting her arms spastically to each side. It was uncomfortable to watch.

Trailing Amanda, I felt a swift tug from behind on the collar of my sweater as if lassoed by a cowboy. I turned around to find one of the few people my age that would enjoy this scene: Casey.

"I thought it was you!" Casey shouted, her eyes dancing with excitement (and God only knows what else). "Did you come with Haden?"

"I was at dinner with him, but I don't know if he's here yet," I yelled into her ear. Her silky hair tickled my neck and I was acutely aware that our cheeks touched while we spoke. And yet, she didn't move away. Amazingly, above the stench of beer and sweat, I got a strong whiff of her shampoo. She smelled sensual, like a blossoming pomegranate.

Casey squeezed my shoulders with both hands. "Wait here, okay? I have to do a quick favor for a friend, but then we'll find them together."

She flashed an award-winning smile my way and left. I turned around to find Amanda missing. Strangers jostled around me. *Fuck.* Was I supposed to stay here or look for Amanda?

As I debated this conundrum, I saw the lead singer pull Casey up onto the small makeshift stage. The band sang a cover of Meatloaf's "Paradise by the Dashboard Lights" with Casey taking the female vocal. She sang well, but it was her stage presence that caught my attention. He held her hips as she swayed suggestively, both singing into the microphone, never removing their eyes from each other's. She oozed sexuality. It was playful and erotic and a complete turn on.

"There you are!" Amanda appeared at my side, trailed by Rachel and Haden.

"Here I am," I mumbled, in need of a cold shower.

When the song ended, Casey jumped off the stage and ran straight for Haden where he enveloped her in a gigantic hug. Rachel interrupted their reunion, telling Haden she was ready for a drink.

"I didn't know you sang," I shouted to Casey as we followed the gang to the bar. "You're good."

"I have a lot of hidden talents," she replied, once again reducing me to a hormonal teenage boy. Maybe it was a game to her: *how fast can I make Joshua blush?*

Casey fought her way up towards the bar next to Haden. "Shots?" she called to us.

"Yes," both Rachel and Amanda chorused, while I shook my head.

Casey frowned at me. "Come on, live a little."

"I'm driving," I replied, but she couldn't hear me. I made fists with both hands and moved them side-to-side in a terrible pantomime. "Sorry."

The night carried on with the girls taking shots and dancing, while Haden and I sipped beer and talked at a nearby high top table. Amanda bounced over to me a few minutes before midnight, alit with the hazy pleasure of drunkenness. She stood smiling between my legs and I wrapped my arms around her waist.

The clock struck midnight and the band started to play "Auld Lang Syne." I kissed Amanda deeply, tangling my hands in her hair. But as I pulled away, I saw we had a small audience. Rachel and Haden stared at us. I smiled sheepishly and wished them a Happy New Year.

"What do you feel like doing?"

"Doing?" Amanda repeated.

"Yeah. Do you want to stay or go home?"

Her mouth dropped open. "Stay," she snapped and walked away.

In fact, *stay* was the last word she said to me for two hours. Whereas before she used dancing as foreplay, smiling at me as she twisted and dipped, now she didn't even look my way. The unpredictability of her emotions tonight rivaled a strung out prostitute, but I naively blamed it on the liquor.

"I'm dizzy," Amanda complained, stumbling her way into my arms.

"Do you want to leave?" No answer came. I peered around at her face and saw her eyes closed. I gently shook her awake before guiding her narrow hips out of the bar and towards our car.

Upon arriving home Amanda ran straight for the bathroom. Seconds later I heard the tell-tale splash of puke hitting the water. I filled a glass with water and rustled up a couple of Advil.

I knocked and opened the bathroom door. A putrid aroma wafted towards me. Amanda's head rested on the toilet seat, while her arms clutched to the base like a lifeboat. She looked comatose.

"Open up." I bent down and placed two Advil on her tongue like a priest giving communion. I slowly poured water in her mouth. I turned to leave, anticipating a breath of fresh air, but I heard Amanda mutter something indecipherable. "What did you say?"

She tried to hold her head up, but it was too heavy and quickly tumbled back down onto the toilet. "This is your fault."

I let her words sink in. *My fault?* I went out in the cold tonight because that's what Amanda wanted. I watched her dance and drink for hours, while I stayed sober. And now, after I've brought her water and Advil, she tells me this is my fault.

I closed the door on both her and an argument, giving her the benefit of the doubt. Puking makes everyone vengeful.

A few minutes later Amanda staggered into our bedroom.

"You know, I realized tonight that you don't care about me. You may think you care, but you're not capable of truly caring." She paused, giving me time to contradict her, but I continued to undress, too tired for a fight. "I'm the idiot. I keep thinking things will change but they never do. You never change."

"What do you want me to say?"

"Oh that's classic," Amanda spat. "Can't you figure out what to say without me feeding you lines?"

"Right now? No. There's nothing I could say to make you happy."

She collapsed into the fetal position and emitted a guttural sob. "I thought you were going to propose tonight. I told everyone!" She sobbed heavily between each word, which eventually caused hiccups. "I waited at dinner. Nothing. Again at midnight. Nothing. How could you embarrass me like that? *How*?"

"What made you think I would propose tonight?"

"Do you want a list?"

"A list?" I sputtered. "Even one reason would suffice."

Amanda sneered, in no mood for sarcasm. "I overheard you telling your mom that you were going to propose soon."

"When was this?"

"At Thanksgiving!" she screamed through another round of hiccups. "I don't know if you used the exact word *soon*." She used air quotes. "I'm not a wordsmith"—hiccup, hiccup—"but that was the gist of the conversation."

I wracked my mind but came up empty. "I honestly don't remember saying that."

"So what's up with the bank account you opened at Chase?" she accused. "What are you saving all that money for if not a ring?"

When I started at Baker & Carlson I transferred the difference between my two salaries into a new account. Call me boring and practical, but it was insurance against spending more because I was making more. I had no plan for the money. But now that she said it, I could see how her brain, which thought only of marriage and babies, made the jump.

"How do you know about that account?"

"You left your mail lying around and I happened to notice."

If by lying around she meant filed away in my desk, then sure, it was lying around. But I didn't want to argue semantics. "Why didn't you ask me about it? We could've prevented this whole scene."

"Because finding that account was like finding a ring," she explained. She spoke slowly like I was the one intoxicated and finding it difficult to comprehend simple ideas. "We've been dating two years. It made sense to wait for the proposal. When it didn't happen at Chanukah, I figured New Year's was the obvious date because we would be with friends."

"Whatever." I collapsed face-first onto the bed, exhausted beyond words.

"You can't ignore me!" She hit me with her pillow. "I'm a real person."

"Yes I can!" I roared back. My patience resembled a dried up pond in the middle of the Sahara. "This is self-inflicted drama. Logically, you know I'm not ready to get married and yet you constantly look for clues that I'm going to propose. I'm sick of it. I don't care anymore."

"So you don't care that I'm upset? You don't care that I looked like an idiot in front of our friends?" Amanda screamed, verging on hysteria. "You don't care about how gutted I felt when Amelia announced she's pregnant and I couldn't even say I got engaged?"

"You need to accept responsibility for your actions," I reasoned with forced calmness. "You overheard a meaningless conversation between my mom and me and inferred exactly what you wanted to hear. You looked through my mail, *without my permission*, and decided the money I saved from my new job—that I took *for you*—was to buy a ring. Then, to top it all off, you told your friends I was going to propose tonight. If I were you, I'd feel embarrassed too. So no, I don't feel bad."

"That's right," she spat. "Everything is always my fault."

"Amanda, I'm tired. Tired of listening, tired of talking, and frankly, tired of you."

I walked out of the room and directly into the second bedroom. I fell asleep at some point, allowing Amanda's sobs to lull me into slumber. I knew she wanted me to comfort her with promises that we would be alright, but I stayed put. I didn't feel bad about that either.

Chapter 19

Joshua – September 22, 2012

"**I**'m officially confused," Casey said, rubbing her temples as if bogged down by an SAT question. "You told me you guys broke up a few months ago, but now it sounds like things ended in January."

"You should know better than anyone that relationships don't end overnight. You need to drain every last morsel of potential until you can't stand the sight of the other person and even a friendship isn't possible."

Casey laughed. "So you spent five months watching the relationship circle the drain?"

"In retrospect, it seems obvious we weren't a great match, but I loved her. It took a series of events, with the highlight being New Year's Eve, to realize how fucked up our relationship had become."

"Every relationship is fucked up," Casey commented with her trademark cynicism. "It comes down to whether the two people developed a good enough base to handle the occasional bout of bullshit."

"I suppose that's one way of looking at it."

"Why did you breakup with Amanda?"

"You really don't know?" I deadpanned.

"Indulge me."

"I didn't trust her. She tried to control and manipulate every aspect of our relationship instead of letting it progress naturally. I couldn't trust whether her actions were real or manufactured to produce a certain outcome. You know what I mean?"

"I do."

"There were times when I saw a future together but every few months it felt like the veil was pulled back and she would become unrecognizable. She'd say one thing, but entirely different thoughts were running through her head." I shook my head, remembering some of our more difficult conversations. "I freaked out on New Year's. I realized I could never make her happy because she would always want something more."

"Okay. I'll grant you that she has major control issues, but the obsession with marriage and kids is probably normal." I started to interrupt, but Casey held up her hand. "Hear me out. Amanda took things to the extreme, but people usually see and hear what they want. Something dramatic has to happen for reality to smack them in the face."

"What, like telling all your friends that your boyfriend's going to propose on New Year's Eve?"

Casey smiled slyly. "That might be one example."

"If all girls do this then I quit. It's crazy and exhausting."

"I think girls do it to varying degrees if that helps. We assume we can get what we want in the end, one way or another."

"That's not helpful," I said mildly.

"My point is every relationship is fucked up because you're dealing with two human, flawed people. Maybe Amanda was too involved with the fantasy life she created in her head, but that wasn't the biggest problem here."

"Then what was?"

"You never understood each other," she said. "From the beginning, you guys ignored what the other person wanted, hoping it would fade or was an aberration, instead of taking the time to get to know each other. You guys trekked along, writing off fights but growing increasingly miserable."

"Miserable is a strong word."

"Oh my God!" Casey shouted, throwing her hands up in the air. "She was miserable because all she wanted was to get married and make babies. You were miserable because she pressured and manipulated you at every turn. So no, I think miserable sounds pretty accurate."

"You think I'm sugarcoating the relationship to feel better?"

"No one wants to dwell on how they wasted years in a relationship where alarm bells rang most days." Casey tiled her head to the side and smiled. She ran her right hand through my hair, keeping her coffee colored eyes locked on mine. "Seriously though, why did it take so long to leave?"

It was only a few months ago, but it already felt like another person lived with Amanda. I remembered the events but struggled to recall the feelings. It was almost as if I needed five months to drain my emotions so that there was nothing left.

"As long as I still loved her, I felt I owed our relationship a chance. If she would've left on New Year's Day, some sadistic part of me would've felt like I let the best thing in my life walk away. I needed time to fall out of love with her."

Casey brought her drink up to her lips, softly brushed them against the glass, but then set it back down without taking a sip. "That makes sense."

"Have you noticed that our memory of events tends to gloss over the bad stuff? It's easy to convince yourself a relationship was great or someone was perfect when it's over. But when you live with someone, it's impossible to avoid reality. Staying with Amanda for that time was a daily reminder of why our relationship couldn't work."

"So you're saying I could've saved myself years of heartbreak by simply asking Ryan to move in?"

"Well, I've *heard* that some relationships actually flourish by living together. So who knows, maybe shacking up would've helped."

"Probably not," she conceded. "We still would've had to deal with his wife and the resulting trust issues. No thanks."

I felt like doing a victory lap! Although this evening ambiguously started out somewhere between a friendly drink and a date, I was officially tapped out as far as lending a supportive ear about Ryan. Whether she still harbored feelings for Ryan, the most important point was Casey no longer wanted to be with him.

"So how did the breakup finally happen?" Casey pressed.

"You really are nosy."

"I'm curious. Amicable breakups are on par with Santa and the Easter Bunny. I've heard about them, but I've never actually experienced it."

"Whoa!" I held my hands up. "I don't remember saying it was amicable. The relationship petered out over time, but I guess I was the only one who realized the severity of the situation."

The worst part was Amanda truly believed I loved her enough to come around to her line of thinking. She never lost faith. Even through all the fights, the dwindling sex and the silence that permeated the house, she didn't realize we had become strangers.

"Shocking," Casey deadpanned. "It seems so odd that Amanda didn't realize the relationship wasn't going well."

"I know, right?" I pulled off my glasses and cleaned them with my shirt, stalling to clear my thoughts. "This next part makes me sound like an asshole. I freely admit I messed up on the timing, but I really believed our relationship was over."

"Oh God," Casey moaned. "You cheated. I never would've pegged you for the type, but that's the thing with cheating, there really isn't a type."

I lifted her chin up so that our eyes met. "Never. Absolutely not."

"So what happened?"

"I left my job. Babysitting the clients drove me crazy and dealing with the huge egos of the partners was even worse." I worked there roughly nine months but the stories I could tell would cause law school enrollment to plummet faster than the stock market after 9/11. "Bottom line, I missed the PD office. I had drinks with my old boss. Drinks turned into dinner, which eventually led to a new job offer."

"Which was?"

"Leading the team for juvenile felonies."

Her eyes widened. "And this appealed to you?"

"Working with kids is the one area where I feel like I can make a difference because you catch them early in the system. Depending on the crime, if you can get them into the right program, there's still a chance to turn around their lives."

"Teenagers scare me," she confessed. "When I think of how wild I was..." She shook her head. "And I wasn't ever arrested!"

"It's a small wonder how you avoided the system."

She rolled her eyes. "Seriously, I give you major props."

"It's challenging at times," I said, thinking of the fifteen-year-old boy last week that held up a Domino's with two of his friends. The police report claimed that two boys threatened the employee while one was the lookout guy. I was pretty sure as the youngest that he was the latter, but he refused to speak to me in anything less than broken sentences laced with four-letter expletives. He'd known me two minutes and his friends his entire life. He would never rat on them. "Half the battle is making them realize you really do want to help."

"Does it work?"

I scoffed. "Our definitions of the word *help* tend to differ. They view help as me getting them off and I view it as avoiding the maximum penalty and getting them into a facility where they can get an education and treatment."

"Wait, so the goal isn't to get them off?" she asked, scrunching her face up like a sun-dried tomato.

"Casey, most of my clients are guilty." People always seemed shocked that I was willing to admit this. My goal was to defend them within the bounds of the law—not skirt it like some professional vigilante. "The DA usually has some solid evidence if they make the charge. I go over the evidence with a fine tooth comb, but most of my job is finding mitigating evidence to get my client the best deal."

"That's disappointing," she pouted, sticking out her lower lip. "I was picturing you as this character out of a John Grishman movie, chasing down the real criminals on the streets of Milwaukee."

"You know John Grishman actually writes books, not movies, right?" "I should've known better than to comment on a John Grishman *movie* to someone as educated as yourself." She rolled her eyes. "I'm sure you always read the book first and then complain about the authenticity of the movie."

"I had that coming," I mused, secretly loving her feisty attitude. It was one of the initial reasons for my attraction and I was glad to see it lived up to the billing.

"You should probably finish telling me what happened before your ego sucks all the air out of the room."

"Right." It was well past one and most people had left the bar. It felt darker and more forgiving in the wake of desertion—perfect for unleashing unfavorable news. "A couple weeks later I got the formal job offer. I accepted it without even talking to Amanda."

I know now that I should've talked to Amanda before resigning and explained my reasons like I did with Casey. In fact, my relationship probably would've been infinitely better if I was as honest with Amanda as I was with Casey tonight. Maybe Casey was right when she said our biggest problem was the lack of friendship. Friends talked. But discussions with Amanda inevitably led to fighting and I learned the words were better off left unsaid.

"When did you tell her?"

I rubbed the back of my neck with both hands and held them there. I smiled lazily even though there was nothing to smile about.

Casey narrowed her eyes at me. "Please tell me she doesn't still think you work for the firm?"

"No. Of course not! I just procrastinated a bit..."

"But eventually you told her," Casey prompted.

"It was a Sunday night in May and we just finished watching *Desperate Housewives*." I wagged my finger at Casey to stop her from interrupting. If her gigantic smile was any indication, she was about to lay into me about the show choice. "It was one of her shows."

I distinctly remember Amanda lounging on the couch, wine glass filled to the brim in one hand and her phone in the other. I sat on the other side of the room, reading my book. This was our life: spending time together but not really talking. Friendly roommates, but roommates nonetheless.

"Anyways, I was set to start at the PD office the next day, so I knew I had to tell her. After the show ended, I turned off the TV and sat next to her." Two unprecedented moves in our relationship. "She flipped out, as expected, regurgitating her usual complaints about me."

"Such as?" Casey smiled sweetly to offset her fishing expedition.

"Oh you know, quality gems like I didn't care about her, I wasn't serious about us, I was selfish and incapable of love."

"A preloaded arsenal."

"Yeah, but for the first time, I agreed with her. My decision was selfish. My willingness to exclude her showed I didn't care about her—at least not enough. Instead of defending myself, I told her she was right."

"Which pissed her off even more."

"Naturally; although I don't know why. Given that she accused me of not caring during every fight we had, it shouldn't have come as a surprise that it was true."

"Really?" Her question was laced with sarcasm. "Come on, Joshua. You said earlier that she wasn't living in reality and yet now you're saying she should've realized you tapped out. You can't have it both ways."

"Fair point," I conceded.

"So that was it?"

I shrugged. Amanda was delusional enough to think there was something worthwhile to salvage, but looking back now, I think it was just the shock of the end. I wanted to believe, *had to believe*, that she is happier now. "She moved out a week later."

"Last call," the bartender interrupted.

"I'm probably done," Casey said, cocking an eyebrow in my direction.

"Yeah, we'll take the check. Thanks."

Casey pulled out her iPhone where I couldn't help but notice she had a litany of missed calls and texts. "I can't believe it's almost two."

Was that her cue to leave or did she want to continue talking?

"Normally I'd be in bed hours ago, but for some reason I'm not tired," I ventured, hoping she might feel the same.

"I wouldn't share your geriatric bedtime with anyone if I were you," she leaned forward and whispered. "That's pre-t-t-y uncool."

She was kidding, of course, but she had this confidence about her, like she was the authority on everything cool. I would always be a step (or several) behind, but I no longer considered that a fatal flaw. Tonight led me to believe she didn't either.

The check came and I quickly handed the bartender my credit card.

"Let me help," Casey offered, pulling out her wallet. "That tequila's expensive and we drank *a lot*."

"How about you get the next time?" It was the first mention of a second date, but I felt confident she saw spending seven hours talking about our darkest secrets as more than just a companionable way to pass an evening. Between the kisses and touches, witty banter and flirtations, I'd bet money there was a substantial connection brewing beyond the chemical effects of the tequila.

"Sounds like a plan." As she stood up, her body swayed slightly. She quickly steadied herself on the barstool with a laugh. "Funny how standing up makes you realize how drunk you are. It feels like someone put an IV in my arm containing several more shots of tequila."

"Let's walk," I said, holding out my hand. "We could both use some air to sober up."

"I love this neighborhood," Casey said as we strolled towards the lake. She swung my arm back and forth, reminding me of a little girl. It was odd imagining Casey so young and innocent. She seemed like she came out of the womb primed for the catwalk—beautiful and dangerous. But tonight added so many layers to her story. She grew up too fast and made countless bad decisions and yet a childish sense of adventure and optimism remained. "So much character."

I looked around at the gigantic houses set off from the street. Each house was a study in geometry—half of an octagon, semi-circle, rectangle, cone—jutting out from the tops and the sides. One house had something akin to a princess tower. It was made out of red brick and had a single window on the tower painted black. I was half-expecting to see a trail of Rapunzel's hair streaming from the window.

"It's beautiful," Casey continued, "but I don't think I could live here. It has a vintage Stepford feel, like it represents a bygone era of perfection before the rich fled to the suburbs."

"I agree. Everyone would immediately know I was an imposter when I put my Obama sign on my unmanicured lawn."

"Oh the scandal!" We both laughed.

"Then again, they probably don't let democrats move here."

We reached the deserted roundabout; a fork in the road if you will. One way led down a steep hill towards the lake while the other route ran downtown. We could have turned around, but I wasn't ready.

"Let's sit," I said, pointing towards a bench positioned roughly five feet before the hill plummeted down towards the majestic lakefront. The shimmering lake looked black in the moonlight. Given the late hour, virtually no cars passed on Lincoln Memorial Drive. It felt like we owned the beauty of the landscape. "So let's pretend money's not an issue. If not in one of these lakefront homes, what neighborhood would you choose to live in?"

She turned towards me, wide-eyed with a dreamy excitement that can only arise when answering a hypothetical. "The 8th Arrondissement in Paris. They have the most amazing fashion and art. Walking in that neighborhood is like watching a runway show. And if we're really straining reality, I'd like my own store on the Champs-Elysees between Dior and Fendi."

"I actually meant in Milwaukee."

"Oh-h-h," she said.

"Way to dream big, though."

"I like living in the Third Ward, but my place is too small. My apartment looks like it's in a perpetual state of emergency."

"I've been there, it isn't that bad."

"Oh, it's gotten worse since I left school. I have drawings pinned on the walls, fabric, clasps and closings everywhere, half-finished looks hanging from racks. I constantly cart my work between the studio and home because I never know when inspiration will strike." Casey sounded genuinely stressed. "I want something big, industrial and open. Maybe a loft for designing and then I can live below. Save money on studio rent."

"So definitely the Third Ward then?"

"Not necessarily, but I like being downtown. How about you?"

"The 8th Arrondissement in Paris," I deadpanned. "I'd like to live above a small gallery where I can display my work."

"What an *original* dream." She giggled. "Have you been to Paris?"

"Nope." Heat crept from my cheeks and slowly expanded towards my ears. "I've only been to three states: Wisconsin, Minnesota and Illinois."

"That's so sad," she said, tracing small circles with her thumb in my palm.

I shrugged. "We never really went on vacations as a kid."

"We never went anywhere cool either, but I made it my goal to see something beyond the Mid-fucking-west." Casey laughed. "In fact, I said those exact words to my parents when I was thirteen and they tried to get me to go camping in Lake Superior. They ended up leaving me behind. It was the best week of my childhood."

I stared at her, shocked that her parents would acquiesce to such an arrangement. "I felt lucky on the rare occasion my parents went to a movie."

"Yeah, well, my parents didn't really enjoy my company. They once told me I had an uncanny ability to make every situation worse." Casey threw her hands up in the air. "The feeling was mutual."

"Most people I know would agree you make the party *better*," I argued.

Casey was always the center of attention when I saw her out. She danced, drank, joked and told off-color stories while everyone laughed along. But as snapshots breezed through my mind, I struggled to determine whether Casey was *everyone's* focal point or simply *mine*. Drinking has a funny way of realigning events and feelings. Had I always been drawn to Casey? If not, why would I have such vivid memories of her? She paid me little attention and yet I could choreograph her movements like a ballet dancer.

"To be fair, I was a nightmare to parent. Part of me feels bad for them, but that's probably just me being selfish."

"Selfish?" I asked, not understanding the leap.

"Before therapy I blamed my parents for everything that went wrong with my life. But with Dr. Kate, I started having flashbacks of all the shit I put them through. God, I felt"—she shook her head—"horrible. But it's a selfish guilt because I'm pretty sure it's due to the fear that karma is going to bite me in the ass and give me a terror of a teenage daughter one day."

"But you'll know all the tricks," I pointed out. "I'll be lost. My kids will run roughhouse on me and I'll have no idea since I never disobeyed any rule beyond staying up late to read with a flashlight under the covers."

"You did that?" Casey's smile spread across her face like the rising sun. "That's adorable."

I spread my arms out wide on each side of the bench, flexing my muscles. "I was a rebel in my own way."

"Let's hope you marry a girl with a wild streak. Otherwise you'll think you're raising a Brandon Walsh but end up with a Dylan McKay."

"I have no idea who those people are," I said.

Casey's mouth gaped open. She tried to speak, stuttered and then started again. "*Beverly Hills 90210*?"

"The TV show? Never watched it."

"No wonder you were so well-behaved. You probably watched *Full House*."

"D.J. was pretty hot."

"Oh my God," she whispered.

"So you're saying I need to marry a bad girl turned good?" I smirked. "Do you have anyone in mind?"

"Me? It's debatable whether I've turned good." Casey turned to stare out at the lake. She bit her lower lip, fighting her emotions.

I wished I knew what she was thinking; I could only hope I'd be around long enough to find out. "Besides, I'm sure all the tricks have changed. Other than being able to tell if they're drunk or high, I'd probably prove pretty useless. I'd just end up imposing my bad karma on you."

I wrapped my arm around her. "I think you're worth taking a chance."

"You say that now," she whispered. For a moment I thought she might cry, but she coughed instead.

"When were you in Paris?" I asked, eager to leave behind a subject that obviously upset her.

"Twice actually. I took a bus tour through Europe a couple summers ago. We went to all the major cities—Paris, Rome, Prague, Berlin—but we only spent like two days in each place. Most of the trip was spent on the bus sleeping off a perpetual hangover. It was basically a three-week long party."

"Sounds like fun. Who did you go with?"

"No one," she said breezily. "I thought it was better to go alone. Give me some time to think, you know?"

"Sure," I said, matching her nonchalant tone, but inside my mind was reeling. I wanted to study abroad in Australia during college, but I chickened out because I didn't know anyone else going. I feared I'd spend four months holed up inside while everyone else went out and had a grand ole time. The idea of leaving college, the first time in my life I had an active social life, for a repeat of high school was terrifying. It never occurred to me that anyone else would go alone. I envied the ease with which Casey moved through life. She assumed she would make friends and, if not, made her own fun.

"But the second time I went to Paris was last fall for fashion week."

"Were you showing your clothes?"

She laughed heartedly. "I wish! Only the biggest designers in the world show there. I had to sneak in to watch. It's invitation only."

I was still confused. "So why did you go?"

"A couple of years ago I started a fashion blog. Initially, I did it to post my designs online in the hopes of getting my name out there," she explained. "But people kept sending me fashion questions so I started blogging about trends, what's hot, what's not, how to reuse last season's wardrobe. It blew up a bit and I got a few advertisers. I took that extra money and went to Paris and New York to cover the events for my blog."

"Wow," I said, genuinely impressed at her entrepreneurial spirit. "A fashion designer, businesswoman *and* a writer. I'm a bit out of my league."

"It's a fashion blog. It's hardly worthy of a Pulitzer."

"You're too hard on yourself," I admonished her. "You started your own fashion line—"

"It's not a big deal," she interrupted, evidently uncomfortable with my praise. "Really."

I rolled my eyes. "Tell me about Paris—without the party bus."

She smiled serenely. "It was lovely."

"You can do better than that," I said, wrapping my arms around her and pulling her close.

"It felt like every one of my senses, dormant since birth, blossomed. Everything I was and wanted to be in the future suddenly seemed possible." She turned to me, wide-eyed and serious. "Paris changed my life."

Chapter 20

Casey – September 29, 2011

"**R**éveiller quelqu'un!" I pried opened my eyes and saw a woman shaking my arm. I was caught somewhere between dream and reality, unsure which side had won. "Vous êtes à Paris!"

She ripped open the window to my left, allowing sunlight to flood my seat. I shielded my eyes with my hand as I squinted outside. We evidently landed in Paris, but it could have just as easily been another planet. The airport was silver and had tunnels jutting from the middle like the legs of an octopus. It looked like something out of a sci-fi movie.

After grabbing my bag from baggage claim, I jumped into a cab. I missed the descent into Paris—my sleeping aide was far too effective—but the view from the ground was majestic as we made our way towards my hotel. I grabbed my camera and started snapping pictures of the street fashion. I didn't want to lose a single memory. Women strutted in three-inch heels, leather jackets and cigarette pants while pushing strollers. (A far cry from the mommy apparel donned back home.) Others sported leggings with ankle boots. Hats and sunglasses appeared mandatory.

When we arrived at my hotel, I found a dilapidated room perfect for budgeted travelers. It contained two single beds, each with a bright orange and red bedspread circa 1970, wall mounted headboards and a chest of drawers sized to hold doll clothes. The stale smell of smoke and dust led me to believe the room was last cleaned when *Saturday Night Fever* premiered. I'd probably have emphysema by the time I left.

I began unpacking my clothes to prevent wrinkles from setting in. Since I didn't have a ticket to any of the shows—it was an industry wide invitation only event and I wasn't *yet* considered a valuable part of this industry—I hoped my clothes, looks and personality could barter my way in.

I threw on a pair of black leather pants, a vanilla jersey tank-top with a plunging cowl neck and black ankle boots. I wrapped my hair in a loose bun, pulling out tentacles to give it a tussled look. Mascara, a hint of blush and a mute pink lip and I was good to go. The effect was chic but elegant.

As I approached the Louvre, the excitement bubbling inside me was so intense that I thought the pyramid marking the entrance was a mirage. I struggled to look casual but my heart strummed at the same pace as a cheetah hunting its dinner. When I reached the bottom level of the Louvre, it quickly became apparent that sneaking into the shows wasn't a possibility. Security guarded each door, slowly flicking down lists and marking off names.

I straightened my shoulders (bad posture was a dead giveaway for an American), walked down the hallway and leaned against one of the walls where it was not as crowded. I needed to attract attention while also impressing upon people that I didn't care. Thankfully, I perfected that look at the precocious age of seven.

I pulled out my iPad and began writing an update for my blog. A half-hour later, a deep voice interrupted me. "Are you free to accompany me to the show?" he asked in accented English.

I looked up, unsure my ears heard correctly. He was roughly my height, with dark brown hair buzzed on the sides, longer on top and styled heavily with product for texture. He wore tight dark jeans rolled up a few inches at the bottom, unlaced combat boots, a black t-shirt, a black suit jacket and a grey scarf. It was impossible to tell whether he was gay or straight. The cultural divide was too great.

"Which show are you going to?" I asked, as if it mattered.

"Alexis Mabille." Was he kidding? Alexis Mabille was one of the hottest designers in Paris. He had the type of drama and eccentricity people would sell their kidney to see.

When I was positive I wouldn't squeal like a teenage girl at a Justin Bieber concert, I accepted his invitation. I expected him to admit he was joking or needed a line to chat me up, but he held out his arm instead and escorted me down the hall.

"Adrien Monreau and guest," he told the security guard, who waved us through.

Color me impressed.

The room was grand beyond comparison. It was long and narrow, with white marble floor and rows of chairs flanking the runway. Gigantic stone statutes, probably twenty feet high and ten feet wide, lined one side of the wall, while the opposite side had stories carved into the stone.

Adrien led me to a set of chairs a few rows back. Moments later eerie music bled out of the loudspeakers as the first model sashayed down the runway. Mabille's attention to detail, from the impeccable tailoring to the consistency of jewelry, hairstyle and makeup, was remarkable. Like Madonna or Michael Jordan, this type of greatness is best appreciated in person.

When his wedding gowns trailed out, I felt faint. Each dress was a blinding white, draped like a Greek goddess and fastened with different bow placements. He took risks with the length and the cuts, which gave the dresses a sensual feeling. The eerie music worked in opposition to the beauty of the designs, as if we were observing something illicit.

"I watched you during the show," Adrien said after the models finished their last lap. "The way you reacted—the mesmerized look in your eyes with each new piece—you cannot fake that."

I searched for words to explain my profound longing but I felt depleted, like a marathoner on the last mile. "I'm in love."

He held out his hand. "Come. You'll explain this love to me over wine."

I didn't abide by many rules in life, but I knew this: When a handsome Frenchman offers to buy you a drink, you go. I felt like a twenty-first century Cinderella, except instead of rescuing me from indentured servitude to go to a ball, Adrien took me to a priceless fashion show.

We settled on a small café a few blocks from the Louvre. Adrian greeted several people on the way to our table, all obviously on a stopover from fashion week, which allowed me a moment to study him discreetly. He was made of rough angles: chiseled cheekbones, a squared jaw and slanted lips as if he was in on a joke the rest of the world misunderstood. The crinkles on the side of his eyes when he smiled put him in his mid-thirties, but the sheer number of people he knew betrayed connections well beyond his years.

Adrien pulled out my chair, a truly foreign gesture to me in more than one sense of the word. He stared at me intently, studying every pore on my face. "Are you a model?"

"Is that your best line?"

His forehead creased. "A line?"

"Yes; a way to flatter me into liking you."

"No, no, no." He laughed. "I work with models. I'm a casting director at DDD."

I shook my head.

"It's an international modeling agency and PR firm," he explained.

"How did you get interested in fashion?"

"I was born," he said with a laugh before telling me how he grew up in a fashion powerhouse. His mother was a model and his father a photographer, which meant he spent much of his childhood travelling to exotic locations. Despite his privileged upbringing, he remained surprisingly humble when I pressed him for insider stories.

He named dropped reluctantly and always with lavish complements. If I wanted industry smut, Adrien was not the guy to ask.

"You are very beautiful," he announced suddenly, as if discovering a new fact. The sun rose in the east and I was beautiful. End of story. "The camera would grab these cheekbones"—he lightly traced my cheek with his index finger—"and never let go."

"I've never modeled."

"What a pity," he said, frowning. I quickly learned he used this phrase to describe any and all bad news ranging from *The building is on fire* to *I overslept by five minutes*. "When I saw you, I assumed you were an aspiring model that some casting director shamelessly tossed away."

"I'm actually a designer," I confessed, sipping my wine. Back home wine felt pretentious and inefficient compared to tequila, but here it felt potently romantic. Paris made even the most ordinary events—walking in a park, sipping wine in a café—extraordinary. "I came over here to see if I could get into any of the shows."

"How have you fared?"

"Rather well for my first day," I smirked.

He smiled back as the server set down an array of bread and cheese. Adrien picked up my plate and arranged me a small sampling.

"Tell me about your work."

"I like to think of it as street infused vintage with a hint of glamour," I explained. "Boho chic, if you will."

Adrien nodded slowly and deliberately, refusing to veer his eyes away from me as I spoke. "I would like to see these designs."

"I don't have a full collection yet," I admitted, silently cursing my impulsive nature. I should have finished my collection before jetting to Paris where it was possible to meet important industry people. "I only graduated from fashion school last year."

"And?"

"I've sold some pieces in a boutique back home," I quickly added, my confidence shattering like a glass vase. "As well as on my blog, but given your job, I just worry..."

His forehead crinkled. He interlaced his fingers together, leaned forward and peered intently into my eyes. "About what?"

"Compared to the portfolios you're used to seeing, it's rather amateur." I wanted to crawl underneath the table. "A friend of mine that dabbles in photography shot the pictures, while a couple of other friends modeled. Needless to say, we're not professionals."

"Everyone has to start somewhere. It's important that you are working and trying new things. Please," he smiled and put a reassuring hand on top of mine. "Show me."

I pulled out my iPad, directed it towards my website and reluctantly handed it to him. I watched his eyes scan each outfit in fastidious detail, feeling exposed and vulnerable.

"Well done here." He pushed his index finger and thumb on the screen to enlarge the image of a thin, almost sheer, purple jersey dress. "It's a hard fabric to manipulate to hang like this, but the seams look nice and clean."

But with the good, I also had to take the bad.

"These pants are disastrous," he muttered. Adrien maximized the picture to reveal that one of the back pockets of the jeans was a good quarter-inch higher than the other side. I dug my nails into my hand. How had I not noticed that before?

He flipped to the next look, my crème dela crème, a maroon cocktail dress. I side-pleated the bodice of the dress to give it a sexy sweetheart neckline. "You did this by hand?"

"Yes," I breathed, awaiting his criticism. It was a difficult hand-pleating stitch that took hours to make.

"Your work is impeccable. I can't see any puckering and the pleats are perfectly straight. But always be aware of the fabric you are using. The dress looks heavy in the picture. Don't push forward with a design that doesn't fit the fabric."

I nodded, feeling the heat growing on my face. He was doing me a favor. People paid him for advice. But it was impossible to erase the disappointment I felt as he levied each criticism. Just once it would've been nice for someone to recognize my talent without equivocation. But I also knew if he fawned over my designs—when they were clearly light years below his usual clientele—the praise would have been disingenuous. To get to the next level I needed to embrace and incorporate his criticism into my work.

"There are a lot of good ideas here," he added. "But you need to match the right model to the right piece. Look here. Why would you put that dress on her?" Adrien pointed towards a picture of my friend Betsy. "She looks like she's drowning. The dress was obviously cut for someone taller. That hemline should hit the middle of her thigh, yes?"

"Yes."

"It changes the feeling of the dress when it hits her knee. Now she's meeting her boyfriend's parents for brunch instead of going to a party." He turned to me, his pupils dilated to the size of dimes. "You do not design conservatively, so make sure it does not photograph that way. You need to convey the attitude of the girl you design for in the styling."

I started to thank him but he covered my mouth with his, clearing up the questions of whether he was gay or interested in me.

"Such beauty," he whispered as he pulled away. His accent sounded thicker, his voice heavier, like he was emerging from a deep sleep.

"Everyone looks beautiful in Paris."

"Some more than others."

He kissed me again. It was the type of kiss that usually disappeared during high school when sex entered the equation. But tonight began and ended with a series of dizzying kisses that felt more like dancing.

As Adrien walked me back to my hotel, I smiled at the traffic racing by and even the dog shit that littered the sidewalk. It was impossible to dim my mood. Today was a perfect day; one that I couldn't have dreamt if a genie presented me with a single wish.

TWO DAYS LATER THE blaring ring of the telephone jolted me towards consciousness. I lunged towards the phone, instantly feeling dizzy and nauseous. A sea of red liquid sloshed in my stomach, courtesy of the several bottles of wine I polished off last night with some random French businessmen.

"Hello?"

"Casey, what are you doing?" My foggy brain pushed its way through the haze and registered Adrien's clipped voice.

"Sleeping," I croaked.

"Meet me in the lobby in a half-hour. And pack your designs."

He clicked off and I scurried into the shower. Forty-five minutes later, I rolled a suitcase of my clothes into the lobby. Adrien sat waiting, flipping carelessly through a magazine.

"I have a surprise," Adrien announced, after greeting me with a kiss on each cheek. I assumed it was another fashion show, but he led me to a black Mini Cooper parked outside. "And, no, I will not give you a hint."

As we drove, Adrien sprinkled in his personal history of Paris. I saw the hotel where he lost his virginity (*a bit overwhelming*), the school he sporadically attended (*very boring*) and the street corner where he broke his arm trying to impress a girl while skateboarding (*I have never skateboarded before or since*).

I was laughing so hard at one story that I didn't even notice we pulled over. A girl knocked on my window and I jumped back. It was hard to see her face beneath the bug-eyed sunglasses she wore, but her skin was the color of a porcelain doll.

Adrien reached over and opened my door.

"Bonjour," she said, kissing Adrien on both cheeks, before crawling into the backseat. Adrien introduced her as Celine and said nothing more. For the rest of the ride they conversed in French, which left me with little to do but look at the scenery.

The shadows of the buildings began to fade away in favor of tree-lined houses and open green spaces. We pulled into the driveway of a three-story white shingled house. Half the house had vines crawling up the side, while the other half stood white and pristine.

Adrien exited the car, stretched his arms above his head and inhaled a deep breath. "This is the best air in France!"

Celine crawled out from the backseat like an elegant giraffe. She removed her glasses to reveal a heart-shaped face, wide eyes and a snub nose. Not classically beautiful, but striking nonetheless.

"Ah, Papa!" Adrien called as a slightly older version of Adrien came down the front steps. He had the same cut cheekbones and jaw line, dark eyes and skinny physique. But his age was apparent from the sprinkles of grey in his hair and the three deep-seated lines adorning his forehead. "Casey, Celine, this is my Papa, the great Rene Monreau."

Rene's eyes lingered on me a beat too long before he took my face into his hands, kissed each cheek, and declared me beautiful. Much like Adrien, his father exuded charm and I knew he had no trouble, even at his age, finding the company of beautiful women.

Rene linked my arm in his and we walked into a sprawling back yard. Privacy trees marked the boundaries, but otherwise it was a blank canvas. He led me to a patio table filled with different lights and camera equipment.

"I like an open landscape. It encourages the viewer to focus on the clothing," he explained to me before winking at Celine. "And the beauty of the model."

"Have you figured out your surprise?" Adrien asked a few moments later when Rene and Celine disappeared inside.

"My surprise?"

"Yes." His eyes sparkled mischievously. "My father will photograph Celine in your clothes."

"But why?" I sputtered.

He shrugged, full of self-satisfied confidence. "I told him I met this young, talented, American designer that needed a keen eye to photograph her clothes. My father volunteered."

"And Celine?"

"I helped Celine back when she was poor and could not book a single job."

I was speechless. I wrapped my arms around his neck and kissed him deeply, trying to harness my gratitude into a single gesture. "Thank you."

We went back to the car to gather my suitcase. I briefly regretted leaving most of my pieces back in the States. But who could have predicted this scheme of events? A second was all I allowed myself to wallow. I had a famous photographer, a beautiful model and some of my clothes. I would use every moment to my advantage.

"Do you have a sewing machine?" Even though Celine and I were similar in height, her swanlike frame required some alterations.

"You have come to the house of fashion," he said, leading me inside.

Adrien wasn't kidding. He showed me his mother's closet, which was roughly the size of my apartment. Three of the four walls were filled with clothes, shoes and accessories, all organized according to item, color and season. It was a fashion mecca: Chanel, Dior, Louis

Vuitton. I felt faint as my fingers brushed against the different silk, cashmere and wool garments.

Adrien opened a large cabinet that included a sewing machine, a dress form, a tape measure, pins, buttons and zippers, as well as numerous thread colors. Apparently his mother had sporadic aspirations of designing when her modeling career ended but could never quite muster the dedication.

My heart pounded with both fear and excitement. This was my first photo shoot with a professional model and photographer. It felt unreal.

I went into the attached bathroom to take Celine's measurements. She stood clad in an ivory colored lacy bra and thong. Her rib and hip bones popped out like knifes, making her already flat stomach appear concave. Most people would probably consider me thin, but model thin was a different breed. In any other scenario but fashion you'd rush this girl to the doctor for malnutrition.

An hour later I dressed Celine in a skimpy, dark blue jersey knit dress with a platinum colored sheer tank-top underneath. I borrowed a pair of hot pink Christian Louboutin heels from his mom's closet, as well as some bangle bracelets, and we made our way outside. I couldn't imagine how Celine and her one-hundredth of one percent of body fat dealt with the cold and I immediately apologized.

"She's a professional," Rene consoled me. "She does not feel the cold."

I smiled back, doubting whether someone could really master such a skill. But maybe he was right. While Rene snapped pictures, Celine morphed into the trendy hipster I strived to create in my designs. But when the camera was off she drew into herself like a turtle, locking her legs, hunching her shoulders and hugging herself.

Adrien alternated between looking at Celine and the computer screen that displayed each new shot. Sometimes Adrien would call out a direction when the garment wasn't photographing the way he wanted or her pose wasn't translating well on camera, but mainly he left the direction up to Rene. They made quite the duo.

Meanwhile, I worked frantically to tailor the clothes to her non-existent curves, shuffling her in and out of outfits with the speed of a pit crew.

A couple hours later we finished. I kissed Rene on both cheeks, ignoring his hand that trailed down my spine to the top of my ass, and hugged Celine tightly, thanking her profusely.

The drive into Paris was silent as the heat of the car and the hours of hard work mingled together to make us drowsy. I felt both relieved and perplexed when Adrien dropped me off. It was impossible to ascertain his intentions through the cultural barrier: friend or lover? In America, no man would help out a girl he just met unless he had romantic designs on her.

"I find it is best to go over the pictures with a fresh mind. Are you free tomorrow night?"

I nodded. "But I'm leaving the day after."

Adrien brushed his lips against mine, letting his tongue briefly flirt with the idea of more, before pulling away. I exited the car, bewildered by the sensuality of the kiss and his lack of persistence. One thing was for certain: love had a whole different set of rules in Paris.

I SPENT THE NEXT AFTERNOON walking around Paris, breathing in the culture, memorizing the vibe of each changing neighborhood, hoping it would inspire some new designs. I inhaled the smells of freshly baked croissants and warmed myself with decadent hot chocolate. The chaotic pedestrian traffic passed by me with nary a glance while I sketched and blogged and cataloged in my memory the smallest of details.

As sunset neared I made my way onto the Pont des Arts Bridge. I could see the Louvre and the Cathedral of Notre Dame lit up in the distance and heard the calm waters of the Seine below. I stood near the spot where Carrie and Big reconciled in the final scene of *Sex and the City*.

I wasn't asking for such a storybook romance, but it would be nice to share this with someone. My mind drifted to Ryan, but I quickly stopped those thoughts. His wife and baby girl shared his life, not me. Luckily, that thought no longer gutted me.

I walked back to my hotel, wondering what was next for me. I felt flooded with ideas and inspiration. I could already feel the weight of the fabrics in my hand, the calluses from late nights sewing and the ache in my back from standing over a dress form all day. I may have wanted love, but I was willing to wait for that.

I wasn't willing to wait to take my career to the next level. I might never show at Paris fashion week, but I wanted to reach a broader market and test my design abilities. No more coasting by, working half-days, pleased to sell a few pieces. I needed to devote myself—mind, body, soul—to my craft. I needed to *believe*.

By the time I returned to my hotel, the air was tinged with drizzle. My feet throbbed as if I spent all day starring in a rendition of *Chicago*, but I felt embraced by the magic of the city. I was sad to leave but even more anxious to get home. I was ready for the challenge of becoming more.

I pulled on a pair of electric purple leggings, a short dark grey sheath dress and black booties. I wasn't the type of designer that embraced patterns, but I loved a pop of color. I flat ironed my hair and decided to go for a bold lip with minimal eye makeup.

Adrien stood outside my hotel clad in dark jeans, a grey sweater and a light pink scarf. I loved men that wore pink; it suggested rebelliousness against the confines of masculinity (and perhaps other wild behaviors).

Adrien gestured towards a silver and lime colored scooter—a toy, really. Back home we called this a moped and deemed it unfit for city traffic. In Paris it was a bargain in terms of price and storage.

"We are *not* riding on this thing."

"Of course we are," he said, handing me a flimsy plastic helmet.

I dropped it on the sidewalk, expecting it to split in half. "This wouldn't save a squirrel's life," I muttered.

"A what?"

"Never mind."

I reluctantly climbed on board, clawing my fingers into the spokes of his ribs. Adrien drove like Evel Knievel. He swooped through side streets narrowly missing jay-walking pedestrians, gunned the gas to make yellow lights and weaved through traffic lanes as if they were a suggestion. My equilibrium was entirely out of whack by the time he parked.

Adrien jumped off the bike. "That was fun, yes?"

"I'm alive," I conceded.

"Welcome to Pigalle," Adrien announced. I nodded towards the sex shop to our right. He laughed and slung his arm around me. "Not tonight my dear."

As we walked, I noticed that Pigalle was a neighborhood at odds: a bit rundown with homeless people but also hopping with hipsters, vendors and street performers. People sang, danced and skateboarded. Promoters solicited us to enter every club we passed. Everyone appeared drunk and happy, but it was still early. Experience taught me that in a few hours the drunken and drugged would become tired, bitter and possibly violent.

Adrien led us to a café where a man stood outside playing "In My Life" on his guitar. How apropos. It was the first time I gave credence to the idea that everyone enters your life, however fleeting, for a reason. Adrien exposed me to the fashion industry in a way I only dreamt about and provided me with talent that sat light years away from my bank account. There was a reason.

Inside the café, the hostess weaved us through a web of small wooden tables, painted in every color of the rainbow. Our table was a purple circle, with a pink and blue chair. I bucked stereotypes and chose blue, which also gave him a chance to color coordinate.

Adrien ordered for us, choosing crepes, eggs with truffles and butter, and, of course, croissants. Back home I would've felt insulted if a man ordered for me, but in France it felt chivalrous.

Over dinner we went through the pictures from yesterday's shoot on my iPad, debating which ones flattered the clothes best. His dad was truly a genius behind the lens and Celine knew exactly how to work her angles.

"Why did you help me?" I asked after we tackled the last picture.

He linked his fingers through mine and rubbed the inside of my palm with his thumb. "I like you."

"Oh." I wasn't used to men giving such straight-forward answers. It could be that simple, but that hasn't been my experience. "How are you still single?"

"I was married once." He tipped his wine glass back until every last drop scurried into his mouth. "Too much fuss."

"When did you get divorced?" I wanted to ensure he was, in fact, divorced.

"Almost two years ago."

"Was it messy?"

"Messy?" Adrien repeated, his eyebrows furrowing.

"You know, screaming fights, broken dishes, veiled threats."

"No, no, no. Isabelle is a dear friend."

"How very French," I muttered into my wine glass.

"We never fought. Originally, I think this is a good thing, no?" I nodded. "But over time I see there is no passion. We were like brother and sister. No good."

"I'm sorry."

He shrugged. "Now we are free to find new love."

It sounded far too easy given my experiences, but then again, the French had a different philosophy towards love. They understood that relationships were finite and flawed, whereas romances were exquisite and rare and therefore needed to be embraced even if the timing was inopportune.

"I like the idea that the end of a relationship is really another opportunity to find happiness," I said. "It feels a bit improbable given my experiences, but it's something to aspire to."

The candlelight flicked across his face, highlighting his mischievous grin. "Perhaps American men are blind and stupid."

"You might be onto something there."

"You are lovely; beautiful, smart and talented," he whispered, gently tracing my lower lip with his thumb before kissing me.

You don't know me that well, I was tempted to say. But what would it have proved? I was leaving tomorrow. It wouldn't hurt to leave him with this illusion. So I let him kiss me. There really are so few chances in life to make-out with a gorgeous Frenchman in a Parisian café.

WHEN WE GOT BACK TO my hotel, Adrien walked me to my room. He pulled me close, running both hands through my hair before stopping at my neck and cupping my head. He kissed me, his tongue slowly exploring my mouth like a window shopper with an afternoon to kill. I was the passive mannequin accepting his advances without complaint.

I opened the door and we fell onto the bed together. The mattress, hard as a rock, sent shock waves down my spine. Adrien rolled onto me, probably assuming my moan was released in excitement rather than agony.

The impact of my body hitting the bed was both painful and sobering. I wasn't sure I wanted to have sex with Adrien. The old Casey would have ignored my confusion and forged ahead with fake enthusiasm. I was many things, but a prick tease was not one.

But questions inside my head continued to loom large. Did I *want* Adrien? Yes, I was attracted to him, but if I really wanted him, wouldn't it have happened already and not as some last night, carpe diem, scheme? And was it really a good idea to mix business and pleasure? Kissing was innocent but sex irretrievably changed the landscape of a relationship. Did I want to risk losing his friendship given the multitude of ways he might help my career?

Completely unaware of my wavering desire, Adrien pulled off my leggings and began kissing up the inside of my thigh.

"Stop," I mumbled.

Adrien looked up. "What?"

"I don't think I want to do this." The words tasted like curdled milk.

He frowned slightly.

"I'm sorry," I whispered, covering my eyes with my hands. "I'm leaving tomorrow and it just doesn't seem like the best idea."

Adrien zipped up his pants and refastened his belt. I hadn't recalled undoing them, but apparently I did so out of habit. He reached out and brushed my cheek with his thumb. "You really are lovely."

"Thank you," I whispered, hating myself. "For everything."

Over the years, I had sex with countless losers who probably couldn't remember my name the next morning. Yet here I was turning down the man that believed in me enough to organize my first professional photo shoot. Maybe one day I'd feel equipped to discriminate between sex that might lead to a relationship and sex that was little more than a release, but I wasn't there yet. I acted irresponsible for so long, devaluing my body and mind, that I no longer felt able to let go even when a good part of me knew this wouldn't be one of those regrettable mistakes.

"Promise me one thing," Adrien said. "One day, when you show your collection at Paris fashion week, you will hire me to manage your show?"

I laughed. "Of course."

"Keep in touch, my lovely." A single, sweet goodbye kiss and he left.

I stared into the sparse hotel room, finding it inconceivable that I was leaving tomorrow. But I felt gratitude, not sadness. Adrien was a blessing; my Parisian guardian angel. He helped reenergize my passions while simultaneously confirming my talent and challenging me to make so much more of my life. For this, I was forever in his debt.

Chapter 21

"**A**re you going back to fashion week this year?"

"No," I said, staring out wistfully at the lake. Adrien asked this very same question two days ago. "Any money I make goes right back into designing new clothes."

"Designing clothes isn't very profitable?" Joshua's voice sounded drawn and tired. His lips vibrated as he tried to suppress another yawn.

"At times. I've established a bit of a clientele, but fashion is cyclical. Unless you're designing for a specific person, it's hard to know whether what you find edgy and exciting will appeal to the masses."

"One day you're in, one day you're out," he said in a terrible German accent.

"Thanks for the advice, *Heidi*."

"Paycheck to paycheck. I don't know how you do it."

"It all works out. In good months I save for bad months. Besides," I added, "I think being poor is worth waking up excited to work."

Poor was a relative term. Thanks to Ryan I didn't have crippling student loans hanging over my neck like most of my classmates. Allowing Ryan to pay for school wasn't one of my prouder moments, but it was a means to an end. I was able to start my own line, make studio payments and travel to support my blog without drowning in the red.

"I admire your courage and passion."

"Stop," I said, refusing to accept praise when it was people like Ryan and Adrien that provided the stepping stones towards success.

After Paris, Adrien quickly became my most trusted fashion advisor. Unlike my friends, whom lavished praise upon my designs for fear of either hurting my feelings or impeding my artistic license, Adrien never sugarcoated his opinions. He stayed supportive but firm and pushed me to try new things. "It's easy to be brave when you have people willing to help. Adrien has been a Godsend."

"I can't believe he set up an entire photo shoot for you. That's insane."

"Surreal," I agreed. "His dad is so talented. The way he manipulated those photographs made my work look like Valentino or Carolina Herrera."

"I'm supposed to be impressed by those names, aren't I?"

I shook my head. "You disappoint me."

He tugged on his well-worn Jimmy Hendricks t-shirt. "I hate to break this to you but I'm not exactly an authority on fashion."

"Really?" I deadpanned.

"And to think, people buy your designs for your style sense. That's the real shame here. The rouse you're playing on the public."

I laughed, delightfully surprised again by Joshua's sense of humor. He didn't take himself too seriously, which was refreshing after some of the men I've dated who thought the world started and ended on their timetable.

"So you didn't want to make a go of it long-distance with Adrien?" Joshua asked. He had a gentle and yet authoritative way of lobbing personal questions. It felt like a soft, subtle tap on the shoulder; I found myself answering seconds before I realized it was a topic I would rather avoid.

"No-o-o," I emphasized.

Clips from our time together flashed in my head. A casual fling with a burgeoning friendship was perfect...for me. But I could never figure out Adrien's intentions. Friend, colleague, fling or girlfriend? Adrien remained a mystery. He was overwhelmingly kind in all of our conversations, but I still felt a barrier between us. I didn't know how much of that was his personality, the cultural difference or whether he kept me at a distance because I made my intentions for friendship so clear. I probably would never know.

"He's a collage of divergent personality traits," I continued. "Respectful yet seductive; passionate about work yet laid back personally; responsible yet fun. It would take much longer than a week to get a hold on what he wanted from a woman, but I don't think it was a long-distance relationship with me. We're much better suited as friends."

"I doubt that." He nudged his shoulder against mine and smirked. "You have no idea the effect you have on men."

"You keep saying that, but I'm curious, what's my effect on you?"

"No way!" He shook his head emphatically. "You've already learned too much about me tonight."

"I could say the same to you."

"So no one since Adrien?"

"In what way? You infer that I *had* Adrien, which clearly I did not."

"That was my favorite part," Joshua confided. It could have been the cool breeze or the alcohol making his cheeks rosy, but it appeared he was blushing. "It was nice to hear a story that didn't involve details of sleeping with a sex god."

"I never said anything like that," I retorted. I purposefully kept my stories strictly PG-13, even though the unedited version would need a bit of leniency from the MPAA to get an R rating.

"Ryan?"

"Well, if I had known..." I stopped. I knew Joshua liked me, but I felt nervous admitting it. *Joshua Shaw made me nervous.* Wonders never ceased. "If it helps, I'm not really that girl anymore."

He raised his eyebrows. "I hope a little bit of that girl is left."

"What I meant is that I've lost my ability to have meaningless sex."

"You tell me now, what, seven hours into the date?" Joshua looked around, making as if he was going to escape.

"It's the tragic effect of Dr. Kate," I jokingly mourned. "But don't worry. My bad girl persona still makes occasional appearances."

Truth be told, I hadn't had sex for a good six months. For fear of stating the obvious, I missed the sex but it was nice to feel in control of my life and body. I didn't immediately flip out if my period was a few days late or if I saw a suspicious pimple near the territory covered by my panties. I no longer woke up in random apartments, unable to remember how I got there, who I was with, whether we had (protected) sex and how I was going to get home. It wasn't nearly as exciting but my trusty vibrator helped pass the lonely nights.

"I'd personally have words with Dr. Kate if she lobotomized your entire bad girl persona." Joshua's smile faded. "But seriously, don't give Dr. Kate credit for turning your life around. You did the work."

"God, you two should meet. You sound just like her."

"I'll take that as a compliment."

"I'm cold," I confessed, curling into the warmth of his chest.

"Do you want to head back?"

I saw in his fluttering eyes, heard in his strained voice and felt from his jerky movements that he was exhausted. But I loved how he fought both his body and mind to spend time with me. He'd stay until sunrise if I wanted.

"Yeah," I said, saving him from himself. "We probably should."

We strolled back on the quiet streets towards Mission Bar. Maybe tiredness had set in or perhaps we had exhausted our conversational abilities for one night, but either way, we walked hand-in-hand in companionable silence. It was a silence far too mature for a first date, but I wasn't worried. The one takeaway from tonight was that Joshua didn't overthink situations or his feelings. He let his life unveil organically.

"Are you okay to drive?" He cupped my head in his hands and scrutinized my eyes like an ophthalmologist.

"I think I've sufficiently sobered up."

"Good because you owe me a ride," he grinned.

I looked up and down the deserted street. "How did you get here?"

"I met a friend for drinks after work and he dropped me off," Joshua explained. "I knew very little about you except that I should come with my drinking shoes on."

I clicked open the car, smiling at his utter lack of self-consciousness in using such a colloquial phrase. "Get in."

"Can you recite the alphabet backwards?" he asked. I gently banged my head against the steering wheel. "I'm kidding! Although, you might want to sit up. If a cop drove by right now he'd probably think you passed out."

"I'm not worried," I said, turning on the car. "I have my attorney here to defend me."

He laughed. "You could never afford me."

"You work at the public defender's office!"

"Details, details."

We drove through the sleeping streets of downtown Milwaukee and made our way into the Third Ward. "Where is your studio?" Joshua asked.

I pointed out one of the converted warehouses a few blocks away. "It's a pretty eclectic space. A bunch of artists, designers and photographers."

"Sounds a lot more entertaining than my coworkers," he muttered.

"It's great when I'm stuck because there's always someone willing to take a coffee break." I made more genuine girlfriends via my studio than I had during my entire life. It was probably the biggest reason I didn't feel the need to go home with random guys. It's hard to feel lonely when you have a girlfriend you can call on a moment's notice. "But challenging when I'm in the middle of creating a piece and someone stops by wanting to chat."

"That's the worst," he agreed wearily.

We turned off Kinnickinnic and pulled onto a residential street with a bunch of older character homes. He pointed towards the third one from the left, a large brick duplex. It was hard to see in the dark, but I recognized a porch swing and two entry doors. The second floor had a spacious wood balcony overlooking the front yard, which was made up of a single large hill.

"It looks nice," I said. Joshua stared up at the house, perhaps trying to imagine how a stranger would view it. Or maybe he just fell asleep with his eyes open. "You're not used to these late nights, are you?"

The hours I worked changed based on when I felt inspired. It wasn't unheard of for me to stay up the entire night working and go to bed as the sun was about to rise. But Joshua's glazed eyes told me experiencing this hour from anything other than his bed was a first for him.

"I'm fine," he yawned. His eyes looked slightly bloodshot. Dark circles reflected off of his glasses. He looked adorable, like a stray puppy looking for a good meal and a warm bed. "You're worth losing a little sleep."

We kissed a few times during the night but that was when the ambiance of the bar, the intoxicating effects of the liquor and the conversational highs were at its peak. Needless to say, those kisses didn't calm the nervous energy crackling through my veins as Joshua met my eyes and came towards me. He tugged both sides of my vest and pulled me towards him for a slow, luxurious kiss.

I closed my eyes, memorizing the moment: the brush of his whiskers against my chin, the taste of tequila on his tongue and the faint aroma of soap radiating off his skin. I pulled away first, eager to see the look of awe that crossed his face after each kiss. It was enough to make me melt for days.

"Get some rest," I said. "I'm counting on you to help design a few t-shirts for my collection."

It was the best way to let him know that I wanted to see him again without any pressure. If tonight was any indication, we were much better off spending time together informally and seeing what happens.

"I'd be honored—as long as you're honest about whether you can use them."

"I'm always honest—especially when it comes to fashion," I answered. "Besides, something tells me this might be exactly what you need right now."

"I think I already found what I need," Joshua said with a smile and ducked out the car.

The subtle comments he dropped all night, like coins slipping into a slot machine, exposed me to a type of romance I only heard, saw and read about, but had never experienced. Before tonight I doubted the existence of men who so easily and cleverly professed their feelings. I assumed it was a manufactured lie produced by Hollywood; a mythical unicorn for female consumption. But Joshua appeared to be the real deal.

"You might have," I whispered to myself as I drove away. I shook my head in wonder. Who would've thought? Not me. Maybe Rachel. Nah, not even her.

A HALF-HOUR LATER I lay in my bed, curled up between two pillows, smiling, unable to sleep. My brain was wide awake, rewinding the events and conversations of tonight. It had been a long time since I engaged in a post-date analysis with any level of enthusiasm. More often than not the feelings of dread over potentially running into the person caused my stomach to turn sour as the flashbacks skittered across my brain.

But tonight a steady stream of happiness pumped from my heart. Some might diagnose this feeling as infatuation, but it felt more potent than that. I had been through every stage of love to recognize that these feelings held real potential. My giddiness didn't arise from any level of fascination or idolization like I suffered from with John. I understood too well the highly flawed nature of humans to put anyone on a pedestal anymore. Nor was it akin to the desperate longing, heightened passion and insecurity I felt with Ryan, never knowing what our future held. I didn't need Joshua to validate my beauty, talent or worthiness of love as I strived for in so many one-night stands. I needed a partner; someone to compliment my life, not provide absolution to live it.

Best of all, I acted like myself around Joshua. I opened up—the good, the bad and the absolutely disastrous—and he listened with a compassionate (and often clever) ear, refusing to judge even the worst of my indiscretions. He reacted genuinely but fairly, providing a dose of comic relief at all the right times. The old me would have dismissed his sensitivity as weakness, a refusal to see me for what I was: broken. (Who am I kidding, the old me wouldn't have gone on the date!) I would've felt unworthy of the love of a decent man. But I knew that not to be true anymore.

Joshua was a free thinker and an idealist, consistently treading the line between other people's expectations and his passions, but finally at a point where he decided where the line began and ended. He wasn't perfect. Not even close. He acted selfish at times, became too easily depressed, dwelled in his childhood insecurities and allowed people to take advantage of his kindness. He learned at an early age to hide his feelings deeply; so deep that no one could penetrate and consequently spent most of his adult life unthawing in stunted romantic relationships. But with each story he told, I grew attracted to him because of his ability to accept his flaws while consistently working to be a better person. He struck a balance between challenging himself to find happiness while still making the necessary compromises to flourish in a life he might not have chosen with a different upbringing.

There was significant baggage on both sides. Most of it was released tonight in an alcohol-fueled truth session. Neither of us could have foreseen any repercussions from sharing too much; after all, this one date was the beginning and the end—a mere compromise to Rachel. Each of us came in with a faulty perception that the other person had not changed since our first meeting years ago. But our feelings shifted subtly and significantly as the night progressed. I'm not sure who recognized it first. Did it matter?

Imperfect timing reared its ugly head so often in life that it was easy to ignore the few times it worked in our favor. Tonight, on a random Friday night in September, forced into a date years after meeting, fate put both of us, unattached and unencumbered by emotional ties, in a bar together. Fate worked its magic. The rest was up to us.

About the Author

Marisa Rae Dondlinger lives and writes in Milwaukee, Wisconsin with her husband and two young daughters. A graduate of the University of Wisconsin Law School, she is also an avid reader and runner.

About the Author

Marisa Rae Dondlinger is the author of Come And Get Me, Gray Lines, Open, and Scenes From a Bar. She lives in Wisconsin with her husband and two young daughters. A graduate of the University of Wisconsin Law School, Marisa practiced law for several years before devoting herself to writing fiction. When not writing, she enjoys reading, going for walks, and watching her daughters play sports.

Read more at marisaraedondlinger.com.